LINDA ANNE SMITH

Unknown, Unseen

UNDER THE RADAR

Unknown, Unseen—Under the Radar

Unknown, Unseen—Under the Radar is a work of fiction. Names, characters, places, and incidents are the products of the author's imagination or are used fictitiously. Any resemblance to actual events, locales, or persons, living or dead, is entirely coincidental.

Jacket and interior design: Erik Mohr/Ian Sullivan Cant (madebyemblem.com)

ISBN paperback edition: 978-0-9949295-8-7
ISBN electronic (mobi) edition: 978-0-9949295-9-4
ISBN electronic (epub) edition: 978-1-7781601-0-3

For all children and youth
whose hidden trauma goes unknown and unseen.

PART ONE

Chapter 1

Jess, tall and svelte, walked through the cafeteria of Riverbank High. Her hair was braided in curved cornrows that fell down her back in a cascade of curls. Her stylish outfit came from thrift-shop foraging, a skill she had learned at her grandmother's side–a woman who had always looked sharp despite her tight budget.

A few students gazed up as Jess passed by, but most were bent over tables, chattering among themselves, trying to make their voices heard over the reverberating and amplifying effect of the high concrete walls. She didn't stand out among the students, but neither did she blend in. Victor, from Jess's English class, sat with his crew on the other side of the large room. He spotted Jess and meandered through the tables, feigning a chance encounter.

"Eh, Jess!" Victor said as he approached, "You got anything going on tonight?"

"Like I've said before," Jess replied as she continued to walk, "not with you."

Victor followed. "Well, a guy can hope, can't he?"

"Dream on. It's never going to happen."

Victor laughed, "Yeah, yeah, that's what they all say."

"Damn! You *do* have a problem."

Victor strolled back to his group, and Jess slid onto a stool attached to a round table near the rear exit. A boy, earbuds in, sat across from her, sipping orange juice and scrolling through his phone. After a few moments, he left without noticing Jess at all.

Jess nibbled on a granola bar and looked out at the students as though watching a movie. From their mannerisms, she was getting a feel for the characters—the leads, the supporting, the extras—all talking and laughing as they ate. Where would she fit in? With whom? And what would happen once they got to know her?

Although Jess was in Grade 11, it was her first year at Riverbank High. And, as she discovered, much of the forming and culling of BFFs, cliques and clubs were done in Grade 10. In her first few weeks, while the veterans were reuniting or realigning, Jess had been intent on navigating through the sprawling campus and adjusting to the demands of her courses. There was one girl, Layla, who Jess had been surprised to spot among the sea of faces—someone she knew before Riverbank. While friendly toward each other, they had no classes together nor common interests. On the rare occasions when they passed in the hallways, they gave each other a fist pump and went their separate ways. And Layla never came to the cafeteria during her lunch breaks. Like many of the students, she always left the school.

Keenly aware of her solitude, Jess gazed out again at the students chatting, joking, and sharing food. *What did she have in common with them anyway?* she thought. *Two more years. Only two more years.* Jess never went back to the cafeteria. During her lunch break, she either roamed the halls glancing at bulletin boards or went to the library and perused a book.

Chapter 2

"Jess?"

The corridors surged with high school students moving in both directions on their way to their next class or lunch break. Sebastian picked up his pace and followed the girl, his eyes focused on her dark, coifed hair as it bobbed ahead. *Could it be her? Could it be Jess?* As he squeezed through the mob, his frizzy, red hair, spiralling out in every direction, brushed across a student's face.

"Gross!" she exclaimed as she backed away, giving Sebastian a gap to lunge forward.

"Jess?" he called out again. The girl paused, turned around and scanned the crowd. *It was her!* "Jess, it's me!"

Jess looked around and spotted the shaggy, freckled teen. She laughed and gave him a high five. "Sebastian, what are you doing at Riverbank High?"

"I could say the same about you!" he exclaimed. "I'm in a class with Layla. When she told me you were here, I couldn't believe it!"

Their abrupt stop prompted grumbling from those attempting to get past. "Take it to the side, would ya?"

"Follow me," said Jess. She led Sebastian through a series of corridors, and the throng thinned out. "When did you start here?" Jess asked as they walked.

"A few days ago. Moved from Red Deer during the October long weekend. What about you?"

"Started in September."

"This school is gargantuan," said Sebastian as he strolled along with Jess.

"Two thousand students," replied Jess.

"Where are we?"

Jess stopped at a door and tried the knob. "We're in luck," she said as she pulled it open and walked in. "One of the break-out rooms for music practice."

The room was no bigger than a small bedroom with several folding chairs and, against one wall, a keyboard. Sebastian dug his fingers into his hair and smiled broadly.

"I thought you'd like it," said Jess. "What brings you to Calgary?"

Sebastian dropped his backpack on the floor and dragged a chair to the keyboard. "My mom hooked up... again. Actually, she got married this time." He flicked on the switch and adjusted the settings. "What about you?"

"Long story."

Sebastian laughed, "It always is." Jess smiled. Sebastian started to play some chords and looked at Jess. "Come on, come on."

"Don't you have class... or need to eat something?"

"Right now, I have a keyboard. Come on, one song, just one song." He started to play the chords again.

Jess set down her backpack, stood near the keyboard and began to sing, "Five hundred, twenty-one thousand, six hundred minutes...."

~

Ms. Willow Leboucan heard music echoing through the quiet corridor. As she walked down the hall, the music and singing became increasingly vibrant and compelling. From the musical, *Rent*. It was one of her favourites–*The Seasons of Love*. Willow reached the open door and looked in. Both students were oblivious of her presence. Jess, with her head tilted up and her eyes closed, blasted out the song's climax in perfect pitch. "How do you measure a year in the life? How about loooovvvveee?" The pianist, head bent over the keys, was totally absorbed in the moment.

When the song ended, the pianist played a series of chords, saying, "That's what I'm talking about, Jess. Damn, I've missed this."

Willow coughed lightly. Both students spun around and stared at the teacher in the doorway.

"Jess?" said Willow, recognizing her Grade 11 English student.

"Ms. Willow, the door was open.... This is Sebastian. He just moved here. We know each other from another school."

"I see..."

"It's my fault. I–" Sebastian sputtered.

"I think," said Willow, cutting him off, "you should perform at our upcoming *Riverbank Revue*."

"What's the *Riverbank Revue*?" asked Sebastian.

"It's a cross between a talent show and a preview of the spring performances from our drama and choral students," said Willow. "We put on a revue every year, usually in the first week of December."

"I'm in the choral group," said Jess. "We're performing a couple songs, and the drama students are doing a few acts."

"We also insert several performances of students. They may or may not be enrolled in drama or choral," continued Willow.

"But weren't the auditions for the revue over a week ago?" asked Jess.

Willow tilted her head and gazed at Jess. *So, you had been interested,* she thought. "You can consider what I just heard as your audition. I was part of the selection committee with the drama teacher."

Sebastian broke into a wide grin and turned toward Jess. Jess looked down at her feet.

"You can use this room to practice if you like," said Willow. She glanced from Jess to Sebastian. "Come on, you two," she urged. "You could perform this act tonight. It was exceptional."

Sebastian looked at Jess and shrugged with a smile. After a few moments, she slugged Sebastian lightly on the shoulder and said, "Well, okay."

"Meet me here after school," said Willow. "We'll get everything set up with the drama teacher. And lock the door when you leave."

Chapter 3

"He's a new student," said Willow softly as she squatted near the Senior Secretary, June Barnes.

"A few more details would help with the search," June said with a smirk, "such as first name, last name, grade—you know, the minor details."

Willow loved June, quick-witted, competent and accommodating. "First name, Sebastian. And he must be quite new—I've never seen him before."

"You keep track of all two thousand students, do you?"

"You can't miss this kid. Red, curly hair springing out every which way."

June sat up a little straighter, "You're right. He enrolled last week. Can't remember his last name.... Let's see." She pulled up a list of Sebastians. "You're lucky his name isn't among the top ten. Okay, last week's registration... Here he is, Sebastian Miller."

"Thanks, June." Willow gave her a shoulder hug.

"Yeah, yeah, get out of here." As Willow started to walk away, June said, "Don't bother hunting for his file. I doubt we'll see it for another month."

"As a matter of fact, I'm looking up someone else."

"Busy, busy, busy," said June, returning to her work.

~

Willow sat cross-legged in a corner of the room that housed the students' records and opened a file: Jess Gayle. In a class of forty students, Jess was one among many. She had never been a cause of concern nor warranted any particular inquiry. Bright, attentive, punctual with her assignments..., aloof, never contributing to a discussion. Now that Willow thought of it, Jess didn't appear to have any friends, at least not in her classroom. And yet there she was this afternoon, obviously close friends with a dishevelled, gangly teen and hyper-modest about her remarkable musical talent. Who was Jess Gayle?

Jess's school record followed a typical trajectory until middle school. Then absences increased, grades fell, and schools changed frequently. In one two-year period, she transferred to four different schools. Last year in the second term, this trend turned around, and during the past summer, she successfully completed the maximum slate of summer courses. This fall, Jess registered at Riverbank High School as an independent student. Willow flipped through the registration form to the emergency contacts. There was only one: Annisa, a caseworker. Then she saw the flagged alert—a restraining order against her uncle, Rodolfo Tanis.

Willow closed the file and leaned her head against the wall. She taught well over a hundred students per term; two hundred if she included the students in her extra-curricular activities. Who were these kids? Most, like Jess, strolled into class, remained attentive (or a least awake), handed in assignments (sooner or later) and went their way. But who were they? What did they carry to school along with their books? How could she get to know them, really? And if she did, how could she possibly respond to their needs?

Chapter 4

It never got easier, coming to a new school. Mallory Mudford had lost count of the times. Six... eight? It was even tougher after school had started–this time in November. Last night she couldn't sleep, dreading her first day.

Mallory lowered her eyes as she entered the classroom and slid into an empty seat near the back, off to the side. Pretending to glance through the notebook she placed on her desk, Mallory scanned the other students from the corner of her eye. No one seemed to notice her. Success.

This was the biggest school she'd ever attended with the largest classes. Easier to remain unnoticed and yet observe. The classroom was filling up. Friends sat together at small tables that served as desks–two chairs for each table. Amid the hubbub, Mallory noticed another girl enter: tight jacket and jeans; impeccable makeup; large, brown eyes enlarged by liner and mascara; her hair, long, thick, black, chic. She looked like a model and too old to be in high school. A boy near the window elbowed a friend nearby and said to the girl, "Still playing hard-to-get, Jess. The offer's open. Anytime you like."

"Go to hell, Victor."

The girl called Jess continued down the aisle, and Mallory expected her to pass by. Instead, Jess slid onto the chair next to Mallory and pulled a notebook from her pack. Mallory began to doodle.

"You're new here."

Jess's comment caught Mallory off-guard. "Yeah," she replied.

Ms. Willow, their English teacher, walked into the room and rang a chime. The class gradually silenced. Mallory looked up and saw Ms.

Willow looking her way. Instinctively she lowered her head. *Do not introduce me, do not introduce me,* she pleaded internally as she stared at her notebook. Ms. Willow began the class without any introductions, and Mallory breathed a sigh of relief.

Chapter 5

Thursday. The last rehearsal for the *Riverbank Revue* without an audience. Friday afternoon, Riverbank's art classes and a group of students from a neighbouring elementary school would come for the dress rehearsal. And, as customary, the performance would take place that evening on the first Friday in December.

Willow walked into a classroom designated as a holding area for the choral acts. Ever since her chance encounter with Jess and Sebastian in the music room, Willow had kept them on her radar and looked for opportunities to connect. From their records, both appeared to have had erratic attendance and grades in the past, Sebastian more than Jess.

"Sebastian, Jess. Would you give me a hand?"

As they walked down the corridor to the front entrance, Willow said, "The pizzas have arrived. Mrs. Barnes is getting them loaded onto carts at the front door. We need your help to bring them to the auditorium and set them out on tables."

"That means first dibs on the pizza," said Sebastian. "Sounds like a good deal."

"So, what's your favourite?" asked Willow.

"I'm easy—pepperoni," he replied.

"You won't be disappointed. There's plenty of that," replied Willow. Then turning to Jess, "What about you?"

"I'm not too fussy—cheese, I guess. Chinese food is my favourite. I'd go for that any day over pizza."

"What's your favourite Chinese dish?"

"Chicken chow mein."

"Maybe at our next *Revue*, one of the parents will spring for Chinese."

"A parent paid for the pizza?" asked Sebastian.

"Sure did. Since we're rehearsing right after school, one of our parents wanted to make sure you folks had something to eat. Tomorrow another parent is paying for lasagna."

"For real?" said Sebastian.

"Many of you performing, and the staff helping out, aren't able to— or prefer not to—rush home, eat and come straight back. So one of the parents offered to provide dinner so we can remain at the school and relax between the rehearsal and the performance."

As the trio turned into the main entrance, Mrs. Barnes was stacking the last of the pizza delivery onto a cart. "Here you are!" she said cheerfully. "Perfect timing." They each pushed one of the four carts loaded with pizzas, beverages and paper plates to the auditorium and began to unload them onto a row of tables.

As they finished, Willow turned to the two students, "Like you said, Sebastian, first dibs to the assistants. Help yourselves."

"I'll call the other students," said Mrs. Barnes.

Willow, Jess and Sebastian plated their pizzas and walked up a side aisle as the other participants poured through the doors. Something caught Jess's attention. "Check this out." The three gazed at a display of students' art hung on the wall. "There's a girl I sit next to in your class, Ms. Willow," said Jess as she pointed out one of the paintings. "She was making little sketches like this in her notebook. I think it's hers."

"Very cool," remarked Sebastian. "Sorta dark."

"Haunting," said Willow.

"What's her name?" asked Sebastian.

"Mal something," said Jess.

"Mallory," said Willow.

"In my mind, I call her 'Hoodie' because she's always in sweats, a tee and a hoodie, which she pulls over her head."

Willow looked closely at the painting. "You're right, Jess. It's Mallory's. She signed it."

"Yeah, she doesn't talk much, but she draws her reactions to discussions in class," said Jess as they walked to a table. "Kinda like emojis but more detailed. She slides her notebook over for me to see when she's done. They're pretty funny."

As they ate, Willow asked, "Are any of your friends or family coming to the performance?"

"My mom and Max plan on coming," said Sebastian. Then as an afterthought, "Max and my mom got married a couple of months ago."

"What about you, Jess?"

"I had someone–Annisa–who wanted to come, but something unexpected came up, so I'm not sure if she'll be able to make it."

"I hope it works out for her to attend," said Willow. "She'd really enjoy your performance. I'm proud of you both."

Willow's phone chimed, and she looked down at the text. "I have to go. The drama teacher needs me backstage."

Chapter 6

Sebastian stood as he played the final measure. His bushy red hair was pulled back into a small ponytail, his white shirt untucked over dark slacks, the top button undone with a loose necktie, and his sleeves rolled up to his elbows. Sebastian cleaned up nicely for the *Riverbank Revue*. Jess was stunning, from her hair to her makeup to her dress. She blasted through *The Seasons of Love* with the emotion, control and vibrancy of a professional. "How do you measure a year in the life? How about love? Measure in love."

As Sebastian played the last chord, the audience stood and cheered, many dabbing their eyes. Sebastian jumped, his wiry body fist-pumping a "Yes!" He turned toward Jess and clapped with the audience. Jess walked over, took his hand, and raised it up. They bowed together, tears glittering in their eyes. What followed was a blur for both: all the performers out on stage for a final bow, words of gratitude and praise from the principal and drama teacher, bouquets given by the students to their teachers and accompanists, and, backstage, hugs and laughter as the students picked up their belongings and went to join their family and friends in the auditorium or lobby.

～

"You were magnificent, just magnificent," said Sebastian's mother, Stephanie, as Sebastian and Jess walked toward her in the auditorium. She hugged him, kissed both cheeks and hugged him again.

"Mom, this is Jess. And Jess, this is my mom, Stephanie, and Max...

her husband." Jess acknowledged both with a nod and hello.

"Jess, you are a knockout. Just look at you!" said Stephanie, extending her hands. Jess smiled her appreciation. Stephanie turned to Max, "Weren't they marvellous?"

"A knockout," said Max, focusing his attention on Jess. While Stephanie had been gushing about the performance, Max had been eyeing Jess, a gesture lost on Stephanie but not on Jess. Her smile hardened into a glare.

"I've got to be going," said Jess. "See you tomorrow, Sebastian."

Jess walked up the side aisle of the auditorium toward the lobby. Friends and families were gathered in small groups, offering bouquets, taking photos and chatting animatedly about the show. A man broke away from a nearby gathering and approached Jess, extending his hand. "Congratulations! Your performance was astounding!"

"Thank you," said Jess hesitantly as she shook his hand.

"Are you taking voice lessons?"

"No, I just like to sing."

"Jess, Jess, over here." Jess looked up and saw Willow at the auditorium doors.

"Ms. Willow is calling me," said Jess and, with a quickened pace, went to meet her teacher.

"So, I see you've met Mr. Jarod Edgar... or was it Jarrett? Something like that."

"He said he liked the performance."

"He's quite the glad-hander."

Willow and Jess continued to watch the young man as he moved toward a side exit and encountered a family group blocking the way. "Wait. Let's see if he does it," Willow said with a wink. "Here it comes... Out goes his right hand and... the handshake... with his other hand smoothing his curly hair... done!" Jess and Willow smiled, suppressing their laughs. "I watched him with you, and he did the same thing with me."

"Who is he?"

"I just met him tonight when I was congratulating the drama teacher. His aunt's at the Central Office. She and the drama teacher used to work together. She's probably around here somewhere meeting up with other teachers she knows." Willow turned to Jess and handed her a bouquet, "You were outstanding."

"They're beautiful," said Jess smiling. "Thanks."

"Gerbera daisies, my favourite. Such bold, bright colours." Then scanning the room, Willow said, "Did Annisa come?"

"No." Jess looked down. "Annisa *was* my caseworker, but she's not anymore."

"I'm so sorry to hear that," said Willow.

"Yeah. She was really looking forward to my performance. But then, she called a couple of weeks ago. Got a job in Vancouver—program manager for a shelter... something to do with housing, I don't know. It all happened very quickly."

"When is she moving?"

"Sometime soon. Annisa told me she had to fly to Vancouver this morning for meetings and would look for an apartment while she was there. Then she was returning to pack. My new caseworker is a woman called Paige. I haven't met her yet."

"Oh, Jess, Annisa would have been so proud. You and Sebastian are quite a duo."

"Yeah, well," Jess stammered.

"You have a gift, Jess; an exceptional gift. You sing from the soul." Noticing Jess's discomfort with her praise, she said, "It's late. Let me give you a ride home."

"I can take the bus."

"I'm driving Mrs. Barnes home—her car broke down this morning. You remember her from yesterday, right? The carts with the pizzas?"

"Oh, yes."

"So I can drop you off as well. Where exactly do you live?"

Jess gave the address.

"No problem at all. It's right on the way. I'll drop you off first." Willow pushed open the auditorium doors, "Just wait near the office. I'll be there in a minute."

When Willow met Jess at the office, she handed her a white sack. "I picked this up before the performance—it's been in the staff refrigerator. Chicken chow mein—your favourite."

"How did you know?—Oh, yesterday I told you."

"I pay attention," she said, raising an eyebrow. "Just give it a zap in the microwave."

"God... thanks, Ms. Willow."

"Here comes Mrs. Barnes now. You've probably seen her in the office; she's one of the school secretaries.... Mrs. Barnes, you remember

Jess," said Willow.

"Of course," Mrs. Barnes smiled. "And I'll never forget you after your performance tonight. Well done!"

"Do you live here?" Jess teased. "You're always around."

"Sometimes it feels like it," Mrs. Barnes laughed. "But no. I help out with the drama and choral productions. And if you ever need anything from the office–transcripts, class registrations, whatever–come see me."

"Thanks," said Jess.

"Jess is on our bus route, June. She's coming along for the ride."

Chapter 7

Sebastian climbed into the backseat of the truck. Stephanie turned around in the front passenger seat and smiled at him. "I knew from the time you were five that you were a musician," she gushed as Max pulled out of the school parking lot. "The hours you spent playing jingles on that little keyboard I got you."

"Yeah," said Sebastian. He remembered the occasion a little differently. A family, moving out of the apartment next door, couldn't fit all their belongings into their rental trailer. They left behind a keyboard and several other items, most of which Stephanie appropriated with the help of her young son. But with his mother in such high spirits, he wasn't going to squabble over details.

"I remember you, around eight or nine, borrowing my phone so you could learn to play piano from videos you found online." Stephanie laughed at the memory.

Max shifted in his seat as he drove on.

"Now, look at you! The grand finale! And a standing ovation!"

Max slammed on the accelerator to cut through a yellow light. Stephanie stiffened and gripped her door handle.

Directing her attention to Max, Stephanie continued, "And you enjoy Sebastian when he's on the keyboard, Max. You've told me he has an ear for music."

"There are a lot of people who have an ear for music," said Max. "And once I get the sound system installed, we'll be streaming in *professional* music."

Sebastian crouched lower in the backseat behind his mother.

"So," asked Max, "when are you going to bring your jingling little fingers into my shop?" He reached up and positioned his rearview mirror to view Sebastian in the back seat. Sebastian made no reply. Max raised his voice, "I'm talking to you!"

"I don't know... I have school work to catch up on."

"But you have time to 'jingle' away on the keyboard." Sebastian remained silent, and his mother looked out the window. "When I was your age, I spent every spare moment I had in a shop down the road from my home. And look at me now: I own my shop, and I'm the boss of five employees. Music doesn't put food on the table."

"Plenty of musicians make money from music," Sebastian muttered.

"What was that?" yelled Max. Both Stephanie and Sebastian jumped at the sudden outburst. "Speak up if you have something to say."

"Musicians make money."

"Yeah, some do. But you'll never be one of them," Max scoffed. "Learning how to play from some old windbag online, my God." In the darkness, Max couldn't see the flush surging from Sebastian's neck to his face.

"Sebastian's had a late start to school with the move and all," said Stephanie cautiously, her previous enthusiasm vaporized. "He'll be at your shop after Christmas."

"He better be," said Max. "I'm not about to give him a free ride." Then glaring at Sebastian in the rearview mirror, "I hope you're paying attention, Jingle Fingers."

Chapter 8

On Monday, Sebastian strolled into English class and dropped into a seat. A small group of classmates began to clap. "Woo-hoo!" "Way to go last Friday." A couple of girls walked over to him and introduced themselves. "You were A-mazing!" "When did you learn to play like that?"

Sebastian blushed with all the attention and joshed with the students who surrounded him, "Well, it all started when I was six months old, and I was listening to Mozart, and I thought to myself—"

A small group of guys, standing together at the rear of the classroom, looked over at Sebastian and laughed at some remark one of them had made.

Sebastian and the rest of the class turned toward the boys, still snickering. "What?" demanded Sebastian.

"Victor, let's go," said one in the group, moving toward the door. "We have to get to our class." Then he walked out.

Victor remained with the other boys. "Oh, have we upset Mr. Pi-a-no Man?" he mocked.

Mrs. Flint, the English teacher, walked in, "Good morning. Seats everyone." Victor slipped out the door. A remaining teen from the group took his seat behind Sebastian and whispered with a smirk, "Mr. Pi-a-no Man."

Sebastian turned around and yelled, "Fuck you!"

"What was that?" exclaimed Mrs. Flint. "We don't use that kind of language in this classroom. Now apologize!"

Sebastian glanced at the students who had just congratulated him, now staring, stunned and serious. He turned toward the boy behind him, who opened his eyes wide in feigned innocence, then at Mrs. Flint, simmering with disapproval. "Fuck you, too, bitch," he shouted as he grabbed his backpack and strode out of the classroom.

~

"I don't understand it," said Willow, "I've worked with Sebastian—he's... hilarious, vivacious..., just a great kid."

"Well, Mrs. Flint refuses to have him in her classroom," said the principal, Frida Quinn. "She's of the opinion that, with his blatant lack of respect, he needs some sort of serious consequence. An apology, according to her, is merely a perfunctory gesture; his outburst was uncalled for and uncouth—her words. She thinks he's become cocky because of his performance and needs to be brought down a notch."

"Sweet Jesus. So what does she propose?"

"Other than removal from her class? Not much."

"And you?"

"I would like to see a calm conversation with Sebastian to find out what happened and go from there."

Willow rubbed her forehead. "If he joins my class, he'll be in a higher level English course."

"I could lean on Flint," said Frida, "Sebastian is her student. But with her current mindset, I doubt he'll succeed in her class."

"I'll take him.... Where is he? I'd like to chat with him or set up a time to talk later if he's not up to it right now."

"That might be hard today," replied the principal. "Sebastian took off after he left Flint's class."

"Crap! No, wait. I have his contact number—I needed it for rehearsals. I'll reread his file after school and try to set up something for him tomorrow morning."

"Thanks, Willow."

"You owe me."

"As always," said Frida as she walked away.

Chapter 9

Mallory breathed more easily. Despite her mid-semester move, she was soon on par with her classmates. She faded into the massive throng that hustled from one class to the next, just one student among hundreds and hundreds jostling through the high school's labyrinth of corridors. She knew every entrance, emergency exit door, and bathroom. And she had discovered a quiet niche under a back stairway where she could eat her lunch in peace. No one had used this staircase since she had begun hanging out there. Until today.

The doors from the hallway swung open and slammed shut. "Layla, my God, what's the problem?"

"Jess, it's Sebastian. He lost it today."

"What do you want me to do about it?"

Mallory pushed her back against the wall behind the stairs and froze. There was a slit in the staircase where the metal step didn't meet the backplate. Mallory could see two girls standing near the staircase doors. She recognized Jess from her English class but had never seen the other girl. She was slight and sallow-skinned; her hair, straight and dyed jet black; her ears peppered with piercings; her dark clothes draped around her.

"He listens to you! You know he listens to you," Layla insisted.

"Christ!" Jess leaned against the cement wall. She sighed, "What happened?"

"There's this guy—he was bugging Sebastian about playing the piano. Then Sebastian tells this other kid to fuck-off. Then the teacher got on Sebastian for swearing, and he called her a fucking bitch and took off."

"Layla, hold on. I'm not really following."

Layla tried explaining the sequence of events again.

"Okay, okay. Just stop. The main thing is, Sebastian told the teacher to fuck-off and left class."

"Yeah, I guess," said Layla.

Moments went by in silence. Mallory barely breathed.

"I'll try to find him after school. Damn—and I got a paper due."

"You want me to come?"

"Yeah, sure. I'll meet you at the main entrance."

The door slammed. Mallory shifted and started again on her sandwich. Then she heard the boots walking toward the stairwell.

Jess poked her head around the back of the ascending staircase. "Oh, it's you."

To Mallory's surprise, Jess sat down next to her, rummaged through her backpack and pulled out a granola bar. "Nice spot."

"I find one in every school."

"In every school?" Jess said with a laugh. "How many are you talking about?"

Mallory stopped to calculate. "Six... maybe more. Hard to keep track."

"Christ! I think you topped me. Are your parents travelling preachers or something?"

Mallory giggled softly. "No. My dad's an electrician. We just move around in Calgary."

After a few moments, Mallory asked, "Who's the guy you were talking about?"

"Did you come to the *Riverbank Revue?*"

"My art class went to the dress rehearsal."

"The redheaded guy I sang with—he's Sebastian."

"How do you know him so well?"

"We lived together for a while."

"With your family?"

Jess said nothing for a few moments, nibbling at her granola bar. "We lived together in a group home. Layla's still there."

"What's a group home?"

Jess gave Mallory a sideways look. "Where kids go when their families are fucked up."

"Oh..." For a while, they ate silently.

"So," asked Jess, "why did you move around so much if your dad has always worked in Calgary?"

Mallory shrugged.

"Your mom must be sick of all the packing and unpacking."

"She's not in the picture."

"My mom died, too," said Jess gently.

Mallory finished off the last of her sandwich. Although she and Jess didn't hang around together during school, an unspoken bond had been growing between them. Since the day Mallory arrived three weeks ago, they had sat next to each other in Ms. Willow's English class. Whoever got there first placed their backpack on the adjacent chair until the other arrived.

"My mom didn't die," Mallory said softly. "She took off... when I was a baby."

"Sorry," said Jess. Then turning toward Mallory, "If you were a baby, how do you know she took off?"

Mallory looked quizzically at Jess, "My dad told me."

"Oh," Jess said casually. "Well, welcome to the 'fucked-up family' club." She shifted onto her knees, "I've got to go."

"Me, too."

Both crawled out from behind the staircase into the stairwell.

"Is that guy going to be okay?" asked Mallory.

"Sebastian? Yeah. I'll find him after school."

Chapter 10

Sebastian pounded on the keyboard. When no one was home, he blasted the volume, obliterating every thought, allowing the raw emotion of his music to course through his being.

"You're home early," said Stephanie.

Sebastian was unaware of his mother at his door, her words drowned out by the music. She walked to the side of the keyboard. Sebastian lurched, surprised, then lowered the volume. "You're home early," she repeated.

Sebastian continued to play. Rarely did he enter the house before seven p.m., studying at the library or hanging out at a store that sold musical instruments. His mom always came home with Max after the shop closed, never by herself, and he had intended to be long gone before they arrived.

"I was feeling a little light-headed, so I came home," said Sebastian. "I had something to eat, and I'm feeling better. What about you?"

"I have to pick up something for Max."

"Yeah, well, I'll be leaving soon. Need to meet up with some friends."

"Why don't you stay and do a workout with us when we come home? You can blow off some steam. Might help you feel better."

Sebastian played on. "That's your thing, Mom, not mine." His mom was a fitness buff. If music was his drug of choice, body-building and beauty was his mother's. Her *Ima-gram* account was strewn with selfies highlighting her sculpted physique; her coifed hair dyed in her latest hue; her makeup, dramatic; her nails manicured, both fingers and toes. In between relationships, she had eked out a living in beauty salons. Her dream was to become a fitness coach with a popular blog that would bring her financial security—wealth if she was lucky. It was at a fitness conference that she had met Max. He was a weightlifter with a well-equipped gym in his basement: a match made in heaven, she had told her son.

"And," continued Sebastian, adjusting his settings as he played with one hand, "I'm not working at the auto shop. I hate the damn place."

"Sebastian, it won't be forever," said Stephanie, fretting. "You can get a scholarship, go to music school.... It would only be for a year or two."

"Yeah, if I don't succumb to the exhaust fumes before then." For a few moments, music filled the silence between them. "Do you really like the work you do for Max? Answering the phone, trying to keep that grubby reception area presentable... scrubbing the bathrooms?" While he waited for a response, he played the "Jeopardy" theme song.

Stephanie shifted her weight to one leg and stared at her son.

"I didn't think so." Sebastian struck up another tune. "And how much do you get paid?"

"I'm married, for God's sake."

"So you don't have your own money. You have to ask Max for everything."

"We work as a team... and you have to pull your weight, too."

Sebastian hit a dissonant chord, and the music ceased. He turned to his mother. "Oh, is that in the prenup agreement? I work for nothing at the auto shop for the privilege of living with Max?"

Stephanie looked out the window.

"I'm going to Dad's place."

"You know he's in jail."

"He might have been released early."

"Not likely. But if he is and you do track him down, you'll be back in a group home in a month."

Sebastian had always felt closer to his dad; he was more affectionate than his mother, and they shared a passion for music. During his childhood, Sebastian had had a few stints living with his dad, but, unlike his mother, his father could not kick his drug addiction. Sebastian always landed back with his mom. A couple of years ago, Sebastian had located his father and run away, only to be apprehended some months later when his dad was arrested for dealing drugs. Sebastian had stayed at a group home for several months while he and his mom completed a family reintegration program. She was single again, compromises were made, apologies exchanged, and Sebastian returned to his mother. Her "welcome home" gift was the keyboard. Then over the summer, she met Max. Within three months, they were wed.

"Mom, I offered to help out around the house—shovel snow, mow the lawn—but Max won't let me do anything unless 'it's under his direct supervision.' You were there; you heard him. And he's always putting me down."

"Oh, he just likes to tease."

"I'm not working at the shop, Mom. I'm not working with Muscle Max."

"Sebastian, this is the best relationship I've ever had... Max has his own business...." Her voice was becoming frantic. "Have we ever lived in a house like this?" Then the pleading stopped, and her tone chilled, as Sebastian knew it would. "You're going to be out of here in a couple of years. Don't blow it for me."

Sebastian turned off his keyboard and grabbed his coat and backpack. "I'll be back later."

Chapter 11

Jess walked out of the school's main entrance to the broad sidewalk that ran the length of the school. She looked in both directions as other students scurried past. The sharp north wind bit into her thighs, covered only by her leggings. *Layla, where are you?* She whipped her pack around and reached in for a pair of gloves. The temperate weather the Chinook had blown in yesterday was gone. It would be bitterly cold tonight.

"You're Jess! The girl who performed 'Seasons of Love,' right? I came to the show!"

Jess startled. She hadn't seen the woman approach.

"I'm meeting someone today at the school. So happy I saw you on my way in. I'm Lena Lugine." Jess continued to pull on her gloves. "I work for a firm in Toronto. Here in Alberta, I circulate among the schools, choral groups, and dance studios looking to support fresh talent." Lena pulled out a card. "Here's my information. You can check out the website."

"Okay," said Jess, hesitating before taking the card.

"You gave an outstanding performance. Just amazing for someone your age. Look over our website and, if you want to talk further, give me a call. We could have coffee together."

"Yeah, maybe," Jess flipped over the card. "You use *AppChat?*"

"Yes. From experience, I know that most teens use *AppChat*, and their parents often use *YouApp,* so I wrote both of my handles on the back of the card. And it's easier to contact me that way. Well, I've got to be going."

As Jess pocketed the card, she watched Lena head toward the school's main entrance amid the tide of departing students.

"Jess, over here!" Jess turned and caught sight of Layla walking towards her from a side entrance. She hustled to meet her, eager to get on a bus and out of the cold.

~

Jess and Layla stood together on the city bus, hemmed in by restless students. "Where do you suppose he went?" asked Layla. "To the mall?"

"Maybe." Jess jolted and gave a sharp jab with her elbow to a guy who had just brushed his hand against her thigh. He winked at her and maneuvered further into the bus.

"Bastard!" Jess hissed. "We're getting off at the next stop."

"To shake off that creep?"

"No. There'll just be another one on the next bus.... Before we go to the mall, I want to check out that store, *Strum 'n Drum*. Sebastian's mentioned it."

The girls walked through the store entrance to a cacophony of twangs, strums, glides and drumbeats. A plethora of guitars, electric and acoustic, lined the walls and enlivened the displays of drum sets and amps that formed the centre aisle. Several people, assisted by sales reps, checked out the instruments. Jess and Layla scanned the room.

"You looking for something in particular?" asked a bearded, middle-aged man in a cowboy hat.

"Keyboards," said Jess.

"On the other side." He indicated a wide passage that led to another section of the store. This area was notably quieter. Keyboards, banjos, ukuleles, harmonicas and smaller percussion instruments were featured around the room. At a front counter, a sales rep was busy with a mother and her two children. Near the back of the room, red hair springing around a headset, sat Sebastian playing a keyboard.

"Score!" said Jess.

Until Jess and Layla were standing directly in front of the keyboard, Sebastian remained lost in his music. When he looked up, Jess pretended to speak without making a sound. Sebastian pulled off his headset. "You gonna let us hear some of that music?" she asked.

Sebastian shrugged. He unplugged the headset, lowered the volume and continued to play.

"So, tough day at school."

"Layla filled you in, I see."

"Victor's an asshole," said Layla, "and so are the idiots who hang around with him."

"They're all fucking bastards," muttered Sebastian.

"What happened, exactly?" asked Jess.

Sebastian leaned back from the keyboard and gestured emphatically as he related the event. Layla filled in the details while Jess reminded them to keep their voices down.

Sebastian, calm when they arrived, now breathed heavily and resumed playing.

"The dickhead is jealous," said Jess. "He set you up."

"I'm not going back to that bitch's class," he said.

"You don't go back to school, they'll call your mom," said Jess. "You want her involved?" Jess and Layla exchanged a glance.

"I'll go with you, Sebastian," said Layla. "I saw it all…. I'll get there early, meet you at the office."

All the while, Sebastian continued to play. Layla and Jess waited a few moments.

Jess moved around the front of the keyboard to Sebastian's side and gently tapped his shoulder. "So, what are you gonna do?"

"I'll be there," he muttered.

Jess stood behind him, lightly punching his arms. Then lifting up his hands, she playfully brought them up and down on the keys.

Sebastian laughed, "Get lost." He plugged in his headset and resumed playing.

As they left, Layla and Jess waved to the sales rep. "Sebastian sell you a keyboard?" he asked.

"Almost," said Jess.

"Come in again when that guy's here, and you won't be able to walk out without one."

Chapter 12

Mallory put her plate in the sink and scraped the leftover spaghetti into a container. "Fucked-up family club." The phrase looped over and over in her mind like an annoying earworm. She opened the fridge and made a space for the leftovers. Mallory ate alone for most meals. Her dad, Ryder Mudford, was an electrician working for an electrical contractor at construction sites throughout the city. The time he came home from work varied, depending on overtime, errands or a workout at the gym. When her dad did arrive, he had already eaten, or he warmed up leftovers and ate as he streamed a show on his computer. Mallory had never given much thought to their staid, daily ritual. It was what it was, like the frequent moves and his shifting moods. Was this the fucked-up part Jess was talking about?

It hadn't always been this way. After they moved from Newfoundland, Mallory remembered trips to the zoo and movies in the theatre. There had been walks to the playground, tobogganing in the snow, and hot chocolate when they came home. She was his little girl. No mom or pictures of mom. Mallory had no memories of her; her mother—"shallow and fickle," according to her dad—had walked out on them. It had been years since she had even been mentioned.

Life in Newfoundland was murky except for one vivid memory. Mallory had just turned five and was wearing the bright blue dress she had received from her grandmother on her birthday. With their belongings packed and loaded, Mallory crawled into the backseat, crammed amongst the boxes and bags. As her dad drove off to Alberta, Mallory had unlatched her seatbelt and pressed her face against the side window, watching her grandmother on the sidewalk grow smaller and smaller until she disappeared altogether.

"The fucked-up family club." Jess's comment was made without judgment, more as a matter of fact, something they had in common. Nonetheless, it rattled Mallory's complacent acceptance of her reality. Yeah, she and her dad moved a lot, but there was always a reason: cheaper rent, crappy neighbours, better housing. Every move, however, meant a different school; that was the tough bit. Her dad never rented within the same neighbourhood. Then a memory, long suppressed, surfaced with such abruptness that Mallory found herself wiping tears from her cheeks.

~

At the end of Grade 4, Ryder moved into a new neighbourhood, and Mallory was placed in a day camp for the summer. That's where she met Grace Belcourt. Like Mallory, Grace enjoyed drawing, painting and crafting. Organized sports were merely tolerated. Although both were initially shy, by the end of summer, they were, as a camp counsellor remarked, "joined at the hips." Grace was Mallory's first real friend, and when the girls found out they were going to the same school for Grade 5, they jumped and screamed.

~

"Grace! Mallory! Your parents are here," announced the after-school attendant. The girls dropped what they were doing and walked out to the school lobby. "You two as well," the attendant said to Grace's younger brothers.

Ryder and Mrs. Belcourt often arrived at the same time to pick up their children. As they waited for them to put on their jackets and gather their backpacks, Mrs. Belcourt said, "Just look at Grace and Mallory—kids grow up so fast at their age."

"Yeah, it's hard to believe this will be Mallory's last year in an after-school program."

"I still have the two younger boys.... I'm trying to find a part-time job in the morning, so I don't need child care."

"Good luck with that."

A couple weeks later, as Mallory and Ryder were leaving the after-school program, Mrs. Belcourt came bounding toward the door.

"I thought I'd be late for pickup. Let's see—five minutes to spare!"

"I know the feeling," laughed Ryder.

"By the way, I got the job. This is the last week of after-school care."

"Congratulations!"

Mrs. Belcourt made a move toward the door but paused. "I've been thinking—I mean, it's completely up to you—but I would be happy to watch Mallory after school, and you could pick her up at my place. The girls get along so well."

"How much are you charging?" asked Ryder hesitantly.

"Nothing! You would be doing me a favour. Mallory and Grace will be occupied together, and I can concentrate on the boys and dinner."

Mallory's eyes widen with surprise. She had been so disappointed when she heard she wouldn't have Grace to play with after school.

"I know I'm springing this on you," said Mrs. Belcourt. "Don't feel you have to answer one way or the other. But if you are interested, give me a call. If you like, you and Mallory can come for supper and check out our place. I'll give you my number."

"I'll think about it," said Ryder after typing the information into his phone.

Driving home, Mallory said nothing; she knew pleading irritated her father. After a few blocks, Ryder asked, "Would you like to stay with Grace after school?"

"Yeah. She's fun to play with," said Mallory, keeping her voice even.

"It would also save me a bundle," he muttered.

Savings alone would not have been enough to persuade Ryder to consider the offer. An unexpected development at work tipped the scales. His boss won a bid for several townhouses that another electrical contractor had abandoned. Ryder was offered the project with his choice of two apprentices. To complete the townhouse project on time required ten-hour days. Flexibility with Mallory's evening pickup was necessary.

"You know, Mallory, this could work," her dad said at last. He explained the project he'd been asked to head. "My hours will be longer while I complete the project, but after this job, I could be promoted to lead hand! And then foreman!"

And so it was decided. Ryder opted out of the dinner invitation, but he and Mallory stopped by to meet the Belcourts and tour their home. Mr. Belcourt, home from the oil fields for a few days, shook hands with

Ryder. "I've heard so many good things about Mallory. Seems like we have a win-win situation regarding after-school care."

"I appreciate that, but I would like to give you something."

"There's no need," said Mrs. Belcourt. "However, if you want to do something, just bring a bag of apples or oranges every week. That will be plenty." She paused. "And if you need an early morning drop-off, Mallory is welcome here as well."

"No, no, that's fine. For the mornings, she'll continue to use the daycare at the school."

~

As much as Mallory liked Grace, she began the new arrangement tentatively. The after-school program was an equal playing field; now, she was on Grace's turf. Gradually her apprehensions faded. The Belcourts were relaxed and welcoming. At times, even the younger brothers vied for Mallory's attention. Mallory was fascinated by a hideaway desk in the main living area that housed the arts and crafts materials, a treasure trove that kept Grace and her busy for hours. Until the snow fell, there were scooters and bikes and a backyard where they could kick around a ball. The family had plenty of board games and, of course, video games— rationed by the half-hours.

One day when Grace and Mallory were busy at the crafting desk, her younger brothers began squabbling over the Lego structures they were constructing. Grace's mom was helping her dad with a plumbing problem in a bathroom upstairs. Grace stomped over to the boys, trying to resolve the issue by out-shouting them. Grace's intervention only exacerbated the situation—Lego were flying across the room, the boys were yelling at each other, and Grace was stomping her feet and raising her voice to get their attention. Mallory watched in stunned silence, but when Grace's father came hollering down the stairs, she froze.

"What the hell is going on down here?"

All three children yelled out their responses together.

"Grace," he bellowed, "do the Lego concern you? I thought you had other things to do!"

"But, Dad—"

"No buts. This does not concern you," he barked. "Go back to your crafts."

Turning to the boys, he said sternly, "Now what's the problem here?" and he began to sort out the disagreement.

Grace returned to the craft desk and resumed her project, muttering, "Stupid brothers. You're lucky you don't have any."

Within minutes the Lego warriors had come to a truce, and Grace's dad went back upstairs. The boys went about their play; Grace, her art. Only Mallory remained on edge.

"Is that it?" she whispered to Grace.

"What do you mean?" said Grace, confused.

Mallory shrugged and continued her work but could not dismiss a sense of foreboding. In time, Grace's mom and dad came downstairs. While her mom prepared supper on the kitchen island, her dad sat on the floor near a heap of Lego, put together a car and raced it with his boys. It really was over. No brooding silences that lingered hours—or days—when Mallory disappointed her father. Grace's family was a whole new world.

~

Mallory's dad and his team finished their work on the townhouses at the beginning of December. The general contractor was impressed with the results. He offered Ryder's boss a similar project which, again, was given to Ryder. The new project was estimated to finish in late February. So Mallory was with the Belcourts all day during the Christmas break. And during this period, she discovered a new passion: cooking.

Grace and Mallory were at the kitchen island painting with watercolours. Across from them, Mrs. Belcourt was chopping vegetables for a chilli dish. Grace was bent over her artwork, but Mallory was intent on the food prep.

Noticing Mallory's attentiveness, Mrs. Belcourt asked, "Would you like to help?"

Mallory smiled and joined Mrs. Belcourt. Hands washed, an apron donned, a cutting board and knife laid out, and Mallory was on her way. During the Christmas break, with Mrs. Belcourt's encouragement, she ventured into grilled cheese sandwiches and spaghetti, lettuce salad and hard-boiled eggs, pancakes and oatmeal. The most magical moment happened when the cupcakes she helped bake were cooling on racks, and Mrs. Belcourt pulled out a frosting decorating kit. Mallory was mesmerized. All the kids were given a few cupcakes to decorate. Mallory waited until after Mrs. Belcourt demonstrated a few designs that could be fashioned from just one tip and then made her first attempts. The frosting was wobbly and uneven, with some globs hanging off the sides, but Mallory was hooked.

When school resumed, Grace and Mallory continued their after-school activities together, but once Mrs. Belcourt began to prep in the kitchen, Mallory was at her side. Sometimes Grace joined in, but generally, she worked on her crafts or played a video game at the island, joining in the conversation as Mallory and Mrs. Belcourt cooked.

Ryder's busy schedule didn't leave father and daughter much time for leisure. But Ryder, happy at his job and anticipating a promotion, and Mallory, content in the Belcourt family, eased any inconveniences. At the end of February, the townhouse project was complete. Back at the worksite as part of the regular crew, Ryder was commended for his work, given a modest bonus, "but not a damn mention of a promotion."

~

It was early March, and today, as planned, Mallory would make chilli by herself. She and Grace raced home after school, urging Mrs. Belcourt and the boys to hurry up. Once inside, Mallory set to work. Mrs. Belcourt coached from the sidelines, and Grace sat at the island with her sketchpad drawing up a certificate. Mallory chopped the vegetables, browned the ground beef, opened cans and combined all the ingredients in a pot, carefully measuring the spices. Soon the chilli was bubbling away, with Mallory stirring it attentively.

In time, Mrs. Belcourt sampled a spoonful. "I couldn't have made it better myself," she said, giving Mallory a hug.

Grace came over for a sample. "Yep, it tastes just like yours, Mom."

Though Mallory didn't say much, she glowed in her accomplishment. "I better get ready before my dad comes."

Shortly after, the doorbell rang. As usual, Ryder stood in the doorway and exchanged greetings while Mallory quickly slipped into her boots and grabbed her coat and backpack. Before they turned to go, Mrs. Belcourt said, "Your daughter is quite the chef. Today she made dinner all by herself! I have some put aside for you and Mallory."

Mallory glanced at her father. There it was, for the first time in months: the glint in his eyes and the tightened jaw. And then, gone. It was so fleeting, Mallory wondered if she had imagined it. Yet, she felt suddenly on edge.

"Thanks," he said graciously as he accepted the covered bowl of chilli. "Let's go, Mallory."

On the ride home, Mallory sat silently in the back seat. Although hectic, these months had been the happiest of her life: she had a friend—a whole family of friends— and a place to laugh, play, and learn to cook. She didn't want to do anything to upset her dad and her life.

"So, you made dinner for the Belcourts," Ryder said blandly.

"Yes, but Mrs. Belcourt was watching the whole time. She's teaching me how to cook."

"I should have known she wanted you for a maid," he said brusquely.

"Oh, no, Dad. I wanted—"

"My food isn't good enough for you?"

"It's good. I just like cooking. It's fun."

When they arrived home, Ryder popped a frozen dinner in the microwave and left the chilli for Mallory. Life resumed as before. Whatever had riled Ryder had flared up and dissipated.

～

Spring break was late that year, toward the end of April. Mrs. Belcourt promised Mallory and Grace that during their week from school, they could each decorate a cake. For the first few days, they drew up their designs and practiced with various frosting tips on the bottom of cake pans. On the last day of the break, they baked two cakes and, in the afternoon, set to work. As Mallory was applying her finishing touches, the doorbell rang. Ryder walked in and stood by the door.

"Oh, Ryder, you have to see what the girls have done!" said Mrs. Belcourt.

Mallory and Grace were standing side-by-side, the younger brothers leaning over the kitchen island to watch the completion of the cake art. Mrs. Belcourt squeezed the girls' shoulders and praised their creations; both girls beamed.

Mallory tilted up her cake, "Dad, come and see!" she exclaimed. But as she looked up, she saw the determined glint, the tightened jaw.

"I can see it just fine from here," he said coolly. "Hurry now; we have to get home." All activity paused. The joy emanating from the decorators and their admirers iced over. Even the younger brothers turned toward Ryder, perplexed.

Mallory rinsed her hands quickly while Mrs. Belcourt made small talk to lighten the mood.

Ryder gave a brief nod toward Mrs. Belcourt as Mallory scooted past him with her jacket and backpack, and he shut the door.

"God, that woman is beginning to annoy me," said Ryder in the truck. "What does she want? Another daughter?" He began to mimic her, squealing, "'Look what the girls have done!' A fucking phony."

Mallory brushed away a tear and swallowed hard to keep others from falling.

Nothing more was said about the cake decorating, but an aura of uncertainty left Mallory off-balanced. When her dad made a comment, was it merely an observation, or was he being sarcastic? Did that smile at the cashier indicate her dad's appreciation, or was it a cap on a volley of complaints that would explode when they brought their groceries to the truck? At home, Mallory spoke less than usual, afraid to set off her dad and entrench the deepening gloom. Even ordinary, everyday remarks could trigger a rebuff. Yet, saying nothing could also prompt a reprimand.

One day, attempting to break the silence, Mallory said, "I got 'excellent' on a story I wrote."

"Oh, and did Mrs. Belcourt give you a big gold star?" said her father dismissively. "You always get excellent for writing. We'll celebrate when you get published." He paused and flashed her a smile, "Wouldn't that be something. The father of an author."

In the subsequent weeks, Ryder chatted pleasantly with Mrs. Belcourt for the couple of minutes it took Mallory to gather her things and depart. The cool indifference he had shown toward the cake decorating project was never repeated. However, in the truck, he'd make snide remarks about something Mrs. Belcourt said or what she wore, the mess the two boys had made, or the daft expression on Grace's face—"Is she backward or challenged? They should have her checked out."

~

"Someone's birthday is coming up next Tuesday," Mrs. Belcourt said as they walked home one Friday afternoon. "If the weather keeps up like today, we might be able to have the party outside."

Mallory's birthday was the following Tuesday in the last week of May. When Grace's two brothers had celebrated their birthdays, they came home to a special "snack" that the celebrant had chosen—for one, tacos; the other, hamburgers. And a decorated cake, of course.

"What are you going to have for your birthday snack, Mallory?" asked Grace.

Mallory laughed. This would be her first real birthday party. "Hmmm," she said. "Chocolate cake with butterscotch ice cream!"

"And how should I decorate the cake?" asked Mrs. Belcourt.

Mallory thought a moment. "Like a kitchen counter!"

That Saturday, Mallory woke with a start to a loud beeping from the rear of the house. Dazed, she walked to the kitchen window that faced the alley. Dread, then numbness pervaded her being. The large plastic containers they used for moving were stacked in the kitchen. Most of the cabinets were open and empty, already packed. From the window, she saw her dad directing a rental truck as it backed toward their yard.

Mallory was standing in the same spot, looking blankly out the window, when a young guy from work and her dad walked in. "Go pack your things. We're moving."

On Monday, the day before her birthday, Mallory was enrolled in a new school. That evening her dad lectured her on home-alone safety and gave her a house key. She never saw the Belcourts again.

~

Mallory sat in the dark kitchen, weeping into the crook of her elbow. *Yes,* she thought, *"fucked up" summarizes it quite nicely.*

Chapter 13

After her last class before Christmas break, Willow called over Jess and her new student, Sebastian. "So, what are you up to over the holidays?"

They looked at each other. "Not much," replied Jess.

"Same here," said Sebastian.

"Well, enjoy your break," said Willow. "Before you leave school, I'd like you to stop by the office and ask for Mrs. Barnes. She has a couple of gift cards for you. Take it easy, and I'll see you in the New Year."

"Ah... thanks," said Jess nonchalantly.

"Yeah, thanks," said Sebastian as they walked out of the classroom. When they reached the door, Sebastian turned and said, "Merry Christmas, Ms. Willow."

~

After their visit to the school office, Jess and Sebastian walked to the back staircase, sat on the bottom steps, and opened their envelopes.

"What did you get?" asked Sebastian.

"Let's see...," said Jess. "Gift card for groceries–fifty dollars! Woo-hoo! And a gift card for the cinema! What about you?"

Sebastian glanced at his cards, "The same."

"Sweet," said Jess.

"Yeah," said Sebastian. "This is a first."

"So, what are you doing for Christmas?"

"Max got invited to a lodge for a week of sledding–something to do with an uncle in British Columbia. So, we're having an early dinner on

Christmas Eve, and then he's driving off, thank God. He's even closing his fucking shop from Christmas to New Year's, if you can believe that. It'll be great to have him gone. Wish it was permanent.... Do you have anything up?"

"On the Sunday before Christmas, the Youth Foundation has something planned—you know, for those of us from the group home who don't have any relatives. Dinner in one of their conference rooms with some of the staff. That's it."

"Want to get together for Christmas?" suggested Sebastian. "We could go to a movie together."

The door to the stairwell opened, and Mallory walked in. "Ah, sorry. Didn't know you were here."

"It's okay. Come in, Mallory. You know Sebastian."

"Yeah. I saw you at the dress rehearsal. You played the piano."

Jess turned toward Sebastian. "Mallory and I eat lunch here. You can join us if you want."

"Yeah, sure," said Sebastian, "What do you got?"

"Should have known," Jess laughed.

The three teens ducked under the staircase and sat against the wall, Jess in the middle. She riffled through her backpack while Mallory unwrapped a sandwich. "You want half?" she asked Sebastian.

"Thanks."

Jess unearthed a handful of snacks. "Help yourselves." She noticed Mallory's sketch pad poking out of her backpack. "May I look at your creations?" she asked. Then turning to Sebastian, "Mallory's the artist I told you about."

"That's pushing it," said Mallory.

"We spotted your picture in the auditorium display," Sebastian said. "That qualifies you."

"Mallory's always doodling during class. It's quite entertaining, especially when the doodles appear to be a commentary on the discussions going on, right Mallory?" Mallory smiled, pulled her pad from her backpack and passed it to Jess. Slowly Jess flipped through the pages, Sebastian looking over her shoulder.

"These are really good," he said, as the pages were turned, "Very cool. Like Ms. Willow said, 'Haunting.' She saw your painting, too." Mallory made no reply.

When Jess reached the blank sheets, she passed the pad back to

Mallory. "Sebastian and I were talking about Christmas," she said. "What do you have planned?"

"Planned? If it's like any other year, Dad will get off early on Christmas Eve. I'll have a nice dinner prepared, maybe sketch him a picture if I get inspired. He'll pass me a twenty or two. Then we'll watch a movie. On Christmas, we just lay back."

Jess glanced at Sebastian, who shrugged. "Want to get together with us on Christmas? We'll probably go to a movie and then have something to eat at my apartment."

Mallory jerked her face toward Jess in disbelief. "You want me to hang out with you?"

"You don't want to?"

"Well... yeah. I really do. I'm just... Yes. What time?"

"We don't have to figure that out now. What's your number? We'll text each other closer to Christmas."

They pulled out their phones and exchanged information.

Chapter 14

"You have a lovely place here," said Paige, Jess's new caseworker, as she lay her coat on a chair near the front door.

Jess had spent the morning thoroughly cleaning her apartment and running out to a local bakery for fresh pastries.

"Yes, it's quite comfortable."

"I apologize for not coming sooner. Annisa left big shoes to fill. I've been busy getting acquainted with everyone in her caseload. But I wanted to see you before Christmas. Here's a little something for you." She handed Jess a gift bag.

"Thanks," said Jess as she took the gift and set it on the kitchen counter, "We can sit at the table. I have tea and cinnamon rolls."

"Just water for me, thanks."

"You sure? The cinnamon rolls are still warm from the bakery–they're so good."

"No, that's fine."

As Jess filled a glass with water from the tap, she asked, "How is Annisa doing in Vancouver? Have you called her?"

"No, I haven't called, but I assume she's doing fine. Probably very busy. Being the coordinator of an outreach centre in East Vancouver is quite a feat. I would imagine it will be some time before she feels she has a handle on things."

Jess set the water on the table and sat down.

"Do you have any plans for Christmas?" asked Paige.

"On Sunday, the Youth Foundation is having a Christmas dinner for some of us who went to the group home."

"That's good of them." Paige took a sip of her water and put the glass to the side. Jess watched as Paige reached down to her shoulder bag, pulled out a laptop, set it up on the table and tapped in a code. "Let's see now... Yes, I phoned you a couple of weeks ago." Paige peered at the screen and scrolled down. "You told me about your performance at school." Pushing the screen down halfway, Paige looked across the table at Jess. "That was just an introductory call. But now, how are you doing?"

"Okay."

"How's school going?"

"I do well enough in my courses."

"Any friends?"

"A couple, but I mainly keep to myself after school. I don't want to fuck this up."

"That's wise." Paige took a sip of water. "I called the Independent Living staff before I came here. They're quite pleased with you." Paige lifted up the laptop screen and scanned Jess's file once again. "You respond to their calls... your place is kept tidy—as I can see for myself." Paige looked up, smiled at Jess, then turned back to the screen. "Yes... yes... I called the school, and an assistant principal told me that you're keeping up with your classwork.... Except for a couple of sick days, you have perfect attendance...." Paige scrolled down the screen, "You're living within your budget.... Jess, this is outstanding. It shows a great deal of focus and maturity. You're one of our superstars!"

"Like I said, I don't want to fuck this up."

"Is there anything you would like to discuss? Anything on your mind?"

Yeah, Jess thought, *I want to get a job, earn some extra cash.* Instead, she asked, "What happens after high school?"

"Well, that's not for a few years."

"Actually, a year and a half."

"Jess, you're working toward independence and showing that you are quite responsible. Completing high school is very important if you want to get further education or a job. Concentrate on that for now."

"But after high school, will I be able to go to college or a trade school? Will I have housing and support?"

"It's all decided on a case-by-case basis... and what funding is available at the time."

"The girl who lives upstairs told me that a government program to help kids like us continue our education has been cut. She knows a single mom who is scrambling to find help to finish a business course."

"Not cut; reduced. But by the time you graduate," Paige said placidly, "there may be other programs available. Like my mother says, 'You'll cross that bridge when you come to it.' Doesn't pay to worry about it now."

Jess said nothing, sipping her tea. Last June, she acquired her independent living status and spent the summer taking remedial classes to achieve class level. Currently, she was keeping up with school and could probably handle a job on the weekends. She'd look into it. But in the meantime, Jess knew the drill—no problems, no drama, less hassles. Paige had enough to worry about, all carefully stored in the laptop lodged between them.

"Anything else on your mind?" asked Paige, snapping Jess out of her musing.

"No, not right now," Jess said with a smile.

Chapter 15

The mall swarmed with holiday shoppers, and the food court was filling up. Jess sat at a table near a vendor famous for fries and waited for Lena Lugine. Jess had checked out the website for InTrend Agency and discovered it was a large, reputable firm in Toronto; Lena was the agent for teens and children. It wouldn't hurt to meet with her and hear what she had to offer. And with government programs being cut, banking some money seemed like a good idea–Jess had experienced life on the streets and didn't want to end up there again. After her meeting with Paige, she'd messaged Lena. Now Jess waited at their designated spot, watching intently for Lena. Soon she saw her approach: stylish, hair and makeup flawless, leather satchel hanging from her shoulder. Jess waved.

"Oh, Jess, I'd recognize you anywhere," said Lena as she approached the table. "So happy you could make it."

After the introductions and comments on the snowy weather, Lena said, "I'm going to get some coffee. Can I pick one up for you?"

"I can order my own," said Jess.

"Oh, no. My treat. You hold the table."

"Are you sure?"

"Absolutely. So what will it be?"

"Hot chocolate."

"With whipped cream? And drizzled with salted caramel?" Lena smiled encouragingly, "It's delicious."

"Sure, okay."

When Lena returned with the beverages, she asked, "Did you have a chance to look over the website?"

54

"Yes. It was interesting."

"As you saw, we cover a wide range of talents from modelling to acting and singing. Quite frankly, you would qualify for all."

Jess sipped her cocoa. "Yeah, maybe, but I'm still going to school."

"What grade?"

"Eleven."

"So that makes you, what? Sixteen, seventeen."

"Sixteen."

"Have you ever modelled before?"

"No."

"That's surprising. You must be a natural."

Jess laughed a little. "You can thank my Grandma. She always told me to stand tall and proud, like a ballerina."

Lena smiled, "She sounds wonderful. Do you see her much?"

"No, no. She died a while back."

"Well, perhaps, from up above, she let our paths cross."

"Maybe."

"Would you be interested in some modelling jobs? Small gigs, of course. A few hours, now and then."

"What would I be modelling?"

"Like I said, these would be small jobs. Today, for instance, I just finished a shoot for eyeglasses. A new online eyeglass company is starting up and wants shots of various faces wearing their frames." Lena paused and looked thoughtfully at Jess. "In fact, if you're interested, I could pay you a hundred dollars today for a few hours of work."

"Seriously?"

"Sure, if my photographer is available. Do you know where Devonian Gardens are? Downtown? Plus 15?"

"Where all the stores are?"

"Yes, the CORE shopping centre. The gardens are on the top floor near a food court. They make a great backdrop for photoshoots."

"Is it hard to find?"

"No. If you go by train, get out at the TD station and follow the signs..., or ask anyone."

"Yes, I guess I could hop on a train."

"Let me give my photographer a call."

Within fifteen minutes, everything was arranged. "Now I have an application form to fill out, but before we begin, let's get some lunch—

again, it's on me." Jess protested. "No, no, I don't want to hear it," Lena persisted, "If you're going to work, you need to eat."

Again, Jess held the table until Lena returned with the meals. Lena ate a couple of bites and then searched her satchel for a form and pen.

"So, let's get started." Lena went through standard questions: full name, address, cell, email, birthdate. "Social insurance number?"

"What?'

"Your SIN number? You need it for paying taxes and other things."

"Oh, that. I don't remember it."

"Don't worry about it. If you get permanent work with the firm, you'll need one, but I'll be paying you cash." Lena looked back down at the application form. "Now I have some personal questions I need to ask regarding size, you know, for modelling clothes. Height and weight?"

"About five feet seven inches and, I don't know, somewhere around 125 pounds."

"Bust, waist, hips?"

Jess paused. "I wear a size eight if that helps."

"That's perfect." Lena continued to scan the application. "I think we have everything for now. I just need you to sign down here." Lena made a big X near the signature line. Jess quickly looked over the form and asked about the last paragraph.

"Oh, that just states that the rate of pay will be decided before each job."

Still staring at the form, Jess asked, "So how does this work?"

"I scout for local jobs, and if I find one that fits your profile, I give you a call and see if you are interested."

"I'm only free on weekends."

"Okay." Lena scribbled something on her notepad. "Actually, you're approaching this very prudently. Start small and gradually build up. With your talent, you could be living quite comfortably on your own by the time you're twenty. Isn't that what we all want? Earning a decent living and not having to answer to anyone but ourselves?" Her cell phone dinged a text, and she glanced at her phone. "Seth is getting ready to walk out the door with his equipment. Are you in?"

Jess signed the form, and Lena shook her hand. "Smart choice. I'll meet you in an hour and a half."

"How will I find you?"

"Just message me when you arrive at the gardens, and I'll find you."

Chapter 16

Mallory unzipped her coat as she entered the mall. People of all ages bustled in every direction. Mallory smiled; just the way she liked it–packed. Mallory often came here on the weekends. When her father was caught up in a video game, he barely registered her request to go to the mall before waving her off. And Mallory would have a few hours out of the house and abundant inspiration for her artwork. There was always something to observe: trees and flower displays, a joyous reunion, a vacant stare, a pestering child, bored clerks at kiosks, weary shoppers and sleeping babies. The stories she imagined as she stepped through the looking glass of her sketch pad into the world of her subjects. Life in the mall never disappointed.

Mallory usually settled into one of the stuffed chairs clustered sporadically throughout the broad corridors. Shrouded by her solitude and the hood of her sweatshirt, Mallory faded into the background and drew. The challenge today would be finding an empty chair.

A middle-aged man, watching over a cache of bags, waved to a woman leaving a store. "This is it," she said, lifting a shopping bag. "We're done." The man and the woman gathered up their parcels, and Mallory slipped into the seat he vacated. With her pad in hand, she inconspicuously scanned the scene before her. A few seats away sat an older woman, a grandmother perhaps, cuddling a sleeping baby; Mallory began to sketch. That's when she saw her–Jess coming down the corridor with a woman in a tailored coat, her long hair curling gently over her shoulders. Mallory couldn't hear their conversation as they passed, but their smiles and gestures suggested some familiarity. *Probably her caseworker,* thought Mallory, and she returned to her drawing.

Chapter 17

"This is cozy," Mallory said. She slid off her shoes and hung her coat on a hook near the door. Jess lived about twelve blocks from Riverbank High in the ground-level suite of a four-plex.

"Yeah, it's okay," said Jess, yawning, still in her pajamas.

The front door opened immediately into the living room with a kitchen in the rear and a small dining table midway. Although neat and clean, everything was worn, from the furniture to the cupboards and appliances, right down to the linoleum, scratched and colourless where foot traffic was the heaviest. But Jess had attempted to brighten things up with colourful throw pillows and posters hung on the walls.

Mallory grabbed her backpack and walked toward the kitchen.

"You weren't supposed to bring anything!" scolded Jess. "Sebastian and I were getting the food, and you said you'd cook!"

"I didn't bring any food," said Mallory as she placed her backpack on the kitchen counter. "I brought my tools." From her pack, she pulled out a hand mixer, a pan and a spatula.

Jess laughed, "I do have some pots and pans."

"Yeah, I wasn't taking any chances."

The trio had decided on a Christmas brunch followed by a movie. Sebastian was free all day, but Mallory wanted to leave her house before her dad woke up and be home early in the afternoon to avoid an intense interrogation. So she arrived at Jess's shortly after nine to begin her prep—a little earlier than planned. The menu was French toast with strawberries and whipped cream, scrambled eggs and bacon, and a fruit salad.

"I'll give you a hand," said Jess. "Give me a few minutes to get dressed. In the meantime, make yourself at home."

Mallory pushed up the sleeves of her sweatshirt and surveyed the contents of the fridge. "Nice," she muttered to herself and began to pull out the fruit.

~

"Sebastian, there's not enough room for all of us in this kitchen," said Jess. "Besides, we're almost done. Why don't you pull out my keyboard from the storage closet near the bathroom and play us something."

"Oh, you still got the baby keyboard?" Sebastian jested as he walked toward the closet.

Mallory turned to Jess, "You sing *and* play the piano?"

"Nah. When I was in the group home, I was given a keyboard for Christmas and learned to play one hand. I use it when I'm trying to nail a song."

"Isn't this cute!" said Sebastian, holding up the keyboard. "All twenty-four keys!"

"Forty-five," corrected Jess.

Sebastian set the keyboard on the dining table and plugged it in. Jazzed-up Christmas carols filled the room, and they sang along, even Mallory.

~

"I got a job at *Strum 'n Drum*," said Sebastian as he dove into his French toast. The small round dining table was just big enough for their three mismatched plates and bowls piled with food and their mugs steaming with hot cocoa. The stove and oven, just behind them, kept the remaining food warm for seconds. "Craig, the boss, said I helped sell a few keyboards last week."

"How did you do that?" asked Mallory.

"I play them!" said Sebastian. "It's so much fun."

"You also know a lot about keyboards," added Jess. She turned to Mallory, "Don't get him started."

"Well, Craig, you know, the boss–"

"Yeah, you just told us that Craig was the boss," said Jess. "You got that, Mallory? Craig's the boss."

Mallory giggled softly.

"Okay, okay. Craig—I don't have to mention he is the boss because you already know that—he told me that if I wanted to get a foot into the music industry, it's good to get some kind of job in the field. He says it builds up your resume for the future. He also told me to volunteer somewhere as well."

"Are you going to?" asked Jess.

"For now, I'm sticking with *Strum's*. Craig lets me go in anytime to play the keyboards, *and* three days a week for three hours, I'll get paid for it!"

"When do you start getting paid?"

"First week of January!"

"Sounds like Craig likes you," said Mallory.

"What's not to like," he jested, standing and taking a bow.

Jess rolled her eyes. She turned to Mallory and asked, "What about you? Do you want to get a job?"

"I guess... I probably had one. I just didn't get paid for it."

"Like you volunteered?"

"My dad volunteered me."

"What!" exclaimed Jess.

"When I was around thirteen, sometime around then, my dad didn't want me staying home during the summer, but the types of summer programs I had gone to before had an age cap, and I couldn't get in. Somehow he discovered a local church with day camps for low-income families."

"So you joined the church and got in free?" joked Sebastian. Jess and Mallory laughed.

"No, anyone could go. You didn't have to belong to the church. But for all the time I spent there, I could have been a member."

"So what happened?" asked Jess.

"They started the day with a Bible story and prayer. Then the kids were divided into groups and went from station to station throughout the day—like games, songs, arts and crafts, hula hoops..., that kind of thing."

"Yeah, but what happened to you?"

"I was getting there," said Mallory.

"Yeah, Jess," said Sebastian as he got up for seconds, "let her finish her story."

"Sooo, groups of kids came for a week at a time—it wasn't meant for the whole summer. Moms from the church brought their children and volunteered for a week, then another set would come the next week. But the coordinator told my dad that I could come all summer if I helped the younger kids with their lunches and snacks and spent the day with whatever mom was stationed with the arts and crafts. So my dad volunteered me every year after that."

Sebastian's eyes went wide, and Jess exclaimed, "Are you kidding me?" Mallory lowered her eyes. "Mallory, I'm not putting down your work at the day camp. But shit! Didn't your dad give you a choice?"

"Not really. But what could he do? He didn't want to leave me alone at home, and he didn't have money for any summer program."

"You know," said Sebastian, "your dad gets government money for you every month. Just saying."

"And electricians are well-paid," added Jess.

Mallory shrugged. "That day camp wasn't all bad. I mean, it got boring at times, but if the kids didn't need help with their crafts, I came up with my own creations. Some of them turned out really cool. Besides, I didn't have friends like you guys."

"Ahh," said Sebastian. He got up and hugged Mallory, and Jess reached over and squeezed her shoulder.

"So, would you like a *paying* job?" asked Jess.

"I don't think my dad would let me. You know, 'Dan-ger-ous.'"

"If you could, what would you like to do?" asked Sebastian.

Mallory raised her eyebrows. "I've never thought about it.... Something with food or Art, I guess."

Jess and Sebastian looked at each other. "Fast food joint?" said Jess.

"Dishwasher at a restaurant?" added Sebastian. "You know, just to get in, then move to food prep."

"Grocery store?" said Jess.

"Or help out someplace, like an art supply store—that's how I got in at *Strum's*. I asked to try out the keyboards. Then a customer came over, and I showed her how it worked, and she bought one. I kept hanging out and helping people. Craig noticed."

"I'll think about it," said Mallory, perking up.

"By the way, what movie are we going to see?" asked Sebastian.

"About that," said Mallory. "I have to get back home. I won't be able to come with you."

Jess gave Mallory a peculiar look but didn't push for an explanation. "That's too bad."

"Yeah, it would have been fun," said Sebastian.

"What are you going to see?" asked Mallory.

"We haven't decided," said Jess.

"Well, I could help you choose," offered Mallory.

For the rest of the meal, the three scrolled through the selection of films, debating which would be the best.

Chapter 18

Mallory opened their apartment door and called out, "I'm home." From the sound of machine-gun fire, she knew her dad was gaming in the living room. She left her backpack near the door and tossed her coat on top. She'd been counting on her dad giving her a twenty for Christmas so she could go to the movies, but last night, his wallet never opened. He'd brought home a small ice cream cake instead.

"Where have you been?" asked her dad when she walked into the living room.

"I took a long walk. I left you a note."

An explosion went off in the video game. "I just blew through level six. I'm warming up before Jack and Wade come online. We are going to kick some ass!"

~

When she was younger, Mallory and her dad had occasionally played video games together, but Ryder bored quickly: "This crap is mind-numbing." As she grew older, her games were more challenging, and her dad enjoyed joining in. However, when online gaming took over, Ryder's enjoyment took a competitive twist: he and Mallory could play against gamers from all over the world. They would become a formidable father-daughter duo taking on other teams. This self-imposed pressure triggered constant frustration on Ryder's part and dread on Mallory's: "Watch out! Northwest, Northwest! LOOK NORTHWEST, DAMN IT. Shit! He destroyed you. And I told you right where he was–northwest.

You're useless! We're out again!"

When Mallory was thirteen, she and her father spent a week of evenings drilling for an "epic takedown" of a rival team.

"Hurry up with your dinner, Mallory. This is our last night to practice. Since when did you become such a slowpoke?"

"I'm not very hungry."

"Are you sick?"

"No."

"You'll have your appetite back after we practice. You can eat something then. Let's go."

Mallory put her head down on the table, "I can't."

"You can't what?"

She swallowed hard, "I can't–" Her voice broke. A surge of emotions, sudden and intense, broke through her customary restraint. Overwhelmed by the onslaught, she began to cry uncontrollably, choking and gasping for breath.

"What the hell?" said her dad with both disbelief and concern.

Several minutes passed before the sobs subsided. Mallory's dad brought over a glass of water and a box of tissue.

"Drink some water."

Mallory took a sip and blew her nose.

"What was that all about?"

"I don't want to play," she whispered, her head bowed.

"I can't hear you," he said, sighing heavily.

With her head still bowed, she said more clearly, "I don't want to play."

"We don't have to play tonight. Go rest."

"Ever. I don't want to play ever. It's just... too much."

"Fine," her dad said, standing. "I thought you had more grit and stamina. My mistake."

That was the end of the dynamic duo. Jack and Wade, previously a team Ryder competed against, were looking for an additional partner and invited him to join. And Mallory's relationship with her father drifted more and more into that of an indebted roommate who kept the place clean and tried to stay out of the way.

～

"How long before Jack and Wade come online?"

Mallory's dad checked his watch. "About a half-hour."

"I'm going to make a grilled cheese sandwich. Do you want one?"

"Sure. Make me two."

Mallory hummed about the kitchen, beaming. Even though she missed out on the movie, this had been one of the best days ever. Her dad was content, and she had friends—people who actually liked her. And her dad would not sabotage these friendships because she had no intention of ever letting him know they existed.

Chapter 19

Craig, a large, bearded man with a cowboy hat, sat in his office at the rear of *Strum 'N Drums*. "Make yourself comfortable," he said when Sebastian arrived at his door, indicating a chair across from the desk. Sebastian sat and rubbed his hands together rapidly to warm his fingers, still tingling from his bone-chilling walk to the store.

"You know there is an invention to help with that problem," said Craig, giving a sustained look at Sebastian's hands, pale and chapped. "Mitts."

"Yeah, yeah," said Sebastian with a chuckle.

"With your talent, you want to take good care of those hands." Craig sat at his desk, opened a drawer and pulled out an empty form. "So let's get you on the payroll, young man." The two had gone through the usual questions of name and address when Craig asked, "What's your phone number?"

"I don't have a phone number."

"You don't have a home phone?"

"My mom has a cell phone. Is that what you mean?"

Craig sighed and repositioned his cowboy hat. "Is there a phone in your house connected to a wall? Some are wireless, but you can only use them in the house. Like the ones we use in the store." Craig lifted up a phone from its charging station.

"No. We don't have one of those. But," Sebastian fished out a phone from a pocket, "I have a phone—my mom gave it to me when she bought a newer model. I can only use it, though, with Wi-Fi, like at school or home or the mall where the Wi-Fi is free. I don't have cell service."

"So, while you're working here, your mom can't get ahold of you?"
Sebastian shrugged.

"I can give you Wi-Fi access, but I don't want to see you farting around on your phone in the store."

"Got it," said Sebastian. He tapped in his pin and passed the phone to Craig, who typed in the store's Wi-Fi password.

"Okay, moving along, do you have an email address?" Sebastian furrowed his brow. "You gotta have a school email address."

"Yeah, right." Sebastian rattled it off.

"What's your SIN?"

"My sin?" repeated Sebastian, baffled.

"Yeah, I want you to confess your sins," Craig said with a grin. "I'm talking about your S-I-N—Social Insurance Number."

"I have one?"

"If you want a job, you need one," said Craig leaning back in his chair. "Geeze, maybe along with 'reading, writing and 'rithmatic,' the schools should be helping you guys get set up for life." Craig shook his head and sat back up. "Your social insurance number is for taxes, benefits—all kinds of things. Some parents apply for it right after their kids are born. You might want to ask your mom and dad."

Sebastian blew past the suggestion. "How can I get one? Is it hard?"

"I don't think so... let me check." Craig opened a laptop and made a few entries. "Okay, here we are...." Craig shifted the laptop screen so Sebastian could view it as well. "Looks pretty basic," he said as he scrolled through the form, "Name, address, birth date, parents info... Yeah, looks like you just need to submit a birth certificate."

"Christ," muttered Sebastian.

"Your mom must have it," said Craig encouragingly.

"Ah, she has a hard time keeping track of these things." Which was true, but even more, Sebastian didn't want his mom or Max interfering with this job.

"She needed a birth certificate to register you at school. I know the drill. I have kids."

Sebastian brightened up. "Right!"

"Now, do you have a bank account?"

"I don't have enough money for a bank account," exclaimed Sebastian.

"If you have a nickel, you have enough money to open a bank account."

"Why do I need one?"

"I send all paycheques to my employees' bank accounts—electronically," explained Craig. "When you go to a store to buy something, you tap your bank card to pay or go to an ATM and get cash. Without a bank account, you'll be carrying around a wad of cash, and that's not a good idea, especially at your age."

"What do you mean, 'at my age?'" asked Sebastian.

"Do you have any money on you right now?"

"I might have a couple of bucks." Sebastian checked his pants pockets and then started to search through the pockets of his coat.

"You can stop now," said Craig. "I made my point. You forget where you put your money and then leave your stuff around, and someone rips you off."

Sebastian stared down at his hands, "So does that mean I can't have the job."

"The job is still yours," said Craig. He picked up Sebastian's partially filled employment form and put it into a file folder. "Look, I'll pay you in cash for the next few weeks as long as you promise to get started on your application for a SIN and get a bank account."

"Thanks! Yes, I'll get right on it."

Chapter 20

Mallory sat slumped in a chair at the kitchen table. A local deli had a "Hiring Now" sign taped on its front window, and she had finally worked up the courage to apply. The owner wouldn't even give her an application form. Didn't even ask her name. Alone in the empty house, Mallory pulled out her phone and texted Jess: *Job interview: FAIL.* Within moments a text popped up: *Come over.*

～

"So the guy is a jerk. It doesn't mean you won't get a job somewhere else," said Jess.

Mallory sipped the cocoa Jess had ready for her when she arrived. Both sat for a few moments in silence.

"Mallory, I'm going to tell you something," Jess said. "Take it or leave it, whatever." Mallory looked up, curious. "Your chances of getting a job will be better if you do something about...." Jess made a circular motion with her hands towards Mallory.

"Something about what?"

"Like... your look."

Mallory glanced down at her clothes, "What's wrong with my clothes? They're clean."

"Right. And they look really comfortable, but have you ever thought of wearing something other than sweatpants with a tee shirt and a hoodie?"

Mallory's face fell.

"I'm not dissing you. You can wear your sweats all the time, it's fine with me. But you might want to put on something else when you are out looking for a job, that's all I'm saying."

"These are the only kind of clothes I have."

"I know a place where you can get clothes super cheap." Jess typed on her phone and pulled up a map. She leaned close to Mallory, sharing her screen. "Here," she pointed, "Not too far away."

"Yeah, I've seen that store."

"Have you been inside?"

"No. Everything is used."

"So."

"My dad says it's grubby to wear clothes other people have worn."

"Clothes *can* be washed. Besides, where do you think I get my stunning outfits?" Jess teased. She stood and strutted to the kitchen area, grabbing a bag of chips while she was there. She took a handful and passed the bag to Mallory.

"You get all your clothes here?" Mallory said, pointing to the storefront on the phone.

"Everything but my underwear. I've been going to stores like these since I was a kid with my grandmother."

"My dad would flip if I bought clothes there."

"Does he go shopping with you?"

"No."

"So, he doesn't need to know. You're sixteen, Mallory. Buy your clothes where you want. Just saying, you can get some decent things really cheap at this place."

Jess crossed her legs and bit into a chip. "One more thing. Your hair."

"What about my hair?"

"Your bangs cover your eyes, and the rest of your hair hangs into your cheeks."

"So."

"So, the guy at the deli? Where you went for the job? He could barely see your face."

"I'm not cutting it."

"You don't have to. Can I show you something? It'll be real quick."

Mallory said nothing, so Jess dashed to the bathroom and returned with a comb, a few clips, and hair spray. "All you need to do is pull one side over your ear." Jess took Mallory's shoulder-length hair, tucked one side behind her ear and clipped it in place. "Then comb your bangs over just a little." She parted Mallory's hair and combed her bangs toward the side. "Spray it all down... and a new look." Jess pulled Mallory to the bathroom mirror. "What do you think?"

"I feel naked."

"Okay, but how does it look?"

"All right, I guess."

"You can clip back both sides if you want." Jess tucked some dangling locks behind the other ear.

"Ah, thanks." Mallory took the comb from Jess, removed the clips and combed her hair back to its usual position, the hair spray still damp.

"Yeah, just a suggestion," said Jess as she walked toward the kitchen. "I'm having a sandwich. Do you want one?"

"Sure... okay."

When they had finished eating, Jess said, "I'm thinking of heading over to that store I just showed you. Do you want to come?"

Mallory hesitated.

"You don't have to buy anything. Most of the time, I don't. I just look around, see if something new stands out."

Mallory glanced at the time. "Can I meet you there in about a half-hour? I have to pull something out of the freezer for dinner. I forgot to do it before I came."

"Meet you there."

~

As Jess made her way across the parking area of the strip mall toward the thrift store, she stopped abruptly. Could it be? Coming out of one of the shops was Seth, the photographer, carrying two long, narrow boxes. She walked closer to the store to make sure it was him. "Hey, Seth!"

Seth seemed startled to see her but regained his composure. "Oh, Jess! Hi. How are you doing?"

Jess walked up to Seth. "Fine. I didn't expect to see you here. Do you live nearby?"

"No, no." Then shrugging with a grin and holding up his boxes, "I'm lighting up my life!"

"What?" asked Jess.

"Portable, battery-run lights with adjustable stands," he said like a salesman. Then in his normal voice, "Equipment for my photography course."

"Oh, you're studying photography."

"Photography and videography. At the moment, I'm focusing on portrait photography."

"How did Lena find you?"

"Ah... she put up an ad online, and I sent her some of my material and got the gig. Helps with the bills." Seth paused and looked intently at Jess. "I've been working with Lena for a few months now, and I've taken pictures with other models. Jess, seriously, they can't compete with you. You are the real deal."

Jess lowered her eyes and crossed her ankles.

Seth set down his boxes. "What I'm trying to say is, you can start to build up your portfolio now."

"I'm not sure I want to be a professional model."

"You don't have to be. This could be a way to make some money while you train for something else. You got what it takes."

Absently, Jess began to look at the camera shop in front of her, a big "Closeout Sale" sign prominently displayed in the window.

"Just think about it. I could take the pictures. It would be a win-win for both of us. I'll have portrait material for my course, and you'll have a portfolio for the future.... You don't have to decide now. Do you have *YouApp*?"

"Yes."

"What's your handle?"

As Jess gave her handle, Seth typed it into his phone and sent Jess a message. "Okay, good. I'll message you when I'm free, and you can let me know if '*YouApp*' for it."

"Ha, ha," said Jess smiling. "I'll think about it."

〜

As Mallory walked toward the entrance of the thrift shop, she spotted Jess chatting with a guy on the sidewalk of the strip mall. After watching them for a couple of minutes, she turned and retraced her steps to the main road. Back at the bus stop, she texted: *Something came up. Not able to meet. C u at school.*

Chapter 21

"Mrs. Barnes?" The school secretary swivelled in her chair. "Ms. Willow told me you could help me out... about the birth certificate."

"I've been expecting you," she said with a smile. "Ms. Willow gave me a heads up. Have a seat." Sebastian sat on the edge of a chair, stowing his backpack underneath. His right foot tapped incessantly. "Here's a copy of the birth certificate we have on file."

Sebastian gazed at the document. It was the first time he had read this formal acknowledgement of his existence, *Sebastian Glenn Miller.* "Thanks."

"And just in case you need it, here's the document giving your mother full custody."

Sebastian scanned the document. His dad had not been present for the hearing; his mother reformed. Slam dunk for mom.

"Do you need help with anything else, Sebastian?" asked Mrs. Barnes as she took both forms back from Sebastian and placed them in an envelope. "Ms. Willow said something about an S-I-N."

"It's supposed to be real easy to get online," said Sebastian, perking up.

Mrs. Barnes handed the envelope to Sebastian and turned toward her computer. "Let's check it out." After a quick search, she opened the appropriate site and studied it for a few moments. "You need an *original* birth certificate."

"Shit!"

"They're not that hard to get. You have all the information right on your copy." Sebastian's foot-tapping picked up speed. "Sebastian, we can help you. We've got this." Mrs. Barnes made another search:

birth certificate duplicate. "It says you just have to fill out this form," she said brightly, "and... ah, wait.... You also need a government-issued document... with a photo."

"Shit, shit!" muttered Sebastian.

"Hold on while I read this.... Okay, if you don't have a document, then someone who's known you for a year can stand up for you."

Sebastian bent his head and covered his eyes with his hand.

Mrs. Barnes pushed over a box of tissues and, from a lower desk drawer, pulled out a water bottle. "Have something to drink while we figure this out."

Sebastian quickly wiped his eyes with the back of his hand and took a few sips of water.

"Okay, let's think this through. It's your first year at this school, right?"

"Yeah."

"Did you come with your mother when she registered you?"

"Yeah, we moved, so I came here after school started."

"When your mother came, she had to have had your documents because we have copies. Do you remember that?"

Sebastian thought a few moments. "My mom filled out the form.... Someone else was talking to me, then showed me around. I didn't see any documents."

"Those documents," Mrs. Barnes continued, "must be somewhere at home. And from the quality of the copies, it looks like they're originals. Ask your mom."

Sebastian's demeanour changed, and the foot-tapping slowed. "Yeah, they must be at home."

"Come back with the birth certificate, and I'll help you with the SIN number. *And* if you don't find your birth certificate, don't panic. We'll move to Plan B."

"Sure, and thanks," said Sebastian as he carefully tucked away the envelope in his backpack. "There's just one more thing. Once I get my SIN, I need a bank account to get paid. My boss said they are easy to get, but when I went to the bank, they said I couldn't get one without making it joint with my mom."

"And that's a problem?" asked Mrs. Barnes.

"Yeah, if she needs money." *And,* he thought, *she'll tell Max, and he'll find out about the job, and....*

"I'll see what I can do," said Mrs. Barnes.

~

Sebastian saw the truck lights swing into the driveway and heard the garage door open. Rarely was Sebastian home at this hour, by intent. He hoped his mom and Max would keep to their habitual pattern. He lay on his bed, lights out, and continued to scroll through his phone. After a few minutes, he heard Max climbing the stairs and, moments later, descend them. Max liked to do a workout and shower while his mom cooked. Sebastian rolled off the bed and cautiously opened his door. He could hear his mom clattering about the kitchen but nothing of Max, a sign he had made it to the basement.

"Hi, Mom," said Sebastian as he entered the kitchen area.

Stephanie gasped and then laughed a little, "Oh, it's you! You startled me! Don't usually see you at this hour."

Or most hours, thought Sebastian. "We're doing a project in school," Sebastian said evenly, "about government, taxes, stuff like that. The teacher asked us if we had social insurance numbers—some parents get them for their kids when they're babies."

"Well, I didn't, if that's what you are driving at." Stephanie pulled some celery and carrots from the fridge and began to rinse the vegetables.

"Yeah, so those of us who didn't have them had to do research on how to get one. We're going to apply at school. It'll save you the hassle."

"Good."

"I just need my original birth certificate."

"Well, I can't get it now. I'm getting supper ready."

"I'll peel the carrots while you look," said Sebastian, moving toward the kitchen sink.

"It's amazing how helpful you can be when you want something." Stephanie sighed. "Wash your hands first," she said as she dried her own. "I think I left all your documents in one of my purses. I hope so."

Sebastian had finished peeling and was chopping the carrots when Stephanie returned with a manila envelope. "I want this back *in my hands* by the end of the week," she said, handing Sebastian the envelope. "It's a real pain in the ass to get a replacement, and I don't want to go through it again."

"Thanks, Mom." Sebastian gave his mom a quick hug and ran upstairs. He descended just as quickly in his coat, carrying his backpack and shoes.

"Where are you off to?" asked his mom.

"Meeting up with friends," he said as he slipped into his loosely tied shoes. "I'll be back in a couple of hours." Before his mother could reply, he was out the door and on his way to *Strum's*.

~

A few days later, Sebastian swaggered through *Strum 'N Drum* right into Craig's office. "It's on the way."

Craig looked up from his pile of paperwork.

"My SIN application is done."

"That's great! When do you expect it?"

"The lady at the registry said a couple of weeks."

"So you went the registry route rather than online."

"Yeah. A school secretary came along with me, and they're sending my card to the school. I'll bring it in here as soon as it arrives. And we're working on the bank account."

"I bought you something. And hearing your good news, I'm going to call it a gift to welcome another tax-paying citizen into the community." Craig picked up a pair of mitts from his desk and tossed them at Sebastian.

"Shit! You didn't have to do that."

"Wear the damn things. They won't help you stashed in your backpack. Now, go out there and sell some keyboards."

Chapter 22

"My SIN card came in! Mrs. Barnes gave it to me yesterday afternoon!" said Sebastian as he slid between Jess and Mallory under the staircase. "Mallory, did you find out if your dad got you a SIN when you were a kid?"

"No, not yet."

"Well, if you want a job, you need one."

"Yes, I know. A friend of mine–this guy called Sebastian–he's been telling me all about it for a few weeks now," said Mallory with a smirk. Sebastian gave her a friendly shove.

"You have a SIN, don't you, Jess?" asked Mallory.

"Yeah. Annise set me up with a Health Insurance card, a bank account and a SIN. By the way, how is it going with your bank account, Sebastian?"

"Mrs. Barnes is helping me out with that. But in the meantime, look what she got me." Sebastian paused. "Well, I'm not supposed to show this to anyone, but I can trust you." From behind the waistband of his pants, Sebastian pulled up a thin pouch. "It's like a skinny wallet you wear around your waist. It's to keep your money and important cards from getting lost or stolen. She said to keep change and about twenty bucks in a pants pocket and put all the rest in here–and never take out any money from the pouch in public."

"Very cool," said Jess.

"I think I'll check in with Mrs. Barnes," said Mallory as Sebastian carefully tucked his money pouch behind his waistband. "Maybe she can help me, too."

Sebastian turned to Jess, "Do you ever hear from Annise?"

"No," said Jess dismissively. "She's probably swamped with work. And besides, I wasn't her only client. She had a whole pile of us."

"I went back to the group home and saw DJ."

"Shit! Really?"

"Who's DJ?" asked Mallory.

"He is a counsellor at the group home," said Jess.

"Yeah, DJ are his initials, but, you know, disc jockey?"

"I think she gets it," said Jess. "DJ always kept his cool; upfront about everything. Sebastian and I liked him." Turning to Sebastian, she asked, "Why did you go back to the group home?"

"Well, I didn't actually go into the group home. I just wanted to talk to DJ." Turning to Jess, "You know how he always takes his breaks outside and smokes in that back corner?"

"Yeah," said Jess.

"Well, that's where I talked to him. I wanted to know if I could get independent status like you."

"What did he say?"

"Not likely."

"Why?" asked Mallory.

"Because I have a mother and a stable place to live."

"Did you tell him about your step-dad?" asked Jess.

"Yeah, but when I told him about Max dissing my music, he said I'm probably taking him too seriously. And when I said I didn't want to work in his auto shop, DJ said doing chores is common in families."

"The problem is the way he treats you," remarked Jess.

"DJ asked if he hit me or threatened me... but he hasn't. Besides, he said there are so many teens in worse situations who are waiting for independent living spaces that I would never qualify."

"I guess that rules me out, too," said Mallory.

"Hmm," said Sebastian with a smile, "maybe Mallory and I could come and live with you, Jess."

"Yeah, and we'd all get kicked to the street."

Chapter 23

Seth waved from his seat at the food court as Jess approached their designated spot. "So glad you could make it," said Seth as he shook Jess's hand. "Have a seat." When Jess was seated across from him, Seth continued, "I thought I was free this weekend, but Lena called with a new job. I told her I was planning on meeting with you, and she said it might be a win-win for all of us. She has some jackets that need modelling, and they're your size. If you want, you can have the gig." Then with a wink, he said, "And, if you're okay with it, I'll be able to use some shots for my class and your portfolio." He raised his head and looked past Jess, "Oh, here she comes now."

Lena walked toward the table with a tray of steaming beverages. "Hi, Jess! Can you believe my luck? You, already set up to meet with Seth?" She passed a cup to Seth. "Here's your coffee," and turning to Jess, "You like hot chocolate, right?"

"You remembered?" said Jess surprised.

"Of course." Lena passes Jess a cup, "We had a great time together."

"It was fun," agreed Jess.

"Did Seth fill you in?"

"About the jackets? Yes."

"So, what do you think? Are you up for it? I have the jackets in my car."

"Are we shooting here in the mall?"

"Well, you're our third model for these jackets. The distributor wants a selection of photos to choose from—different models, different settings. Since it's not too cold and the sun is out, I thought we could go to Fish Creek Park. You'll be modelling jackets after all."

Jess was familiar with the provincial park, a wildlife corridor that wended its way through the southern part of the city. "That sounds like fun."

"Wonderful! Jess, you come with me, and Seth can follow in his car."

Within twenty minutes, Lena was driving down the narrow road that snaked through the eastern edge of the park. Dotting the road were small parking areas that spawned into a network of trails. On the east side, the higher elevation of the park's western edge, with its densely packed trees, opened to a broad, flat wetland bordered by steep escarpments. Copses of trees on hilly mounds, devoid of leaves, lifted their bare, spiky branches toward the vast blue sky as if in prayer, pleading for warmer weather to restore their leafy garments. Remnants of other trees, slowly rotting away, raised what remained of their branches but with no such hope. Flattened, brown grasses lay across the expanse, drab and dull. The warm Chinook winds, blowing down from the Rocky Mountains over the last few days, had melted or evaporated all the snow except the drifts that lay protected in the shadows and hallows.

"Kind of bleak," said Lena lightly.

"Yeah," replied Jess absently. Her fifth-grade class had walked through these same dead wetlands; only their teacher helped them discover that they were not dead at all. The decaying blanket of grass protected a host of living organisms, insects and wildlife that would reemerge in spring. Even the dead, hollow trees provided nourishment and shelter. Everything contributed in some way to the preservation of the wetland biome.

"Oof," said Jess as she lurched forward, snapping her out of her reverie.

"Sorry about that," laughed Lena. "I came up a little too fast to this parking space."

As they climbed out of the car, they saw Seth pull in further up.

"Isn't this the area with the restaurant?" asked Jess.

"Yeah, some old rancher's mansion," said Lena as she pulled four large totes of jackets from the back seat. "Can you give me a hand with these?" she asked as she handed Jess a couple totes. Once Seth had retrieved all the equipment he needed from his trunk, they set out; Lena scoped out the sites as they walked. "Here," she would state emphatically, and Jess would pull out a jacket and pose: leaning against a giant spruce, sitting on the steps of the cookhouse, or with her arms crossed in front of the bunkhouse.

"This looks like a great spot," said Jess as they approached the Bow Valley Restaurant. "The veranda is so quaint."

"No," said Lena, without pausing. "It will attract too much attention."

Jess laughed, "It's not like this place is swarming with visitors."

Lena ignored the comment and continued walking. "Here, near the red carriage!"

And so it continued; Lena would point out a spot and pick out a jacket from the totes. Jess would pull it on, pose as directed, and Seth would take several shots. The photos were immediately downloaded to a tablet which Lena would peruse. Once approved by Lena, they would move to the next site. Jess posed on log-carved benches, against fences, and on a small stage. She stepped into the role of a grain-tossing farmer when she joined the bronze statues of a mother and her children feeding chickens and collecting eggs. This quickly gave way to humorous antics that even got a chuckle out of Lena. After a few hours and a dozen jackets, Lena called it a day. Back at the car, Lena handed Jess an envelope and said, "Well done, Jess. That was a two hundred dollar job."

"Shit! That's amazing!"

"You earned it," said Seth

"And the distributor is going to be very pleased with the photos," added Lena.

Jess pulled off the last jacket she modelled, handed it to Lena, and picked up her own from one of the totes. Lena held out the jacket. "This looked really smart on you."

"Yeah, it's beautiful."

"You can take it, you know."

"Don't you have to give it back to the distributor?"

"They don't want the jackets after they've been used. I'm just going to donate them to a second-hand store."

"You agreed to this gig at a moment's notice," said Seth. "Take it."

"Well, sure then. Thanks."

"And now you and Seth can continue your day. I gotta get these photos uploaded and finish the paperwork, so I'm off. You two enjoy yourselves."

Jess followed Seth to his car. "I think we've taken enough pictures for today," Seth said. "They're loaded in my camera." As he popped his trunk and began packing away his equipment, he continued, "If it's okay with you, I'll use the best shots for my class project and your portfolio."

"You're really serious about the portfolio?"

"Absolutely. And once I set it up, I'll teach you how to add pictures to it."

"Ah... thanks."

"I should be able to send you a link within the next few weeks." He closed the trunk. "Now, how about some lunch."

～

"So you've never been to this place?" said Seth as he and Jess sat across from each other, eating their lunch.

"I've been to this park, but I've never eaten at the café here."

"So the first time for both of us."

Seth bit into his Panini, and Jess spooned her chilli.

"Not bad," said Seth.

"The chilli is pretty good, too," said Jess, looking at Seth. She paused, "You've always reminded me of someone, and it just hit me who—Ryan Reynolds!"

"The *Deadpool* guy?"

"That's the one.... Well, not exactly alike, but, you know, close."

"Oh, so now you're going to qualify it. Thanks," Seth laughed. "So, who does Lena remind you of?"

"Hmm... let me think." Jess made quizzical faces and strummed her fingers. "I would have to say... Bella from *Twilight*."

"Never seen it."

"Well, now you'll have to. You'll see I'm right!"

Jess found Seth easy to talk to, chatting about his life and plans for the future. When the conversation veered toward her past and current situation, Jess was evasive and deftly turned the focus back to Seth. He was an only child, he told her. He came to Alberta for work when he was twenty-five but didn't enjoy working in the oil patch. In his spare time, however, he had always enjoyed taking photos and making videos, "and so I thought to myself, why not go professional?" So, he started taking courses in photography and videography, hoping to specialize in portraits and events, such as weddings.

"Who knows, I might be able to make you famous," Seth winked. "The new, break-out model!"

"Yeah, right," Jess laughed. She found his optimism encouraging and his respect and professionalism refreshing. It was a welcomed change from the sexual innuendos and passes she fended off from some of the guys at school—he was like an older brother.

Chapter 24

It was the end of February. The threat of working at Max's auto repair shop lay in remission, and Sebastian did whatever he could to keep it that way. Max and his mother followed their bodybuilding regiment: early morning workout, breakfast, gone for work before seven-thirty. When home from work: supper prep for his mom, workout for Max. After supper, they contorted their bodies through a series of stretches.

In the morning, Sebastian didn't stir until Max and Stephanie were gone. In the evening, he stayed out until he knew they'd be settled in the basement gym. He would then enter the garage through the side door, pause and listen for voices before silently opening the door that led to a mudroom outside the kitchen. He'd put together a plate of leftovers and eat in his room. Outside of his bedroom, Sebastian left nothing personal: not a jacket or a pair of shoes; no dirty dishes on the counter or a dusty footprint on the floor—nothing that would indicate his presence in the house. Laundry and showers were squeezed in when no one was home. He never played his keyboard without his earphones, even when alone, on the chance that Max might come home unexpectedly. And with his new job at the music store, Sebastian never asked for money. He aimed to be a ghost who came and went without notice, not worth the interest or criticism of his stepfather.

~

"Are you fucking kidding me!" Max screamed.

Opening the back door, Sebastian thought this verbal explosion was aimed at him, but a glance showed Max on his cell phone. This time, the absence of voices on the other side of the back door had not signalled an empty kitchen, only a prolonged pause during a phone conversation. Had Sebastian heard this outburst before coming in, he would have sat shivering in the unheated garage until the tirade subsided, but it was too late. His mother, standing near the kitchen counter and nodding sympathetically at Max, looked toward Sebastian as he stood in the doorway. And Max, his back to the door, followed her gaze. He waved impatiently at Sebastian to enter. Sebastian took a couple steps forward and leaned against the doorframe that led to the kitchen.

"So, what's the damage?" Pause. "He ran the car? Christ Almighty! His ass is fired! Tell that motherfucker to get his ass off my property and never come back." Pause. "He padded his damn resume, is what he did," Max roared. "What asshole doesn't know the difference between transmission fluid, engine oil and gasoline. Tomorrow I'll take care of it." Max closed the call and slammed his fist on the counter.

"That motherfucking kid!" Max yelled. "I hire him to change the fluids so my guys can concentrate on bigger jobs, and that fucking idiot poured motor oil into an automatic transmission!"

"My, God," commiserated Stephanie, "the opportunity you gave him—training him on the job."

"These fucking kids! Entitled fucking kids that inflate their resumes. You can't trust them." Max picked up a beer from the counter and noticed Sebastian once again.

"Just like you," he gestured toward Sebastian, sending a spray of beer across the room, "A fucking, entitled kid that thinks he can come in and out of this house as he pleases. Well, that's changing! Beginning tomorrow, after school, you're coming to the shop, do you understand?" Max yelled. Sebastian flushed a deep red.

"What will he do?" said Stephanie timidly. "He doesn't know the first thing about auto mechanics."

"Do you think I'd trust Jingle Fingers under a hood?" he jeered. "He'll be sweeping the shop, vacuuming the cars, and washing the windows!" Then glaring at Sebastian, "Yes, you're going to have to move that lazy ass of yours."

Sebastian had not moved beyond the kitchen door nor removed his winter coat. His backpack was still slung over his shoulder. He glared at Max. "I'm never working in your... stinking... fucking shop."

"Oh, Sebastian, you don't mean that," said Stephanie.

Sebastian's eyes darted between his mother and Max. Then looking directly at Max, he said, "I will never work in your fucking shop."

Max set his beer on a counter. "Really?" he said in a low, measured voice, nodding his head slightly as he gazed at the lanky teenager. Then he turned and walked upstairs.

Sebastian was bewildered. Neither he nor his mother moved. Was it over? He had stood his ground. Had Max relented? Within moments Max returned, carrying Sebastian's keyboard.

"You don't want to work in my fucking shop, eh?" Before Sebastian could react, Max raised up the keyboard, "Well, I don't want to listen to your fucking music." He slammed the keyboard down against a corner of the countertop, cracking the frame open and smashing the display panel. Stephanie gasped. Max sneered at Sebastian and threw the wreckage on the floor.

Sebastian turned from Max to his mother. Stephanie held his gaze, then lowered her eyes and walked next to Max. Max crossed his arms, his veins popping around his well-toned biceps, his shoulders bulging around his neck, and the boulders of his chest pressing against the t-shirt stretched across his torso. Sebastian grabbed onto the strap of his backpack and walked out the door.

Chapter 25

"Hey, buddy, what are you doing here?"

"Is my dad around?" asked Sebastian.

"Seb, you know your dad's not here." The man opened the door wider, "Step in a minute."

Gid was a friend of Sebastian's dad, fighting the same demon, crack. But Gid managed to evade prosecution.

"I need a place to stay for the night, just one night, and I'll be gone."

"Who is it, Gid?" Mara, Gid's wife, walked into the living room holding a child. "Oh, it's you, Seb."

"He needs a place to stay for the night."

"Just for a night," Sebastian interjected. "On the couch... on the floor. I'll be gone tomorrow."

"Gid, a word," Mara said as she motioned with her head towards the kitchen.

Sebastian couldn't make out much from their muttering until Mara raised her voice slightly, saying, "I don't want to deal with his psycho mother. Or the police she'll drag over here."

The couple returned to the living room. "What about your mom?" Gid asked.

"I've already texted her. Told her I was staying with friends for the night. It won't be a problem."

The baby in Mara's arm began to fuss. "One night, Seb," she said. "Then you sort things out with your mother."

Chapter 26

Mallory passed Sebastian a sandwich. She'd packed an extra ever since he joined Jess and her for lunch.

"I didn't know you had cats," Jess said to Sebastian.

"I don't."

"Then where did all this cat fuzz come from?" Looking down her arm, "Shit, you got it all over my sweater."

"Sor—rrry," said Sebastian, scooting over to leave a wider gap between him and Jess.

Jess eyed Sebastian suspiciously. "Where have you been?"

"With friends."

"With friends... not home."

Sebastian said nothing.

"What's she done?" asked Jess blandly.

Mallory stopped eating and looked over at her two friends, trying to follow the conversation with its gaps and tacit understandings.

"She hooked up with a bastard," Sebastian sputtered. A tear slid down his cheek, which he quickly wiped away. He slumped forward and pulled his tightened fists to his forehead, breathing heavily to gain composure.

"Did he hit you?" asked Jess softly.

"No," Sebastian blurted out. "He smashed my keyboard on the kitchen counter."

"Shit!" "God!" exclaimed Jess and Mallory together.

"I wouldn't work in his fucking auto shop."

"You have a job already," said Mallory.

"Which he'll never find out," Sebastian thundered. Then, under his breath, "He thinks I'm a loser."

"He's an asshole!" said Jess. "And I take it, your mom is...."

"What's new there: 'The best thing that has ever happened to me,'" he mimicked.

"Shit!" said Jess. "Soooo, where did you spend the night?"

Sebastian pressed his head back against the wall. "You're not going to like it."

"Christ, don't tell me you went back to Gid?" exclaimed Jess.

"It was just for a night," said Sebastian. "He and Mara were actually quite nice."

"Yeah, yeah. Didn't your dad say the same thing?"

For some moments, the three sat quietly, Mallory deciding to save her questions for another time.

Quietly yet forcefully, Sebastian said, "I'm not going back home."

~

Sebastian did go back, briefly. He knew Max would likely rekey the locks and soon. He skipped his afternoon classes, slipped into the house and hurried upstairs. He dropped his backpack in his room and stole into the bedroom his mother shared with Max. The blinds were lowered, dimming the room, but Sebastian was too leery to turn on the lights. His heart pounded, and every sense was on high alert for the slightest hint of an unexpected return of Max or his mom. If he was caught snooping around here....

His mom had said a purse; all his papers were in a purse. Sebastian walked toward a dresser and opened a few of the larger drawers. He slid his hand underneath the contents, careful to place everything back as he found it. Unsuccessful with the dresser, Sebastian turned his attention to the walk-in closet. He pulled out his phone and turned on the flashlight, casting its light around the shelves and hanging clothes. Two purses sat together on a shelf. Sebastian looked through both— no records, no manila envelope. *Where could it be?* Sebastian began to sweat. The longer he remained in the house, the more his anxiety soared. He left the closet and walked into the room, pausing to take deep breaths. *It has to be in the closet,* he concluded. As he scanned the closet again, he noticed a folding step-stool. Climbing up, he reexamined the top shelves, putting his hands behind boxes. And there he found it, in a corner. *Lookie, lookie,* he thought; *Mom is hiding things from her great guy, Max.* Inside the purse was the manila envelope. He pulled out its contents and discovered not only his birth certificate and custody papers but his health card... and a wad of cash!

Sebastian was tempted to pocket the cash, but in the end, he tucked the empty envelope and the money back into the purse. Meticulously, he put the purse and the step stool back exactly as they were and shut the closet door. Slowly he examined the room, making sure he had left nothing amiss, then he turned and walked to his room. The change of clothes he hurriedly stuffed in his backpack was needed, but he had only returned for his documents and his one treasured possession: a slim photo album with pictures of him and his dad. With these safely stashed in an inside coat pocket, Sebastian picked up his backpack and slipped out of the house.

Chapter 27

Willow Leboucan scanned her classroom. The students were occupied jotting, typing or doodling ideas for their upcoming writing project. Sebastian was printing intently, focused and calm, mapping out a graphic novel. The classroom door opened, and Mrs. M, a learning assistant, walked in. "The student I usually work with isn't here," she whispered to Willow, "so I was sent to this wing to see if anyone needed an extra hand."

Willow knew these infrequent and random offers of help were an attempt to spread out the school's limited resources when an absence made it possible. Today it could not have come at a better time. Since Willow had arrived at school that morning, she'd been called aside by the principal, the drama teacher and several students. She needed a bathroom break and quickly. Though she made it a point never to leave her classes, this was an urgency that could be delayed no longer, and Mrs. M was a veteran.

Willow whispered softly to Mrs. M, "Bathroom. I'll be back in minutes." Mrs. M gave a slight nod, walked to the back of the classroom, and pulled out her phone.

Willow didn't bother with the staff bathroom, halfway across the building and a floor down. Instead, she cruised to the students' restrooms just two doors away. Re-entering the corridor, Willow heard a commotion coming from her classroom. As she sprinted to her door, Sebastian emerged, livid.

"I hate this fucking school and every fucking person in it," he screamed, his eyes filled with pure rage.

Willow was stunned by his raw anger and the roar of his voice. Sebastian stomped down the hallway on a rampage, ripping paper off bulletin board displays and kicking over a waste bin. Students and teachers alike poured into the hallway. Willow wound her way between them, hoping to catch up with Sebastian. She flew down the stairway and saw Sebastian run out an exit door. Pursuit was futile. Turning back, she came face to face with Jess. "He's gone. Back to class."

Willow raced back up the stairs and walked down the corridor toward her classroom. Ignoring the teachers, she turned to the students, "The show is over. Get back to your classrooms." When she reached her room, the majority of her students stood in the hallway, mumbling to each other and pointing out the wreckage Sebastian had left behind.

"Into the classroom!" said Willow as she strode toward her door, but she stopped abruptly at the threshold. Two table desks were upturned; whatever had been on top was now strewn across the floor. Mrs. M stood wide-eyed at the back of the room. Several students sat in their seats, waiting for her reaction.

Willow walked to Sebastian's chair and looked back toward the front of the classroom. From what she could see, he had upended his desk, shoved off water bottles from students' desks as he made his way to the door, and then flipped over the desk at the front of the classroom. As Willow bent to lift up Sebastian's overturned desk, she noticed the writing pad on which he had been so intent as she left the class. What had happened in the two minutes she had been out of the room?

Her students were slowly entering the classroom. Those with desks near the windows went back to their seats. Others who sat within the epicentre of the explosion hung near the whiteboard at the front of the room.

To the students waiting to approach their desks, Willow said, "Let's clean up this mess." And to the whole class, "And not a word. I don't want to hear a word." Willow picked up the writing pad and went to her desk. The principal stood at her door and motioned to her. "Do you need help?"

"Not at the moment, Frida."

Seeing her attention diverted, some students began chatting. "No talking. Read a book, go back to work, or look out the window," she said firmly.

"What happened?" whispered Frida.

"I'm trying to find out. I'll write up an incident report and talk to you later."

Frida gave a glance around the room and left. Willow and Mrs. M helped reposition the desks and collect the scattered belongings. Holding out a binder, Willow asked a student, "Does this belong to you, Ava?" Ava nodded and reached for it. Her hand was trembling.

When order had been restored and all the students were seated, Willow asked, "What happened?"

After a brief pause, one student shook his head, saying, "I didn't see anything. Sebastian just exploded." A few others nodded in agreement.

Victor leaned back in his chair. "The guy is bat-shit crazy."

"What an asshole!" said Jess. "You don't know anything about Sebastian."

"Victor, the facts, not a twisted interpretation," said Willow sternly. "And, Jess, watch the language."

At the rear of the classroom, Mallory glanced over at Victor then shifted her gaze to Willow. It was odd. Mallory rarely lifted her eyes from her notebook. As soon as Willow noticed her, Mallory looked down.

"So," said Willow, redirecting her attention to the whole class, "Sebastian went from quietly writing to flipping desks within a minute of me leaving the room without any... provocation?"

Many of the students nodded in agreement.

"Is anyone hurt?" Every student either shook their head or said no.

"My laptop screen is cracked. My mother is going to be *seriously* pissed," said a student.

"Why is that lunatic even allowed in the class?" said Victor. "He's only here because he went psycho in Mrs. Flint's class. He should be in a psych ward." A few students snickered, but most looked to Willow for a response.

"Enough, Victor! Words like psycho and lunatic are derogatory—"

"Derogatory?" he mimicked.

"You know what it means. Don't use putdowns in my class... or anywhere for that matter." Then addressing the class, "Until a few minutes ago, Sebastian had been doing quite well in this class. I don't know what upset him, but I'll be working closely with him so this doesn't happen again. Remember, Sebastian most likely feels worse about this than anyone else. If any of you would like to talk further about this incident, come and see me or one of our school counsellors. Now, let's start again." Willow motioned for Mrs. M to remain and resumed class on automatic pilot.

The bell rang. Lunch break.

As the students began to leave, Willow called over Ava. "How are you doing?" Tears welled in her eyes. "I want you to feel safe in my classroom. Can you stop by after school?" Ava nodded and left.

Once the classroom cleared, Willow sank into her chair and looked over at Mrs. M, still standing at the back of the room. "What happened?" she asked, bewildered.

Mrs. M walked over to a chair and sat. "I don't know. You left. Everything was quiet. Then that kid just explodes." She threw up her hands. "Just like that, explodes. It all happened in seconds. I don't think you had been gone a minute."

"And nothing happened, nothing at all?"

"If it did, I didn't notice. One of the guys left... I presume, for the bathroom."

"Who was that?"

"You have forty students in here. I don't know these kids. I barely noticed when he left." Mrs. M raised both hands in exasperation. "I have no idea who it was."

"So nothing happened?" asked Willow in disbelief.

"I didn't see or hear anything, okay?" said Mrs. M. "You left. I took advantage of the time to send out a couple of texts and, out of the blue, the kid, the one with a mass of red hair: he explodes!" Mrs. M glared at Willow. "I've heard about him. I don't understand why he's even at our school."

"Where should he be?"

"Not here."

"Then where?"

"Not my problem." Mrs. M got up. "I'm going for lunch."

Though famished a half-hour before, Willow no longer had an appetite. Alone now, she could feel her heart racing and her body quivering. Doubt and self-recrimination seeped through her being. If only she hadn't left. She had read in Sebastian's file that he could be volatile, but she had never experienced this side of him. Maybe Mrs. M was right. Sebastian didn't belong in the class. How could she justify his presence when others felt threatened? Ava already suffered from anxiety, and this incident would certainly set her back. And this time, only a computer had been damaged. The next time would he attack a student?

Willow leaned forward, her head cradled in her hands. She closed her eyes and breathed in deeply to calm herself, but the disparaging thoughts pushed through. What was she doing? She had been accused of coddling challenging students, rewarding before results. Willow saw it differently: kindness forged trust; relationships before results. Was she living a pipe dream? After Sebastian's rampage, did she really see unspoken reproach in the eyes of her neighbouring teachers, or was she becoming paranoid in her uncertainty?

Yet, Sebastian had been doing so well. Paula Flint wrote him off, but the drama teacher considered him a marvel. Quick-witted, he came up with impromptu lines that livened up her classes and got others to participate.

At this moment, Willow knew she was in the eye of a hurricane. By the afternoon, she would be reporting to the principal, fielding emails and texts from parents, facing questions from fellow teachers—some sympathetic, others not—and finding funds for the broken laptop; Sebastian wouldn't be able to cover it. Lastly, Sebastian would need to be reintegrated back to school, facing stares and gossip.

Willow's gaze fell on Sebastian's notebook. Two paragraphs jotted evenly then, mid-sentence in the third paragraph, a dark pencil slash across the page. Willow stared at the slash. This had not been a random outburst. Intentionally or not, Sebastian had been jolted.

Chapter 28

Are you OK? Willow texted Sebastian. *Rough patch today at school. Would like to hear what happened from you. We can work through this.* Willow pocketed her phone and headed to the principal's office for the debriefing.

"As far as we can tell, he left the school grounds," Frida said. "It's probably for the best—let him cool down."

"I've texted him, but I doubt I'll hear back," said Willow, glancing at her phone.

"You have his cell number? We don't have it on file."

"I helped with the *Revue* in December."

"And?" said Frida quizzically.

"I sent reminders for rehearsals—he uses an app. I think Sebastian needs to be reassured that he can try again." The principal pulled down her glasses and gave Willow a look. "He was doing great, Frida, just fine. This will be a real setback for him... Oh! Did you find out how one of my students knew Sebastian had been 'kicked out' of Flint's class?"

Frida sighed, "According to Paula, she warned her class that disrespect was not tolerated in her class and that Sebastian would not be returning. 'I never said 'kicked out'—her words."

"A technicality."

"Willow, Sebastian's behaviour is escalating. What's going on with that kid?"

"Something happened in the classroom that triggered him," said Willow, her voice rising, "I'm sure of it!"

"Okay, okay," reassured Frida.

Willow softened her tone, "I've gone through his file. It's sketchy, but reading between the lines: a custody battle for which his dad does not show up, a stint at a group home, several schools, erratic grades. I wonder about his home life."

"Willow, your hands are shaking. We'll talk more about this later. Why don't you go for a walk? Take a break. I can have someone cover your next class."

"It's a prep."

"Better yet. Now go! Eat something!"

Chapter 29

Willow walked back from the local sandwich shop, sipping her tea. Frida had been right: food, beverage, and fresh air helped calm her. The incident continued to mill around in her mind, but she felt less rattled. As she walked, a thought came to mind: Sebastian and Jess were friends, and Jess was in the classroom when Sebastian lost it; she may have seen something.

Willow walked into the school office and went straight to June Barnes. As she approached her desk, June said, "I hear you had a little excitement in the classroom today."

"Good news travels fast."

"Oh, doesn't it, though," said June with a smirk.

"I need you to look up something for me."

"How unusual." June opened a new screen. "Ready."

"Where would I find Jess Gayle at this time?"

In moments, a schedule filled the screen. June moved her cursor back and forth under a course name with its location.

"Thanks." Willow gave June's shoulder a squeeze.

~

Jess, her head down, leaned against the painted cinder block wall outside the room where the choral music class was underway.

"Jess, if you saw *anything* going on in the class before Sebastian lost it, I need to know." Jess said nothing. Willow continued, "It looks like he might have been bumped."

Jess looked at Willow, "Bumped?"

"I'm not sure. It's a possibility."

Jess hesitated, then said, "Right before Sebastian exploded, Victor walked out of the classroom. Did he bump Sebastian? I don't know."

Willow said nothing.

"Can I go back to class?"

"Do you know where Sebastian may have gone?"

"No."

"If you hear from him, would you ask him to text me? Tell him he's not in trouble. I just want to talk to him."

Jess nodded and said, "Is that it?"

"Yes, yes. Get back to your singing. Most likely, he's at home."

Jess shot a glance at Willow, "His mother's an asshole. His dad's in jail." Then she turned and walked into the classroom.

Chapter 30

Jess heard a faint knock at her door and peered through the blinds of her front window. Wind pummelled the fir trees, and snowflakes dashed horizontally through the domed glow of the street lights. And there, huddled at the front door, was a figure she knew well.

"What are you doing here?" Jess asked sternly as she pulled Sebastian into her apartment. "And, God, what kind of weed have you been smoking? You smell like a rotten skunk! If any of the counsellors walk in, I'm screwed. They'll think I was smoking with you!"

"I need something to eat," said Sebastian in a joint-induced calm.

"Shit! You're stoned out of your mind. You're going to lose your job!"

"I wasn't stoned at work."

"Why are you blowing your money on weed?"

"I didn't pay for it."

"Right. You didn't...." Jess stopped her lecture and stared at Sebastian. "You didn't go back to Gid. Tell me you didn't go back."

"I needed some money; that's the only reason I went back today. It was after work. Just wanted to borrow some money until I get paid. Gid said no loan, but he'd pay me for an errand, a little drop-off. The weed was just a tip."

"A tip to keep you coming back. Sebastian! And who knows what he mixes in with his pot. Wake up! Your dad's in jail because of him, the bastard."

"Jess, Jess," Sebastian slurred, putting a hand on her shoulder. Jess shook it off.

"You told me Gid had your dad hustling drugs outside of homeless shelters," Jess said forcefully. "What do you think his plans are for you? The same thing outside of youth centres!"

Sebastian just looked down. "Go sit at the table," Jess said, her voice softening, "I'll get you something to eat. Hot chocolate and a grilled cheese?"

"Yeah, thanks. You have any Coke?"

"No."

"Yeah, hot chocolate then."

As Jess prepared the meal, she said, "I didn't see you at school this afternoon... or at lunch."

Sebastian said nothing.

"I suppose it had nothing to do with your meltdown in class?" Again, Sebastian did not respond. "Ms. Willow was asking about you. She told me she thinks someone shoved you."

Sebastian lifted up his head quickly. "How did she know?"

"So it is true. Who was it?"

"Who cares." A tear rolled down his cheek. "I'm such a loser. I can't hold my shit together. I can't do school."

"Ms. Willow wants you back. She said to call her."

"I'm not going back."

"What about your mom?"

"She thinks I'm staying with friends."

"Yeah, until a caseworker knocks at her door and asks about you. Sebastian, if you don't show up at school, you'll be back at the group home. Text Ms. Willow."

When Jess brought over his meal, Sebastian was nodding off at the table.

"Hey, time to wake up." Sebastian shook himself awake and began to eat.

"So, where are you staying?"

"Remember Logan?"

"The comedian at the group home?"

"That's the one. He's living with his uncle."

"And his uncle is letting you stay there?" Jess asked incredulously.

"Uh, not exactly. Logan has this *huge* family. The house is packed with people."

"So... you sleep under his bed?"

Sebastian laughed. "They have a garage behind the house–you

know, the kind near an alley—and it's packed with stuff. Like loaded. Logan and I shifted around some boxes way in the back and made like a little igloo."

"Do you eat with them?"

"No. Too much to ask of the guy. Just happy I have a place to sleep. I go through a side door and crawl over stuff to my hidey-hole. But it's been so cold—we could only find some old drapes and a tarp for blankets. I need money to get a sleeping bag. That's why I went to Gid. But he only paid me twenty bucks for the delivery."

"How much do you need?"

"A hundred and fifty more."

"A hundred and fifty more? What's the sleeping bag made of? Spun gold?"

"The garage isn't heated. I need one of those sleeping bags they use in the mountains."

Jess considered a few moments. "Where's the store that sells this stuff?"

"Close to the mall."

"Tomorrow, we'll go buy one together."

"What?"

"I've saved some money. I can help you out."

Sebastian began to cry.

"You can stay here tonight, and let's hope no staff come to chat."

Sebastian got up from his chair and gave Jess a hug.

"Did Gid give you anything else?"

Sebastian reached into a pocket and pulled out a small plastic bag with a pill.

"Can I see it?"

Sebastian handed over the bag, and Jess moved quickly to the sink, turned on the water and washed it down the drain.

"What the fuck!"

"You don't know what's in that shit! Gid's a rat."

"I was saving it for an emergency. I could sell it."

"Stay away from Gid! Now get in the shower—you reek. I'll wash your clothes."

"What am I going to wear?"

"You can sleep in one of my sweatshirts." Then eyeing his pants, "I think my sweat pants will fit, too."

After the clothes were in the wash, Jess opened up all the windows, despite the cold, to air out the apartment. She took the cushions off the couch, pulled it out from the wall and set the cushions behind it. She draped a sheet over the couch, hoping the missing cushions wouldn't be so obvious if anyone came to the door. At least it wouldn't be immediately apparent that she was having a sleepover. Then she brought the blankets from her bed and put them on the cushions for Sebastian. She would turn up the heat, go to bed in her clothes and cover herself with her jackets.

Chapter 31

Mallory waited until her father left the house before she got out of bed for school. He had to be at the worksite by seven, which left her plenty of time before Riverbank's nine o'clock bell. As she laid out the bread for her sandwich, she debated if she would make an extra for Sebastian. He didn't show up on Friday, and she was saddled with an extra lunch. *Oh, what the hell!* she thought as she pulled extra slices from the loaf and set them on the counter.

Sebastian's meltdown was no mystery to Mallory. She knew exactly what had happened. Ever since Sebastian joined Ms. Willow's class, he tried to sit at one of the desks alongside her or Jess. If he arrived right as class started or shortly after, and the preferred places were taken, he found a desk nearby. Such was the case the day he blew up: Sebastian sat a couple desks ahead of Mallory. When Ms. Willow left the room, Victor got up, crossed through the back of the classroom and came up the aisle, passing Mallory. When he neared Sebastian's desk, he bent over and whispered a greeting to a kid who was sitting across from Sebastian. Just before he straightened up, he swivelled his hip quickly, hitting Sebastian's elbow. The movement was almost imperceptible. In the few seconds it took for Sebastian to react, Victor was at the door. But what set off the explosion was the brief moment before Victor walked out of the classroom; he turned back toward Sebastian and put his hand on the doorframe, middle finger up.

Chapter 32

Willow brought in a steaming cup of tea and placed it in front of Sebastian, along with a handful of sugar packets and a stirrer. "Thanks for coming in early. I know it's harder on a Monday." She slid over a paper bag. "I wasn't sure if you would have a chance to eat before you came, so I picked you up a breakfast sandwich. It's yours if you want it."

"Thanks." Sebastian poured three sugar packets into his tea and pocketed the rest.

After a few pleasantries, Willow got straight to the point. "Last Friday, what happened that upset you so much?"

Sebastian stirred and sipped his tea. "I'm sorry. Sometimes I lose it. I'm really sorry."

"Yes, I can see you're sorry. I would like to know what happened that caused you to 'lose it.' You seemed happy enough when I left the room."

Sebastian said nothing.

"I heard Victor passed your desk right before the incident."

"Leave Victor out of this. I got upset. I'm sorry."

After a few more attempts to root out the details, all futile, Willow said, "We have some counsellors at this school–you can speak with them, and what you say remains confidential. They also help students learn how to manage their emotions."

"Like counting to ten?" Sebastian smiled.

"That can help, for sure. There are other tools as well."

"Do I have to?"

"Sebastian, the real question is: do you need help to manage your emotions? This week you flipped over a couple of desks and cracked a laptop. No one got hurt. But I know how awful you would have felt if someone had. You're a wonderful, funny, creative, caring person. You just need some help with your emotions."

Sebastian sipped his tea.

"And," continued Willow, "I understand the counsellors provide some really great snacks."

Sebastian smiled.

"I can introduce you now. Then you and the counsellor can discuss what best fits your schedule." Willow stood. "Why not give it a shot?"

"Okay." Sebastian rose and, Willow noticed, picked up the bag with the breakfast sandwich.

Chapter 33

"Take note of your assigned desks," said Ms. Willow as Mallory entered the classroom with a group of other students. Projected on the whiteboard was a seating plan. "We'll be following this arrangement until the end of the school year."

Mallory scanned the diagram and saw that she was placed where she usually sat, with Jess to her side. Sebastian was placed in front of them. As the desks filled, Mallory noticed several changes, but the students who generally sat near each other were either in the same place or together somewhere else in the classroom.

"What's this all about?" said Victor as he strolled in. His seat was at the first desk in the aisle closest to the door with his pal, Oliver, behind him.

"New procedure," said Willow. "It will save me time taking attendance." Then pointing to his desk, "Take your seat, Victor. I gave you prime real estate. You can be the first one out every day."

Jess arrived and slid next to Mallory. "This is interesting."

"Ms. Willow said it's for attendance."

"Yeah, right." She looked briefly at Victor, and Mallory darted a glance in the same direction.

Sebastian swooped in right as the bell rang. Mallory gave a slight wave and pointed to the desk in front of her.

"Sleeping better?" asked Jess when Sebastian plopped down in his seat.

"Much better," said Sebastian. "Thanks."

~

Sebastian entered the back stairwell and held the door for Jess, "Hard to believe no one else has discovered this place," he said.

"Don't jinx it," said Jess. "But the fact that most students take off during lunch break may have something to do with it."

As Sebastian stooped to sit under the staircase, he said, "Hey, Mallory's already here." Mallory passed him a sandwich as he sat next to her. "Thanks."

Jess settled in on the other side of Mallory and pulled out a water bottle.

"So, did you meet with Ms. Willow this morning?" Jess asked.

"Yeah. She set me up with a counsellor. I'm supposed to check in with her every morning before school starts, which is sweet because," Sebastian bit into his sandwich, "her office is stocked with food."

"The sitting arrangement in Ms. Willow's class was unexpected," remarked Jess. "I guess Victor won't be roaming the classroom anymore."

Mallory looked up at Jess. "You saw it, too?"

"Heard about it."

Mallory turned to Sebastian.

"Victor is an asshole," he said.

"Are you in any other classes with him or his gang?" Jess asked.

"No."

"Good. Stay away from that guy," said Jess. "He just wants to set you up."

For a while, they ate in silence. "Did you hear about Layla?" Sebastian asked as he finished off his sandwich.

"No," replied Jess warily, looking over at Sebastian. "Something happen to her?"

"She's back in detox."

"What's detox?" asked Mallory.

"A place you go to get off drugs," said Jess. "How do you know this?" she asked Sebastian.

"Logan."

"Who's Logan?" asked Mallory.

"Friend of Layla's. We were all in the group home together," said Jess.

"Layla's still in the group home, right?" asked Mallory.

"Yeah."

"Did she get the drugs there?"

"Noooo," said Sebastian. "Not at that group home."

"She probably picked some up here," said Jess.

"Here? At our school?"

"God, Mallory. Yeah, here!"

Mallory lowered her head and continued to eat her sandwich.

"Sorry about that. I didn't mean to get bitchy." Jess pulled out a snack from her backpack. "Layla's an easy target. Some guy probably gave her a few pills, friendly-like, and Layla got hooked again. There's a lot of bastards like that around...." Jess shot a glance at Sebastian. "Here and elsewhere."

"He makes her pay?" asked Mallory.

"Yeah, after she's addicted," said Sebastian. "Even for the 'free' stuff he's already given. The thing is: she doesn't have the money."

"So, how does she pay?"

Jess sighed. "Sex, Mallory. He makes her pay with sex... a blow job. Either with him, or he pimps her out to some other guys at school or after school."

"That's sick," said Mallory.

"When you're desperate for the stuff, you do anything. And the dealer knows it."

The school bell rang sharply. "Nothing like a conversation full of unicorns and butterflies to brighten up our afternoon," said Sebastian as the trio scramble out from their niche.

~

Mallory squeezed through the high school's main entrance amid the rush of students. The sky was brilliantly blue, the sun blazing bright, warming the early March nip. Mallory took a deep breath and walked down the stairs to the broad walkway that skirted the front of the school. Off to the side, she saw Jess leaning against a tree, watching the departing horde.

Mallory leaned on the other side of the tree. "Thanks for telling me about Layla," she said.

"Yeah, it's sad."

They both stood there watching the light-hearted chaos. Friends were getting together and piling into cars. Parents pulled up to the curb, honking or waving to get the attention of their teens. One younger child hopped out of a minivan and ran to greet and hug an older sibling. It was like watching a fairytale, like living in another realm: homes, security, places to go, connections and love.

"Do you ever wonder what it would be like?" whispered Jess, not taking her eyes from the scene.

"I had a little taste once," said Mallory softly.

"Me, too," replied Jess. She pushed herself off the tree. "Want to come to my place? I've got some ham, cheese, eggs and bread."

"Sure."

Chapter 34

A chime rang out as Sebastian pushed through the entrance of '*Strum 'n Drum.*'

"You're early... as usual," said Craig as he turned toward the door. He eyed Sebastian's backpack. "Quite a load you got there, buddy."

"It's not very heavy." The day before, he and Jess had picked out a larger backpack from a second-hand store. Sebastian needed one big enough to hold his new sleeping bag and a change of clothes. He couldn't risk leaving his stuff at Logan's. It might be found, or he might get locked out.

"You know, you don't have to be here until five," said Craig.

"Ah... I like coming early, playing on the keyboards."

"I see. If that's the case, I'd like to ask you to do an errand for me when you arrive."

"Sure."

The boss walked Sebastian back to the entrance. "See that sandwich shop across the street? They have the best soups, salads, sandwiches, and paninis. You ever eat there?"

"Never."

"Well, I like to eat before things pick up around here. Since you are coming in at four, would you mind stopping at the sandwich shop and picking up my order?"

"No trouble at all."

"Good. And while you're there, I want you to get a meal for yourself. I'll tell the owner to add it to my tab."

"Really?" said Sebastian, surprised.

"You're coming early. You earn it." He repositioned his cowboy hat. "And I've noticed you like to come in even on the days you're not on the schedule, so as long as you're here, are you willing to do the pickup?"

"Yeah!"

"So we have a deal."

Sebastian looked around sheepishly, "Like right now?"

Craig laughed, "Right now. Bring that trunk of yours to my office. You can store it there while you work." As Sebastian turned to pick up his backpack, Craig gave him a pat on his shoulder. "And get a meal, not just a sandwich. You know, something to drink, the soup and salad as well."

As Sebastian walked across the street to the sandwich shop, he thought, *I can make this work! At Jess's, I can wash clothes; at school, breakfast, lunch, and showers in the locker room; at Strum's, keyboard practice, dinner and job; at Logan's, a place to sleep. And he had friends. Yes, life was good.*

Chapter 35

The ceaseless ringing from her phone shook Jess out of a deep sleep. It was still dark outside. *Who the hell is calling?* Jess rolled over and looked at her screen. Lena.

"Hello?" she whispered, her voice gravelly with sleep.

"Jess, I'm soooo sorry to call you like this. Seth and I are scheduled to drive to Edmonton for a photoshoot this morning, and our model just called in sick. Jess, I know you don't want any gigs outside of Calgary. I respect that. I'm just asking you for a one-time favour. It's a Saturday-only gig. You'll be able to rest up tomorrow before school. Can you fill in?"

Jess's sleep-fogged mind was struggling to keep up. She could tell Lena was desperate to find someone, but....

Lena barrelled on. "You're the same size. You'd be the perfect fit. And, quite honestly, you're a better model. This catalogue company is going to love you. And I promise you, I will have you back in Calgary by four... no later than five." Lena paused briefly. "I'll make this worth your while—give you some of my commission. It's a great gig: three hundred dollars. We leave here at six-thirty, shoot for three hours, and we'll be out of Edmonton by one or close to it."

Jess looked at the time. "At six-thirty? That's less than a half-hour."

"I know I'm asking a lot, Jess. You'll have time to do your hair and makeup in Edmonton. And don't worry about breakfast. Seth and I are stopping at 'Tim's' before we pick you up."

"Seth's coming?"

"Absolutely, I'm not going to risk this shoot with some unknown, inexperienced photographer. You still want hot chocolate?"

"Yeah."

"And something to eat. What do you want?"

Jess said the first thing that came to her mind, "Ah, grilled cheese, I guess."

"Great! We're on our way. We'll meet you at six-thirty—you know, on the main drag near the corner of your street. Seth said he dropped you off there when he brought you back from Fish Creek."

"Yeah, it's right down the street from my place."

"See you soon."

Jess sat on the edge of her bed for a few moments trying to shake off her grogginess. She had less than fifteen minutes to get ready, leaving her five to walk to the intersection. *Lena has my address, my God. She could have picked me up outside my apartment.* But there was no time for these considerations. She had to hurry.

Jess threw cold water on her face, washed up, and dressed in a pair of jeans and a sweater top. She pulled up her braids, secured them with a scrunchie, then tossed some makeup and hair products into her shoulder bag. She zipped up her knee-high leather boots, threw on her winter coat and locked her door behind her.

Dusk was giving way to daylight as she approached the designated intersection. Seth, smiling broadly, stepped out of a parked car near the corner and walked to meet her.

"I told Lena you would come through!" He shook her hand and whispered, "Did you get my links to your portfolio?"

"Yes. It's a great start. Did your professor like it?"

"He's very impressed."

When they reached the car. Seth opened the back door for Jess.

"Jess, you saved the shoot!" said Lena as she pulled out to the street, "I owe you big time."

"I put your cocoa in the cup holder," Seth said.

"Yeah, thanks, I see it."

"And here is your grilled cheese." He passed back a paper sack.

As Jess settled in, she remarked, "This is a different car."

"Yeah," said Lena. "When I go out of town, I rent a car. It's easier to claim as an expense."

Lena filled in Jess about the photoshoot. "They're going to love you!" she said. "And we couldn't have asked for better weather. This time of year, you never know what you're going to get."

Jess sipped her cocoa, trying to settle after her whirlwind prep. Hearing Lena's and Seth's enthusiasm made her happy she had chosen to come, and she eased into the ride. "This cocoa is really good," she commented."

"I had them put in extra whipped cream and caramel."

The adrenaline surge that propelled her hasty preparation subsided. Within a half-hour, she was overcome with weariness. "I'm so tired," she said, "I went to bed late last night."

"And I woke you up so early," sympathized Lena. "Go ahead and sleep. We'll wake you up before we arrive."

Jess took off her coat, rolled it into a pillow, and rested her head against it. Gazing to the left, she watched the crests of the snow-studded Rockies glow pink and coral with the rising sun until she drifted off to sleep.

PART TWO

Chapter 36

After school Victor and his two sidekicks, Brady and Brock, piled into Oliver's car to pick up some burgers and fries.

"Didn't see you this morning," remarked Victor as the group drove off. Oliver arrived after lunch and had met up with Victor shortly before the last period.

"Dentist. My mom makes cleanings a family affair for my sisters and me."

After they had picked up their orders and were sitting around a table, Victor said, "I was thinking of stopping over at *Strum n' Drum* this afternoon and checking out their guitars."

"Since when have you become interested in guitars?" laughed Brody.

"As a matter of fact, I've been considering it for some time."

"Hey, you gotta check out this video," said Brock. He held up a video of animals playing various musical instruments.

"Yeah, Victor, definitely your style," said Brady. The two roared, causing the other diners to turn and look.

"Kinda quiet, Oliver," said Victor. "You still wasted from the party? Speaking of which—" Victor held up his phone, "Party pics!"

~

The party. Last Saturday.

"Mom, it's just a group of friends."

Oliver's mother had been hesitant about letting him go, but she relented when she heard that the person throwing the party was a friend of Victor's. Earlier in the school year, when Oliver and Victor worked on a class project together, Victor had come over a couple of times to study. He had chatted comfortably with Oliver's parents on a variety of topics, addressing his dad as "Sir" and his mother, "Mrs. Wilson-Patel." Before leaving, Victor complimented and thanked his mom for the sandwiches she had prepared. "A perfect gentleman," his mother had remarked. "Mature for his age." As time went by, Oliver did nothing to adjust his mother's assessment, although he was beginning to feel uncomfortable with some of Victor's comments and antics. But this was the first time Oliver had been invited to a house party, and he was eager to go. "It'll be epic." Victor had encouraged.

Victor gave directions as Oliver drove. "Almost there," he said as they turned down a residential street on the other side of the city.

"How do you know this guy?" asked Oliver.

"Friend of a friend... It's one of these houses coming up."

"Judging from the number of cars, I'd say you're right. In fact, it's probably that house with all the lights on and people walking through the front door."

Victor laughed. "Excellent, Sherlock!"

Oliver dropped off his buddies in front of the house and scoured the neighbourhood for a parking space. Two blocks away, he found one. Arriving at the party house, Oliver walked through the unlocked door into a foyer churning with activity. The walls pulsated with music. Teens holding drinks going up the stairs to the second floor were trying to avoid those hurrying down for refills. Oliver walked into a huge open area. It throbbed with teens dancing in the living room, teens around the dining table cheering a beer pong match, teens dipping into snacks spread out on the kitchen island, and teens lined at the counters mixing concoctions of energy drinks, soda and booze. Talking was out of the question unless you hollered into someone's ear. The energy was intoxicating, and for a few minutes, Oliver raised his arms and danced with the throng in the living room.

Extricating himself from the disco crowd, Oliver looked around but saw none of his friends nor anyone else he knew. He grabbed a beer and followed a couple of people down to the basement. Although the blaring music, hoopla, and stomping pervaded the basement level, the decimal level was lower and the occupants less packed. About a dozen teens were gathered around a foosball table, competing and whooping up encouragement for their friends. A guy hurrying down the stairs behind Oliver opened a bedroom door, and the unmistakable scent of pot wafted throughout the basement. "Woo-hoo," called out the group in the bedroom as the guy tossed around bags of chips and then closed the door.

Oliver went to the foosball table and joined in the fun. He loved the game, and when it was his turn to play, a group of teens he'd just met clapped and yelled his name until he pumped his fist in victory. After that, he was chosen by several competitors to play against them. Cold beers from the basement wet bar were passed around.

Cocooned by avid foosballers, Oliver was oblivious of the time and the growing numbers in the basement. He was jolted back to reality when a herd of young people poured down the stairs, swarmed the basement and took over the foosball table. Oliver squeezed around the mob, moving toward the stairway. The bathroom door swung open as he passed—a guy was parked on the toilet, checking his phone; a girl sat on the ledge of the bathtub, holding the hair of another who was barfing into the tub. The door to the lower deck was open. As teens spilled outside, just as many came in shivering with cold. The potheads had locked the bedroom door against a marauding pack who wanted in. A couple of guys vied to open the door, throwing their weight against it and yanking on the knob. A group stood by, clapping and yelling in unison, "Open, open, open!"

"Shit!!" Oliver exclaimed, but he couldn't hear his own voice. Once on the staircase, he was jostled upward by those behind and pushed back by those descending. Midway he heard the sound of splitting wood and rambunctious shouts of triumph.

Oliver was ejected into the main floor by a surge from those behind him. The open area was now utterly crammed with dancing, hooting teens, the energy at a frenzy. Moving through the room, Oliver quickly scanned for Victor, Brody and Brock without luck. The stairway going upstairs was as jammed as the main floor. Every instinct in Oliver screamed, *Get out!* The foyer was teeming with arriving teens, so Oliver jostled to an open backdoor leading to the top deck. He squeezed out and descended the stairs to the backyard. The light from the windows illuminated enough of the yard for Oliver to locate the gate but not before he saw people defecating on the lawn and vomiting in the garden. He hurried out to the front lawn. The sharp winter wind bit through his shirt. He whipped on the light jacket he had tied around his waist as he ran to his car.

Oliver was driving away from the neighbourhood when three police cars charged past him in the opposite direction.

～

"Hey!" Victor jabbed Oliver with his elbow and snapped his fingers in front of his face. "That was some party!" Victor continued to flip through his photos. "Look at how wasted this guy was!"

"Where were you?" Oliver asked, "I didn't see any of you there."

"We were busy in the bedrooms," said Victor with a wink. "Best part of the parties. A few more notches on my belt. Even Brody got lucky!"

"God, you should have seen it when the cops arrived," said Brock. "It was like watching cockroaches scattering out the doors and across the lawns."

"The secret is to pretend you're asleep," said Victor, "and the cops wake you up and tell you to get lost."

"I left before the cops came," said Oliver.

"We figured," said Victor. "My mom had to call a taxi for us."

"The party had become chaos!" exclaimed Oliver. "People were destroying the house."

Looking steadily at Oliver and speaking like a father calming an anxious child, Victor said, "The party wasn't supposed to get so big, okay? Word must have spread. Yeah, I feel for the guy who had to clean it up, but it happens sometimes." Then banging both hands on the table, he stood up. "Enough of this. Let's go to *Strum N' Drum.*

～

As Oliver pulled into a parking space in front of *Strum's*, Victor said, "You'll never guess who works at this place."

The other three paused.

"The Piano Man!"

"Ah, come on, man," said Oliver, "Leave the guy alone."

"You think I'm coming here for him? That loser?"

Brody and Brock got out, but Oliver remained behind the wheel. Victor looked back through his open door. "You coming?"

"Nah, I just remembered my mom needs the car. I gotta go."

"Shit! So we have to take the bus home! Damn you, Oliver! Just like the party. You're getting useless." Victor slammed the door.

Oliver pulled out of the lot and parked a couple blocks up on a side street. His mom didn't need the car. When his mother bought a new car last summer, his parents gave him the sedan. But he played this charade to have an excuse when needed. *A cop-out,* Oliver thought. He and Victor had been in Mrs. Flint's classroom, hanging out with Brock and Brody the day Victor knighted Sebastian with 'Piano Man.' When the bell rang, he and Victor crossed the corridor to Ms. Willow's class. Brock and Brody, students of Mrs. Flint, relayed the aftermath during lunch.

"What a wimp," Victor had said at the time. "Can't put up with a little teasing."

But Oliver grew uncomfortable after Sebastian's massive blowup in Ms. Willow's classroom. Although he hadn't seen anything, he knew Victor had left the classroom shortly before the outburst. And now, this sudden interest in *Strum 'n Drums*? What did Victor have against this guy?

As Oliver sat alone in the car, his musings shifted. Why was he still hanging out with Victor? At the beginning of the school year, Victor had welcomed Oliver into his group of friends—all high-achievers with big plans for the future. Victor had a razor-sharp mind, easily aced his assignments, and was an excellent study partner. But Oliver was beginning to acknowledge that there was another side of Victor: targeting a guy who posed no threat to him, playing a stud with the girls and, at last, admitting that Victor saw him as nothing more than a ride. So why was he sitting in the car, covering his ass with a lame excuse, instead of standing up to the guy?

Oliver got out of his car and walked back to *Strum 'n Drums*. In the store, he surveyed the displays of guitars. Victor and company were not there. *Don't tell me they left already?* Then he noticed the passageway that led to another section of the store. There, in the back, sat Sebastian in front of a keyboard, head bent, his mass of red hair covering his face. He was surrounded by Victor, Brock and Brody. Laughter spilled out from the group, but Sebastian remained motionless. A large man in a cowboy hat strode down an aisle toward the group.

"What the hell is going on here?" he thundered.

"Oh, we're just having fun with our buddy here," said Victor.

"Fun for who?" the man said to Victor. Turning to Sebastian, he asked, "Are these guys your friends?"

"No. They're assholes."

"Ah, my feelings are hurt," Victor mocked.

The man put his hand on Sebastian's shoulder as he said to the trio, "Get the hell out of this store. I never want to see you here again."

Victor and the two others turned and sauntered up the aisle, laughing among themselves, "'Asshole,' boohoo," laughed Victor. "Hits me right here in the heart." Then he saw Oliver. "Well, look who's here. So mommy doesn't need her car after all?" Oliver flashed him the finger and shook his head with disgust.

"Yeah, fuck you, too, Oliver," sneered Victor.

Oliver walked down the aisle. The man still had his hand on Sebastian's shoulder, and Sebastian was nodding at something the man had said. When Sebastian saw Oliver, he stiffened. The man looked up. "Not another jerk from school?"

Oliver ignored the remark and said to Sebastian, "Sorry, dude. And you're right. They are assholes." Then he turned and left the store.

Chapter 37

The afternoon dismissal bell rang, and the last of the students walked out the door. Willow sat at her desk and typed notes for the substitute teacher replacing her the next day. She was part of a focus group for the school district discussing the future of education. Tomorrow was their final meeting, and a representative of the Minister of Education would be there.

"Ms. Willow?"

Willow turned and was surprised to see Mallory standing in the doorway. Outside of brief interactions that Willow initiated, Mallory had never spoken to her, let alone approached her outside of class. "Oh, hello, Mallory. How can I help you?"

Mallory approached the desk. "Jess hasn't been to school for three days."

"I'm concerned, too." She indicated a chair for Mallory to sit in, but Mallory remained standing. "When was the last time you saw her?"

"Last Friday, at school."

"Did you hear from her over the weekend?"

"No. And I've tried a few times since then, but there's no reply. She usually replies." Mallory paused and stared at Willow.

"Is there something else?"

"Sebastian went by her place yesterday, and she wasn't there."

"Mallory, I know you're her friend, and you're worried, so I'll share something with you. The school called her guardian, and she is looking into it. Hopefully, we'll hear something soon. There's probably a simple explanation."

Mallory shrugged and turned to go.

"Thanks for coming, Mallory. If you hear anything—or need anything yourself—please stop by."

"Yeah, sure."

Willow maintained a calm demeanour for Mallory, but her own apprehension was mounting.

Chapter 38

Officer Wallace walked back to his desk with a cup of coffee and his cell phone vibrating in his back pocket. He glanced at the caller ID—his wife. "Yeah, what's up?"

"Have you seen the numbers? Covid cases are rising. There's a lot of talk that a lockdown is around the corner. Have you heard anything?"

"Nothing," he replied as he sank into his chair and rummaged through a drawer he reserved for his snacks and lunch.

"I had to leave work to pick up Ella at school—she threw up. I hope she didn't pick up that virus. God, this is awful. I'm so worried about you."

"I'll be fine," Wallace said, hoping this would end the conversation; his wife's uneasiness only increased his own. Apprehension simmered within the Missing Persons Unit. Their work was complicated enough without the invasion of a mysterious virus hindering their ability to search for a loved one and creating turmoil in their own families. He pulled out a sandwich from his cooler bag.

"You say you'll be fine, but you don't really know that," said his wife.

"What can I say? No one really knows."

"Well, wash your hands—often." *Too late now,* Wallace thought as he lifted his sandwich from its container and took a bite.

"I need you to pick up some things on your way home, just in case," she continued. "Do you have something you can write with?"

"Can't this wait until the weekend?" Wallace asked as he chewed.

"This is a pandemic, for God's sake! It's been declared a pandemic! Who knows what will happen this weekend."

The office phone began to ring. "Just text me the list. I've got to go."

He abruptly cut the call, gulped down his bite of food, and picked up the phone. "Missing Persons, Officer Wallace."

"I'm Paige Johnson. This morning I reported Jess Gayle as missing. You left a message that I should call you. Have you found her?"

Officer Wallace opened a screen on his computer. "No, I'm sorry we haven't. The call centre forwarded the information you gave this morning, and I'd like to clarify a few points before sending Jess's file to our investigating officers." Wallace began to scroll through the file. "So, Paige, I understand you are the caseworker for Jess Gayle."

"I've only been assigned to Jess for a few months."

"I see that she's run off several times before, the last time about a year ago."

"Yes, that's true. However, from the notes of her previous caseworker, once Jess was placed in the Independent Living Program, she's been fine. In my meetings with her, she seems quite mature and focused."

"How often have you met?"

"Let's see... just checking my notes... yes, twice, right before Christmas and this past Friday."

"So that's, what?" Wallace paused and calculated the interval. "Over two months between visits? How long were these visits?"

"About an hour, maybe less," Paige stammered. "I consider Jess one of my superstars," said Paige, rallying. "She's reliable, sticks to her budget, attends school–rarely absent. No drama, low maintenance, totally capable of living on her own.... Jess has clearly shown herself to be resilient and tough despite what she had gone through."

"Yes, I see she is a ward of the government: PGO, it says in her records–permanent guardianship order. Has she had any contact with her parents?"

"They're dead: drug overdoses, both of them."

"Any other relatives?"

"None that I know of... Well, there's mention here of an uncle, but he's in jail... and he has a no-contact order. Just a moment, I'm skimming through the file... When she was ten, it says, her grandmother died, and custody was given to her mom. Then the mom died, and Jess was placed in foster care."

Wallace typed in a few notes. "You said you met with her last Friday– that was a week ago. How was she?"

"Fine. I picked her up after school, and we went to a funky coffee shop I thought she'd like—you know, something different, outside her neighbourhood. We talked a little about school and her plans to take more classes during the summer. She was polite but not very communicative, so we just chatted about some shows she watches."

"How long were you out together?"

"I dropped her off at her apartment around four-thirty, so... about an hour. She said she planned to stay home during the weekend."

"When did you realize she was missing?"

"Wednesday morning. Someone from the school called to say she had been absent Monday and Tuesday and hadn't shown up that morning either. They were concerned."

Wallace asked the name of the school and her contacts there. Paige continued, "I called Jess yesterday, right after the school contacted me, but didn't hear back. So today, I went to check out her apartment with a staff member from her Independent Living program, and there was no sign of her."

"Why wait a whole day to check out her apartment?"

"Do you want to flip through my caseload?" said Paige curtly. "Right after the call about Jess, I received a call from the police about another client—he'd been apprehended. I spent the rest of the day on that case."

Wallace softened his approach. "Was there anything unusual about the apartment?"

"No, it was clean enough," she said, regaining her composure. "There were some dishes in the sink, the bed unmade, but nothing unusual. We looked for a wallet, her phone... her keys but didn't find them. So it seems she went out somewhere."

"You mentioned a phone," said Wallace.

"Yes." Paige gave Jess's number.

"Do you know her phone carrier?"

"No."

"Does Jess have any friends who might know where she went?"

"Not that I know of. She's never spoken about friends. I talked to the other tenants at the four-plex, but none of them saw her coming or going last weekend."

"Has anyone been out searching for her?"

"I reported her missing," Paige retorted. "Aren't you supposed to search for her?"

"Of course, of course, you're doing all you can," Wallace said evenly.

"Just standard questions."

"Sorry, I'm a little on edge."

"That's understandable. I have a few more questions. Has anything out of the ordinary happened recently?"

"Like I said, she seemed fine to me."

"Does she have any medical or mental health issues?"

"Not that I know of."

"So she wouldn't be taking any medication?"

"Not that I know of."

"Any drug or alcohol use?"

"Not that I know of."

"Has she ever been involved in sex work?"

"What? No! I mean, not that I know of."

"It's just a routine question, nothing more. So, to your knowledge, is there anything that could have upset her?"

Paige let out a sigh of frustration. "I've told you everything I know! Maybe the school knows more."

"Yes, of course, someone will be contacting them. I see we have a photo on file but do you have a recent picture?" asked Wallace.

"Yes. I took one Friday. I can text it to you."

Wallace gave his number. A few moments later, the picture came through on Wallace's phone. "How old did you say she was?"

"Sixteen. She'll be seventeen in a couple of months."

"She could easily pass for twenty."

"Yes, she could."

"Do you know if she had any tattoos? Anything that could help identify her?"

"I have no idea," Paige murmured, "I didn't notice any."

"Okay, I'll be passing this report to our investigating officers. If you recall any additional information before you hear from them, call me."

Wallace strummed his fingers on his desk and stared ahead, focusing on nothing. In the past, Jess had always turned up within a week or two after she ran off: this left him hopeful. Currently, however, she had not shown any signs of being unhappy with her Independent Living program. This worried him. He asked one of his assistants to check all the local hospitals and youth centres for Jess. Then he turned back to the keyboard to finish his report and send it to the investigating officers for further review.

Chapter 39

The representative of the Minister of Education had just finished her presentation to the focus group. After a coffee break, the participants would begin small group discussions.

"That was so invigorating!" said a young teacher as she slid into a chair next to Willow.

"Really?" Willow glanced at the teacher's name tag, "How so, Kara?"

"Weren't you listening to the presentation?" Kara said enthusiastically. "She just applauded the efforts of our school district toward inclusive education; she understands our need for additional support and smaller class sizes."

"Kara, it's one thing to 'understand.' It's another to do something about it."

"Did you hear nothing?" Kara flipped through her notes, "Family liaisons, training for inclusion...."

"Like I said, in principle, we can agree on a lot of things. It's when those principles meet the budget that the shit hits the fan."

Willow gazed at the young teacher, so full of idealism. Though she didn't know Kara personally—Kara taught at an elementary school—Willow surmised that the young teacher was single, lived alone or with her parents, put in several hours after school each day prepping and writing assessments and, most likely, clocked in at least eight hours every weekend. Kara, Willow suspected, arrived early to school each morning, loaded with varying approaches to engage her students. And when these fell apart, as they were bound to do at times; when she couldn't provide the individual attention needed for her lagging students—or those who excelled; when parents sent seething emails unaware of the hours she spent trying to understand and reach out to their child; during those dark moments, she would buoy herself up, remembering that change was on the way. And she was part of the team moving it forward in this focus group.

Willow had been there. Ordinarily, she would have nodded, smiled and tried to stir up the kernels of hope that had settled under a thick sediment of cynicism regarding institutional change. But not today.

"Oh!" added Kara, "Some of us are also going to request a daily component on emotional regulation—not something optional—"

"That all sounds great, just great," cut in Willow. "Now I want to ask you something. How many members of government, or even school trustees, have recently—or ever—come to your school and spent a significant amount of time in a classroom? I'm not talking about a formal walk-through. I'm talking about spending at least a week in the classrooms to experience some of the challenges we face."

"Well, I don't... I've never..."

"I'll help you with that one—none. And the proposals we'll make today? They've been made over and over and over."

"Exactly," said Kara. "The improvements we see in education today came about because teachers pushed for them."

"You're right. Changes have come about because of forward-thinking teachers like you. Schools no longer paddle children for their faults and mishaps. There is a greater understanding of learning differences... and a demand for more personalized education, inclusivity in the classroom.... And as you brought up, the importance of emotional regulation for learning. Teachers were heard and encouraged and, eventually, required to make this all happen. BUT—and this is a big but— with little or no funding to upgrade the teachers and assistants so these changes could be put into practice competently and consistently. AND with few or no additional assistants, counsellors, or learning support specialists to help them in the trenches!"

"We have to start somewhere," Kara retorted. "All change begins at the grassroots,"

"Well, the grassroots are beginning to burn out. What we're up against, Kara, is bigger than 'EDUCATION'—imparting knowledge. It's shaking up the status quo. We lament homelessness, delinquency, addictions, domestic violence, but we do very little early on to assist kids and families in order to prevent these things. So why don't we do it? Do we want to foster continued dependency and maintain power? Have a group of people we can patronize?" Willow leaned forward. "The status quo is hard to break, especially when it's protecting certain mindsets or padded wallets."

"What are you implying?" countered Kara. "Education is in everyone's interest."

"Yes, all parents are interested in their child's education. But the education provided isn't equal. The wealthy tend to send their kids to private, elite schools—most subsidized, I might add, by our tax dollars. And in these schools, the class sizes are small, and professionals are on-site to provide the supports the kids need. And if the kids' families aren't wealthy, then their parents are working multiple jobs to pay the tuition, or they've snagged a rare scholarship. And the best part? The children who don't cut it at these private schools can be expelled or simply rejected. And where are they sent? To us. So the kids ousted from the private schools, land in public schools with no friends, no connections, feeling like failures—and with our resources already stretched to the max. A great combination."

Kara stood. "I need coffee." She picked up her belongings as she went.

"Someone's in a chirpy mood." Willow hadn't noticed Frida Quinn, her principal, sitting close by.

"When did you arrive?"

"Oh, I've been here for a while now.... So this is your new endeavour—to disillusion our rising stars?"

Willow turned to face Frida. "If you wanted to, you could retire this year. Are you holding out to see how deeply the budget will be slashed and then decide?"

"You really have become a cynical bitch," said Frida with a grin.

"We've been through this too many times to doubt the outcome.... And you'll be left to stoke up the sagging morale." Willow started to mimic the gestures of the principal at their staff meetings as she said, "'Remember the kids! Yes, we are continually asked to do more and more with less and less. But we are here for the kids!'" Frida laughed at Willow's imitation.

"After you retire," Willow continued, "you'll collapse in exhaustion from all the cheerleading you've done to bolster up the team. Don't wait too long, or you may never completely recover."

"And when did you get a psychology degree?"

"You know the kids who are affected the most from these cut-backs. And, Frida, you care."

"Does this have anything to do with Jess?"

Willow picked at the dry skin around her nail bed, her fingernails already bitten to the quick. Jess was rarely absent and never past two days. Yesterday, her caseworker was notified. No one knew where she was.

"There's more to education than provincial exams and SAT scores. How well do we even know the majority of our students, what they're struggling with?" Willow shook her head. "We're failing these kids, Frida."

Chapter 40

Sebastian slid into the desk next to Mallory, the one Jess generally occupied. A substitute teacher stood at the whiteboard and wrote her name. "I'll be your teacher today. Ms. Willow is at a district meeting." As she was taking attendance, Oliver came through the doorway and looked around the classroom. He walked past his assigned desk and sat directly in front of Mallory. Victor watched him pass, then ignored him. On the corner of her notebook, Mallory wrote, *What the ??* and pushed it slightly toward Sebastian. He glanced at the message and jotted, *Troubles with V.* Then he drew a stick figure with two x's for eyeballs.

~

At noon, Mallory was the first to arrive at the rendezvous lunch spot, but as the minutes slipped by, she began to doubt Sebastian would come at all. The hallway doors opened and slammed shut. Sebastian poked his head around the staircase, "Still no sign of Jess." He scooted next to Mallory and picked up the sandwich she had set out for him. "I walked around the office area to see if I could find out anything, but no luck."

"Did you check her place again?"

"Yeah." Sebastian's foot jiggled rapidly. "No one's there. She's gone, Mallory."

"Where would she go?"

"I don't know."

"What's going to happen now?"

"Police. At least, that's what happened at the group home when someone ran off."

"You think Jess ran away?"

Sebastian shrugged. "If her caseworker thinks so, she'll call the police."

"Did Ms. Willow talk to you?"

"Yeah. Oliver asked to change his assigned desk and sit next to me instead. She wanted to know if I was okay with that."

"Why does Oliver want to sit next to you?" asked Mallory skeptically. "Doesn't he hang around with Victor?"

Sebastian told Mallory what had happened at the music store. "I guess Oliver has had his fill of bullshitery."

"It shows some of his brain cells are still firing up. Did Ms. Willow ask you about Jess?"

"Yeah, she wanted to know when I saw her last and if I knew where she went."

"Same here," said Mallory.

"Ms. Willow is worried. For sure, they're going to call the police."

"Are you going to talk to the police?"

"Hell, no," said Sebastian emphatically. "There is nothing I can tell them. I have NO idea where she might be…. If I talk to the police, I'll get sent back home."

"You could tell them about your step-father."

"Some police are friends of that bastard. Max fixes their cars for free. Who are they going to believe?"

"If police come to our door and ask for me?–I don't even want to think about the fallout."

After a few moments, Mallory asked, "Why would Jess run away?"

"Maybe something spooked her?"

"But if she was afraid of something and ran off, there are people she could call for help… like you or me… or her caseworker," Mallory said pensively.

"Or Ms. Willow," added Sebastian.

"I don't think she ran away."

Chapter 41

"Think. Is there anywhere Jess may have gone?" It was Friday, and still no word from Jess. Willow had held back Mallory and Sebastian after class to see if any contact had been made.

The two looked at each other and then back at Willow.

"We've been asking ourselves that," said Sebastian. "We have no idea."

"Would you let me know if something comes to mind or you hear from her?"

"Sure," said Sebastian. Mallory nodded in agreement.

"Sebastian, I have your number from the Revue. Is it the same?"

"The *YouApp* contact, right?"

Willow nodded.

"What about you, Mallory? Would you feel comfortable giving me a way I could contact you?"

Mallory gave her a *YouApp* handle as well. "What's happening with Jess, Ms. Willow?"

Willow hesitated. "Ah, come on!" said Sebastian. "Jess is our friend. And you want us to tell you if we find out anything!"

Willow looked at the two youths before her, their eyes wide with worry. "The police have been notified... that's all I know." She began to pack up her laptop and notebook. "I'm sorry for cutting into your lunch break. Go take a walk while you eat, get some fresh air. We can chat again on Monday."

~

Mallory and Sebastian, sandwiches in hand, were headed out a side exit when an arctic blast squelched any desire for a 'fresh air' walk. "I don't think so," said Mallory, backing into the building.

"One deep breath should do the trick!" quipped Sebastian. He filled his lungs and closed the door. As they turned to retrace their steps to their regular lunch spot, they came face to face with Oliver.

"Are you following us?" asked Sebastian.

"Yes, actually. Is Jess okay?"

Mallory glanced at Oliver and said nothing.

"Why do you care?" asked Sebastian.

"I don't know her, really, but I wouldn't want anything bad happening to her."

"Do you think something bad has happened to her? What do you know? Is it Victor?" Sebastian's voice rose with each question.

"No, no, nothing like that!"

"So, what do you want from us?" asked Mallory.

"I can see how uptight you are. Ms. Willow is worried, too.... I heard what she said to you after class."

"What the hell?" exclaimed Sebastian.

"Just cool it and let me explain, okay? I was waiting for you down the hall, and when you didn't come out, I went back and heard the last part of your conversation, that the police have been notified. That's it. I just wanted to know if Jess was okay."

"We don't know anything," said Sebastian. Oliver didn't move.

"So, what do you want now?" Mallory asked softly.

"I have a car. I'm good at tech. If you need my help with something, let me know."

Sebastian said nothing, still trying to size up Oliver.

"Okay," said Mallory, "Thanks." Then turning to Sebastian, "Let's go." And the two walked down the corridor together, leaving Oliver near the exit.

～

That afternoon, as Mallory was leaving the schoolyard, she saw Oliver headed toward the student parking lot. Quickening her pace, she caught up with him as he opened his car door. "Oliver." He turned toward her and smiled. "Thanks for offering to help.... And thanks for standing up to Victor at the music store."

"So you heard about that."

"Why would you even hang around with that guy in the first place?"

"Do you want to talk about it in the car?"

"No. Outside is fine."

Oliver threw his backpack into the car and shut the door. "I'm new to this school. Started in the fall. Victor seemed like an okay guy. He showed me around the school, included me with his friends. Yeah, he could tease, but I didn't think he meant much by it—or that's what I told myself."

"But he's the one who caused Sebastian's meltdown. He shoved him."

"I swear, I didn't see that," said Oliver emphatically. "Yeah, I noticed Victor got up, but when Sebastian exploded, Victor wasn't in the room." Mallory peered up at him. "Okay, I had my doubts," Oliver sighed, "but I hadn't seen anything." Mallory set down her backpack on the pavement and leaned against the car. Oliver continued. "I also began to feel that I was just a ride—Victor's real friend was my car. The last straw came when Victor figured out where Sebastian went after school and wanted to check out the place. I don't get it. Why does he go after Sebastian?" Oliver kicked at the pebble gravel that gathered near the parked cars. "Fuck him!"

A gust of wintry air whipped up dirt and brown, withered leaves, causing Oliver and Mallory to turn their backs against the blast. When it subsided, Mallory looked back at Oliver, "We don't know where Jess is. Or why she would leave. And we don't know where to go from here. Would you give me your number, just in case?"

The two exchanged information.

"Thanks," said Mallory, "Jess and Sebastian are the best friends I've ever had."

Chapter 42

"This is an absolute gong show!" said Frida when Willow stepped into her office. "Moving from in-class learning to online in two weeks?" Frida put out her arms and flicked her fingers forward, moving Willow out of her office. "We're supposed to be six feet away from each other, so let's go to the conference room." As the two walked into the larger room, Frida asked, "What are you doing here anyway? Wouldn't you rather be at home preparing your online lessons?"

"I came in for more of my materials," replied Willow. "It's eerie seeing the school so quiet."

"Yeah, compared to the last couple of days when we had the students scuttling in and out for their belongings."

"How did that go?"

"We'll give the stragglers a couple more days, then we'll be emptying lockers into bags, make sure nothing is rotting. The kids will be able to pick up their belongings—we haven't figured that out yet."

"So tomorrow we have a Zoom staff meeting?"

"That's the plan," said Frida. "We'll see how many manage to tune in."

"A few of us have been practicing together with Zoom, figuring out how everything works before going live with the students."

"Some teachers are prerecording their lessons and leaving the live sessions for questions and answers—we'll discuss all this in the staff meeting." Frida pulled her hair back with her hands and sighed. "One of our biggest challenges now is to find out which students need an electronic device or have no internet service. The IT department is sorting through all their equipment, and June Barnes is formulating a spreadsheet to manage the loans. The phones are ringing non-stop. My email inbox is flooded."

"Well, enjoy your spring break next week," smirked Willow. Both laughed at the absurdity.

"As if!" said Frida. "I wake up in the middle of the night, my mind spinning with all that we need to have in place before this online learning begins in, what? A week and a half? My God."

"I'll leave you to it," said Willow, pulling on her winter coat and picking up a couple of book-packed totes. "You know where to find me if you need anything."

Chapter 43

The door shut, the bolt turned and booted footsteps lumbered down the staircase. Her dad had left for work. Mallory got up as she usually did on a school day and puttered through her morning routine. When she finished, she glanced around, trying to come to grips with her new reality. She had no school... that would begin online sometime the following week. She was home, alone, aimless, anxious about the virus killing thousands around the world, and tethered by the lockdown to a small, aging apartment she had lived in for less than six months. It could be worse, she had told herself when the schools were shut down. Her dad's work was considered essential. She was not tethered all day with him.

Mallory wandered to the front window, idly gazing at nothing in particular. The silence in the room allowed her to sense her heartbeat and opened her ears to the slightest creak. On those rare occasions when Mallory had been left alone all day, she had usually gone to sketch at the mall. Now? It was closed indefinitely. It hit her how comforting the mall had been: she was unknown, yet admitted; alone, yet amongst. In some mysterious fashion, she was connected and, however tenuously, accepted. Mallory opened the door to the side of the large front window and walked onto the tiny balcony. Within seconds the frigid air forced her back into the confining apartment. How long would this last? A few weeks? A month? The end of the school year? Nothing but free-floating, structureless ambiguity in an ocean of solitude—Jess was missing, and Sebastian didn't respond to her texts.

~

Mallory was allowed to be home alone for those few hours after school. Teachers' professional days and the Christmas and spring breaks might have offered more extended periods on her own, but now and again, her dad came home early on PD days. During the longer breaks, his boss gave a few days off to his crew—he liked to ski with his family. Her summers, up to this point, had been tightly regulated. Ryder was willing to forego after-school care, but he did not trust "the dog days of summer." Year after year, Mallory spent her summers at the church day camp. She asked her dad if she could just stay home for part of the summer, but he told her tales of home break-ins, people being held at gunpoint, rapes. It was not safe. As she grew older and Mallory had more access to the internet, she researched the likelihood of her father's sordid tales and found them unlikely, but her father was adamant.

For the past three years, Ryder had rented an RV, and for two weeks, he and Mallory would camp at a site near a lake. This prolonged and concentrated dose of unsought engagement was the worse part of summer. Near the end, Mallory invariably "fell ill" with vomiting and headaches. Ryder attributed it to too much junk food, but Mallory thought differently. Under the constant scrutiny of her dad, she became increasingly on edge until anything she ate came back up. Miraculously, her symptoms subsided as the RV was cleared out and her father left to return it.

And now, here she was, alone, the whole day before her, tethered and untethered, simultaneously, by the Covid pandemic.

Chapter 44

Officer Wallace walked to his desk, now enclosed on three sides by plexiglass. He adjusted his cloth mask, one of several purchased by his wife, and poured himself a cup of coffee from his thermos. His three children, adapting to online school, were home with his wife, whose part-time job had been cut. If his wife had anything to do with it, Wallace would be donning a hazmat suit to work. As it was, he deposited his outer clothing in the washing machine when he arrived home and showered before anyone came near him.

His office phone rang. "A teen was reported missing a few weeks ago," said the hesitant female voice on the line, "Jess Gayle."

"Jess Gayle, you say." Wallace typed the name into his computer.

"Yes, G-a-y-l-e. Do you have any news on her?"

"Who's calling?" asked Wallace. Jess's file popped open on the screen.

"A friend."

"Do you have anything to tell us that would help us in our search?"

"No, I just want to find out how the search is going."

"I'm sorry. We can only release information to authorized persons. However, if you leave me your name...." The call clicked off. "Shit!"

Officer Wallace looked at the file open on his computer. Three and half weeks had passed since Jess's case was sent to the investigators, and no new information had been added. He dialled a number.

"Hey, Jim, it's Wallace. I sent you guys a case a few weeks ago, Jess Gayle. Anything come up? Did she return?"

"Let me bring up the file.... No, nothing's been added from here, so I assume she is still missing. I see her case was reviewed when it arrived....

Since she doesn't seem to be involved in risky behaviour and has always returned, it was deemed a low priority. And compared to some of our other cases...." Jim listed their recent priority cases: a custody battle that triggered a grandmother vanishing with her two-year-old grandson—they had yet to be located, the grandmother was regarded unstable; two elderly persons, separate cases, had wandered off when sub-zero overnight temperatures were expected; a woman fleeing domestic violence had disappeared—the search was still on, her life deemed endangered. "This doesn't include the runaway youths between twelve and fourteen years. And with all the pandemic crap going on, we're stretched to the max. Two of our team got Covid and are home recovering. Some of our support staff had been in close contact with them, so they're isolating. We're trying our best to stay on top of things, but it's been difficult."

"I hear you, Jim," replied Wallace. "Would you mind if I give you a hand and check out a few details on the Jess Gayle case?"

"We'd appreciate it."

"I'll get back to you if I find out anything."

Chapter 45

Mallory's phone rang immediately after her text. "Thanks for calling so quickly, Oliver."

"Not a whole lot going on. Did you call the missing person's line?"

"Yeah. They don't give out information to random, unidentified callers—what a surprise."

"Well, at least we tried," said Oliver. "I've posted a notice on *Imagram* and saw that you did too."

"The problem is neither you nor I have many followers."

"Yeah, but we gotta start somewhere. What about Sebastian? Have you heard from him?"

"I've been trying," said Mallory. "When school was cancelled, we messaged a bit, but now, nothing. I'm worried about him. I gave him your handle. Let me know if he contacts you."

"That's unlikely."

"I'm going to try calling Ms. Willow. She'll have a better chance of getting information on Jess, which brings me to the other reason I texted you...."

"Yeah, what?"

"I got a new Chromebook— well, new for me. It's a refurbished one. My old tablet doesn't interface with the school's program, and I've already missed a day of school."

"No one has a computer in your family?"

"My dad won't let me touch his gaming computer." Mallory laughed a little, "He was convinced he could get the school programs to function on my tablet, so the other night he tried again—and almost threw the tablet out the window! Yesterday he brought home this Chromebook and connected it to our internet. I'm having trouble getting set up on the school site."

"No problem!"

Chapter 46

Willow looked over the attendance of her English classes—over seventy percent had logged in. That was remarkable. She pored over the names of those yet to come online, among them, Jess and Sebastian. Mallory had messaged her to say she'd be online the next day—computer issues. Willow's phone rang. "Frida, thanks for getting back to me. I'm looking over my class attendance. The majority are online, but I have roughly twenty-five to thirty percent missing."

"So, how many are we talking about?"

"Around forty-five."

"We'll give them a week and then see where the numbers stand. We may have to start a phone campaign. How did the classes go today?"

"Well, glitches for sure, but overall, not bad. June Barnes has helped me out a lot. What a computer whiz and so damn unassuming—don't ever let her go. Bribe her, ball-and-chain her, whatever you need to do to keep her at our school!"

Frida laughed.

"Have you heard anything about Jess Gayle?" asked Willow.

"Nothing."

"It's been over three weeks—almost four—since anyone has seen her. Is there someone I can call?"

"Willow, if you're open to it, I can make you the school liaison regarding Jess."

"I'd like that."

"Call her caseworker and find out what's going on—her number should be in Jess's file. Keep me updated."

~

"As I told the police, I've heard nothing from Jess," said Paige, "I don't know what to tell you."

"Is there anything more that can be done?" asked Willow.

"Like what? No one at the four-plex nor the staff who run the Independent Living program knows a thing. No one's heard from her. The fact that she's run away several times before—and returned—suggests that it's likely to happen again."

"But we don't know that, and it's going on a month since she's been seen."

Paige sighed, "Look, I'm sorry for Jess, I am. But I can't control what these kids decide to do."

"If I find new information, whom should I call?"

"Just a moment." Willow could hear Paige typing on her keyboard. "Okay, here it is. I spoke with an Officer Wallace." She gave Willow his number.

~

"You say you worked with Jess, Ms.?" asked Officer Wallace.

"Willow Leboucan. You can call me Willow. The students call me Ms. Willow. And yes, I know Jess. She's one of my English students. Also, our school put on its annual *Revue* last December, and Jess performed. I helped out with the show and got to know Jess a little better."

"Well, this is good to hear. From what I gathered, Jess was a phantom, wafting in and out without anyone noticing."

"Is there any chance I could speak with you? And soon? Jess has been missing almost a month. I'm quite concerned."

"I'm headed to her apartment now. It's not too far from Riverbank High. Can I meet you there?"

Willow had finished her live sessions for the day. "Yes, I know the place. I'll be there."

Chapter 47

Sebastian banged on the doors to *Strum N' Drum* and peered through the glass doors. With the lockdown, Sebastian felt like an unmoored boat being cast about on the shifting tides of Covid. Within days, the minimal degree of stability he had managed to eke out for himself was razed.

First, Jess went missing. He'd contacted some kids he knew from the group home, but none of them had heard a thing. Her disappearance preyed on his mind. Where could she have gone? And why?

A week after Jess disappeared, school was nixed, and with it, friends, food, music and chats with his counsellor. *Strum n' Drums* closed its doors about a week after the schools were shut down. God, he missed his job there, working with Craig, demonstrating keyboards and chatting with the prospective buyers. He missed his one hot meal a day. The Wi-Fi and electrical outlets at school and work had kept his phone charged and his apps functioning. Now his phone was dead, and he couldn't find a place that would allow him to charge it; libraries, coffee shops—he couldn't get into them. Everything was takeout or drive-thru. Day by day, he was trying to outrun a growing panic that threatened to blow up and take over his life.

Sebastian walked to the back of *Strum's* and pounded on the door until he noticed a doorbell. He pushed the button and found it rang loud and continuously as long as he held it down. No response. Sebastian turned and headed back to the main street.

Daytime temperatures, well below freezing, plummeted to bitterly cold levels at night. Sebastian spent his days walking around neighbourhoods and strip malls looking for a temporary respite, if not indoors, at least out of the wind or near an exhaust vent that blew warm air. A couple times a day, he joined the lines outside supermarkets, inching toward their entrances with the other shoppers. Once inside, he would meander the aisles for over an hour, picking up a few items and, always, using the bathroom—it was so hard to find an open public bathroom. He was eyed with suspicion due to his large backpack and, well, he stank. He could no longer sidle into the school's locker room for a shower or drop in at Jess's to wash his clothes. He'd gone to *Strum's* hoping he could pick up some kind of work or, at the very least, use the shower in the employee bathroom. But no one was there, and he had no idea what app Craig used to message or if he even used an app. Sebastian still had some money saved, but it was going fast.

There was one person Sebastian knew would hire him on the spot. He would also be able to pick up a joint to calm his mind and take a break from reality. Instinctively, he began to walk toward Gid's.

PART THREE

Chapter 48

Car door opening. Stumbling on stairs. Thumping. Children playing. Voices. Jess struggled to open her eyes, but her body was paralyzed under a weighted blanket of lethargy, her mind baffled in a fog of confusion. Drifting in and out. Moments? Hours? Voices. Drifting off again.

~

"Time to wake up, girly." Jess's eyes fluttered open. A woman in a stylish, athletic outfit, her long hair swept into an attractive updo, sat on a chair in the corner of the room and kicked at the bed where Jess lay. "Well, if sleeping beauty hasn't finally come out of her slumber." She pulled a cell phone from a pocket and texted.

"Where am I?" said Jess, trying to make sense of her surroundings.

"In trouble."

"What?" Jess leaned up on her elbow. Never had she felt so groggy.

"You messed with Zander. That was stupid."

The door opened, and Seth walked in. "Good to see you awake. I brought you some coffee." He set a mug on the floor near the head of the bed. "Let me help you up." He reached around Jess's shoulder and raised her to a sitting position. She sat at the edge of the bed, dropping her feet to the floor.

"This floor is freezing." Looking around, she said, "Where are my boots?"

"Safely stowed," said the woman. "Do you think we'd put you to bed with your filthy shoes on?"

Seth stood off to the side. There was barely enough room for the narrow bed and folding chair. "What is going on, Seth?" asked Jess.

"I'll tell you what's going on." The woman tossed a handful of photos onto the bed. Jess swiped across them and saw herself posing with eyeglass frames and jackets. "Zander's not interested in this shit," the woman continued. "They're worthless. Your loans are due. It's time to pay up."

"Loans?" Jess struggled to follow.

"Deni, give us a moment, would you?" said Seth.

"Five minutes." Deni got up from her chair and left the room.

Seth handed Jess the mug. "Here, drink something."

"I don't like coffee."

"It's what they gave me."

Jess took a tiny sip and set the mug back down on the floor. "What the hell is going on?"

Seth slid onto the chair Deni vacated. "We've been royally screwed by Lena."

"What?"

"Lena's been playing us. She paid over three thousand dollars for the photography equipment I wanted and told me I could pay it back by taking photoshoots for her."

"Which you were doing? Right?"

"I thought so." Seth shifted in his seat and leaned toward Jess. "Lena had you sign off on receipts for the money you earned, right?"

"Yes."

"She did the same for me when she gave me the money for my equipment. But all the time I spent paying off my debt with photoshoots? Yeah, get this—Lena now says the photoshoots were just practice runs!"

"But she—"

"Would you shut up and let me finish?" Seth snapped.

Jess's eyes widened, and she leaned back against the wall, away from Seth.

"Sorry," Seth said in a calmer tone. "While you were sleeping off whatever you snorted, I've been dealing with some mafioso guy and his sidekick liar, Lena."

"Snorted? I'm not on drugs!"

"That's not what it looks like."

"Lena must have put something in the cocoa."

"Tell that to Zander! You're in some serious shit."

"Who the hell is Zander?"

"He's gotta be some kind of mob boss. There's a buffed-up thug at every door into this house. Deni's his partner."

"But Lena—"

"Lena is a God-damn liar! You got that? A liar. The big photoshoot? It was just a ruse to get you and me delivered to Zander."

Jess's head whirled. "I'm going to be sick." She staggered to the door, and Seth steered her into a bathroom next to her room. She knelt in front of the toilet and heaved until her sides ached.

"Are you okay?" Seth asked softly.

"Give me a minute." Jess crawled to her feet and splashed cold water on her face.

"Here, let me help you," said Seth as he took her arm and led her back to her room. Once there, Jess slouched on the edge of the bed.

"Zander says you owe him a thousand dollars?"

"A thousand dollars!" Jess exclaimed. "For what?"

"For the money Lena gave you—'the loans'—and for other expenses, like the food she bought you, transportation… oh, yeah, get this, for that jacket she gave you!"

"What the fuck! This Zander guy can't hold me here against my will."

"Don't underestimate Zander. I've met him."

"My father is going to be looking for me, and when he finds me—"

Seth locked eyes with Jess. "Zander knows all about me… and all about you."

"What are you talking about?"

"Zander told me you have no parents. They're dead. He said you're a ward of the government and a chronic runaway. Is this true?"

Jess said nothing.

"He also said that if you give any trouble, he will beat the shit out of some redheaded friend of yours. Said when he's done, the kid would never play the piano again. Do you know who he's talking about?"

Jess could feel the blood draining from her face and lowered her head into her hands.

Seth continued, "Zander told me he had connections throughout Canada and would go after my mom if I give him any grief."

Seth and Jess sat in silence, both lost in the mire of their predicament.

"I don't know about you, but I intend to work for Zander until I pay off the debt and be done with it. You can decide what you want to do."

"What kind of work are you going to do?"

"Take pictures... videos, upload them on the web. Like before, just more... God, I feel sick about this, Jess,... just more skin."

Jess's head shot up. "Christ! Is this some kind of porn hovel?"

"Adult entertainment."

Jess broke out in a cold sweat, and her hands began to shake. She clasped them together to hide the trembling.

"Do it and walk away, Jess, or that redheaded kid will be incapacitated." Seth got up and collapsed the folding chair. "We don't have much choice."

"Where are you going?"

"Upstairs to my room."

Jess stood up, "I'm going with you."

"Not unless Zander says so. One of his guards brought me down and is waiting to bring me back up. Stay put until Deni comes back." He walked out the door with the chair.

Chapter 49

Jess lay awake on her bed. The house was eerily silent. There was no window in her room, so she had no idea what time it was, but, not hearing a sound from upstairs, she assumed it was early in the morning. Jess's insides wrenched with anxiety. How could she have been so stupid to believe Lena? More importantly, how would she get out of this mess? Had anyone realized she was missing? Sebastian and Mallory would have texted, but would they have gone by her apartment when she didn't reply? Even if they discovered she was missing, how would they ever find her? No one knew she left for Edmonton–it happened so fast. She couldn't contact them now; all her belongings were gone. When Jess didn't show up for school, would anyone think to look for her? She was one of the thousands of students at Riverbank. Even if someone did search for her, they would never find her. She didn't even know where she was.

And Sebastian, how did these people know about Sebastian? Sure, Lena saw him perform with her, but then what? She tracked down his address? Lena had never even mentioned Sebastian in their chats together. And how had Zander discovered she had run away before? What a massive, fucking mess.

Annisa, her favourite caseworker, had painted a bright future for Jess: independence, stability, a good job. Paige's prognosis was less certain. Everything good in her life withered and died.

Jess's mind wandered. Six years old, sitting with her mother and grandmother in the first pew of the church. In front of them, on a table next to a framed picture, sat an urn with her father's ashes: dead from an overdose. Jess didn't recognize the person in the picture. She wouldn't have recognized her father if she had passed him on the street. From the time she was an infant, she had lived with her grandmother. Her mother made periodic visits but her father? If he had ever come by, Jess didn't remember it. "A good man who was led astray," said her grandmother.

When Jess was ten, she attended another funeral—her grandmother's.

Chapter 50

Jess startled when the door to her room opened abruptly. "No room service for you, girly," Deni said curtly. "You eat with the others."

Jess got out of bed and wobbled into the main room. Her toes curled on the ice-cold basement floor. The room she'd exited was the closest to the stairway leading to the main floor. Next to it, to the left, was the bathroom. Across from her room was a small kitchenette with a sink, some cupboards and a microwave on the counter. Alongside the counter stood some sort of cubbyhole contraption filled with stained cloth boxes. Beyond that, an area rug, covered with heaps of blankets and some throw pillows, filled the corner against the back wall. Near the ceiling was a window, its frame stuffed with pink insulation held in place by strips of grey duct tape. Between her room and kitchenette was a long folding table surrounded by folding chairs. Two women sat with their backs toward Jess and poured coffee from a carafe into their mugs. On the table, along with the carafe, creamer and sugar, were two loaves of bread, a container of margarine, peanut butter and jelly.

"You sit here," directed Deni pushing Jess toward a chair at the head of the table near the staircase. Jess sat. In front of her was a small bowl of rice and a spoon. Jess reached for the margarine.

"Nah, nah, nah," said Deni, "Not so fast. When you start bringing in some money, you can help yourself. Until then, it's rice. We don't run a soup kitchen here." Raising her voice, Deni yelled, "Come on, girls. Up and at it. The food's going upstairs in twenty minutes." Then she turned and walked up the stairs.

The heaps of blankets on the area rug stirred, and two young women sat up. One shuffled to the bathroom; the other lay back down. One of the women at the table poured powdered coffee creamer and a couple sugar packets into her coffee. As she stirred, she looked at Jess. "I'm Star. I'll be showing you the ropes." Jess eyed the bread. "And don't think of eating anything other than your rice. These walls have eyes." Star glanced towards a corner. Following her gaze, Jess stared into the tinted dome of a security camera. "Go ahead, look around," said Star. "There's one in every corner."

Jess ate a spoonful of her rice, lukewarm and unseasoned. She reached for the carafe of coffee, planning to block its taste with sugar and creamer. "Sorry," Star said, "You heard Deni. Rice only. If you want something to drink, get some water." She pointed to the sink. Jess went to the kitchenette and opened a few cupboards until she found a hodgepodge of mugs and filled one with water. As Jess sat back down, Star glanced over her shoulder at a series of grommet curtain panels that ran from the bathroom to the far end of the room.

"Lazy bitches," she said as she stood up. Jess watched as Star yanked open three curtain panels, one after another. Behind the panels were rooms divided by office partitions with just enough space for a narrow bed. "Fifteen more minutes and the food's gone," Star warned the motionless bodies on the beds. She kicked at the sleeping girl on the rug, "Belle, get the hell up."

Jess's attention was diverted from Star by the dark-haired woman who remained at the table with her. "I'm Flower," she said softly as Star repeated her warning and shook a couple of beds. "Eat your rice. You're going to need it."

Star's admonition was effective; three women rolled off the beds and staggered into the main area. "What are you staring at?" snarled one of the women.

"Don't mind Gloria," said Star, who returned to the table. "She's not a morning person."

"Or an afternoon or evening person," said another woman who had come to join them at the table. The women laughed.

"Shut up, Trixie," said Gloria, then to the person in the bathroom, "Hurry up in there!"

"Go to hell, Gloria," said the woman who exited the bathroom.

"I should have known it was you, Angie," said Gloria.

"Coco, come sit next to me," said Star as another late riser came to the table. A young teen took a chair next to Star and leaned her head on Star's shoulder. Star gave the girl a side hug.

Before Jess could stop herself, she blurted out, "How old are you?"

Star answered, stroking Coco's hair, "Old enough, right Coco?" Coco nodded, and Star slipped her some kind of packaged pastry.

"Oh, oh," said Trixie, "Star's little pet is getting a treat."

Coco quickly placed the pastry on her lap and reached for the bread.

As Gloria emerged from the bathroom and Belle, bleary-eyed, pulled up her chair to the table, Star addressed the group, "This is Jackie. She's joining the team."

Jackie? Jess was about to correct her and then thought the better of it. She'd rather they not know her real name.

"Ah, fresh meat," Gloria gibed.

"One of these days," snapped Star, "that mouth of yours is going to get you into deep shit."

"Well, right now, it's making Zander money, so I'm safe for the time being."

Another girl stood up, "I'm Angie." She made a mock bow towards Star, saying, "And this is Star. She's the saint of the team. She makes enough money to have her own car and apartment."

"If you have your own apartment," asked Jess, "why are you here?"

"Oh, she's a smart one," remarked Gloria.

"I train the newcomers," said Star, "and I'm not cheap"—there were a few snickers from the others—"so I hope you're a fast learner. And who knows, if you're as quick as Coco here, I might have you over sometime for a sleepover, like I do with Coco." Coco gave Star a smile, and Star reached over and hugged her again.

There was something off with Coco, noted Jess. She gazed up longingly at Star like a Labrador pup at the feet of its master; she was childish yet smug as the favourite of Star, scarcely giving the others a glance.

Jess finished her rice and ached for more. With no other options, she refilled her mug with water. "You have about five minutes," remarked Star. Activity at the table quickened: bread was slathered with condiments, and coffee poured.

Trixie remarked, "Last night, the club was slower than usual."

"People are afraid of Covid," said Angie. "A guy told me some people think it's a pandemic."

"Yeah, I heard some cruise ship had so many cases, it got grounded."

"The whole city might close down, schools, everything—that's what the bartender told me."

"How are we going to make it?" asked Belle.

"The clubs are still open," said Star, "so we keep at it."

"Yeah, but what if we get sick?"

"Oh, it's just a little virus," replied Star nonchalantly.

The door at the top of the stairway opened, and Deni tramped down with a tray. The last of the bread was emptied from their packages and disappeared onto laps. Star gathered the carafe and condiments onto the tray and went upstairs with Deni.

Flower brought the dirty dishes to the sink while the rest of the girls went to the cubbyholes and rooted through the boxes. Soon mirrors, makeup bags, hair extensions and other paraphernalia cluttered the table where, moments before, they had dined. It was then that Jess noticed the time on the microwave display—2:15. "Is this the right time?"

Flower glanced over, "More or less."

"I thought it was morning!"

"It was... a couple of hours ago," said Gloria.

"Didn't you hear us come downstairs after work?" said one.

"A little." Jess had heard a kerfuffle, shower running, toilet flushing, but she was still so befuddled, she had just turned over and gone back to sleep.

"That was around four a.m.," said Gloria. "It's Sunday, in case you're wondering about the day. We couldn't make it to church, but I'm sure some of our clients were in the pews praying for our souls."

"If they were thinking of us at all, it wasn't our souls," said one, bringing laughs from the others.

"Yeah, we're clubbing our way to heaven," said another.

"More like hell," came the response.

"Speak for yourself," said Gloria. "When I get to the pearly gates, St. Peter and I are gonna scorch the asses of every john on the face of the earth. Wipe those condescending smirks right off their bloated, presumptuous little faces."

"In the meantime, you don't mind taking their money."

"A girl's gotta live," she said.

Star stomped down the stairs. "Get those faces on, girls. We're hitting two clubs today. The first opens at four; vans leave at three."

"We know the drill, Star," said Gloria. "Why don't you stick to your apprentice."

Star went to a cubbyhole and pulled out one of the cloth-covered boxes, scuzzy and frayed. "Come with me, Jackie," she said, "there's too many clucking hens out here."

"Bok, bok, bok, bok, BWAK!" Gloria clucked as Jess followed Star into her room.

Star set the box on the bed. Inside was a mirror with a stand, a few combs, clips, hair spray, toothpaste and toothbrush, and a scruffy cosmetic bag with an assortment of used makeup and another with paraphernalia for fingernails.

"Time to put on your face."

"I'd like to take a shower."

"Shoulda thought of that sooner."

Star left the room and returned with another ratty cloth box. She pulled out a couple of garments. "These should fit," she said, "but if they don't, there are others in the bottom cubbies."

"Fuck!"

"No, you don't need much of anything for that," Star laughed. She lifted another piece from the box, "Club lingerie for dance routines. Get dressed."

"You expect me to wear these to the clubs?"

"Oh, *you're* not going to the clubs—too bad for you. If you know how to play the game, you can make two to three thousand on a weekend." Star cocked her head at Jess, "No, no, I'm going to teach you how to dress and dance for our online clients. Better hurry. Rocky is going to be down soon to film."

Chapter 51

A week later, Deni came downstairs during their afternoon breakfast. "Time for a house meeting," she declared as she descended. Once the girls quieted, she continued, "You're going to hear this when you're out at the club today, so I'm giving you a heads up. The government is creating a lot of hype over this Covid virus. There's really no danger, no more than the flu, but the top dogs have decided to close down the schools." Jess caught her breath. "Rumour is, the clubs might be shut down soon, so make the most of tonight."

"What are we going to do if the clubs close?" asked Flower.

"Just like the schools, go online."

"Shit!" said Gloria.

"We can be happy that Zander has been ahead of the game. We're already online, and now we're going to increase it. To do that, we need more equipment, and everyone has got to pitch in for it."

Gloria threw back her head with a disgusted sigh. "Always something, Deni," she said. "Fence repair, washing machine, freezer–"

Deni cut off the objection with a glare. Gloria pretended to be distracted by some crumbs on the table and swept them to the floor. "The schools will be closed for weeks," continued Deni. "If that happens to the clubs, we're going completely online. Each of you will have your own profile. The best acts will be making the most money."

"You mean the most skin will make the most money," muttered Gloria.

"What was that?" barked Deni.

"Just a little encouragement for the girls," replied Gloria, unperturbed.

"But how will we know how much money we're making?" asked Belle.

"I'll keep track of all that. And since you mentioned it, why don't I look at the accounts and see how they stand now." Deni pulled a notebook out of a back pocket. "Well, Jackie. You're a winner—for the most debt." A few laughed. "Yes, Jackie, you arrived with a thousand dollar debt, and that has now climbed to five thousand." Jess stared wide-eyed, her mouth opened. "No, wait, I forgot to add the thousand everyone is contributing for the electronics and lighting we need." There was murmuring over the thousand dollar charge, which, again, was silenced by a scowl from Deni. "So Jackie, that makes six thousand and climbing."

"Six thousand!" exclaimed Jess in disbelief.

"Meals, laundry, utilities, technical costs, security, training; it all adds up. You've been here a week, and you haven't produced anything profitable for *AppChat Premium*. So you better get busy if you want to pay off your debt."

"Meals? All I've eaten is rice!"

"Unless you start bringing in some cash, rice is all you're getting. We don't tolerate free-loaders." Deni flipped to another page in her notebook. "And our biggest earners are Star and Coco." Star hugged Coco and handed her a chocolate bar. Coco glowed. Deni continued, "Gloria came in second. For the rest of you, I'll have your accounts tallied up by tonight." She put the notebook back in her pocket. "While you're at the club tonight, start thinking up some moves to put online."

Star picked up the tray with the breakfast condiments, ready to accompany Deni upstairs. Jess started to clear off the mugs from the table when she saw Gloria approach Deni.

"Deni, a word," she said.

Deni motioned for Star to continue upstairs, then turned to Gloria. Jess busied herself at the table, straining to hear their conversation above the commotion of the others as they prepared for the club.

"You and Zander know I don't do online. I don't want porn of me on the web."

"Oh, the prima donna is too good for porn? When are you going to get off that high horse of yours and realize you're just a slut, a hustler, a common whore. No one gives a damn about you, not even your own mother—you must have been a really fucked-up kid." Deni shifted her weight to her other foot. "You don't want to do online porn? Yeah, well, I don't want to deal with a pandemic, yet here we are. If the clubs close, porn is your only option." She crossed her arms with a smirk. "That boyfriend of yours is still circulating in Edmonton. Wanna hook back up?"

Gloria lowered her head.

"Oh, by the way, Zander's been informed of your snide remarks, and he's getting tired of them. So if you don't want to wind up in the backwoods somewhere with coyotes licking your bones, you better keep that mouth of yours shut."

As Deni walked back upstairs, Jess moved to the sink.

Chapter 52

During the past several days, Jess had become acquainted with the rhythm of her bizarre basement dwelling. She slept on the area carpet with two other girls—beds were an earned privilege—and Deni assigned her to help Flower clean the basement before recording. The clubbers were the first to leave after rushing through their hair and makeup. And today, Star and Coco would resume their escort services right after the clubbers left. Until now, they had been Jess's constant companions, coaching her during recordings.

As the clubbers glitzed up, Flower and Jess would clean, starting with the dishes and the bedrooms, then moving to the bathroom and main area. By the time they finished, the clubbers were gone. Flower would bring the laundry upstairs, and Jess scurried to prepare herself for recordings. She wouldn't see Flower again until later at night when she returned with the clean laundry, did her hair and makeup, dressed and went to one of the rooms for an online session. Once, during a pause in recordings, Jess heard a guard tell her she was needed upstairs for "VIP service."

Flower was an enigma to Jess. Other than Deni and Star, she was the only one who spent significant time upstairs. Well, Seth did as well, but he told Jess he wasn't allowed out of his room without a guard and spent his days in his room editing and posting photos and videos. From the chatter among the girls, Jess gathered that the clubbers were herded upstairs to a mudroom, then straight to the garage. There they piled into an SUV and were driven to the clubs. When they returned, they were marched directly downstairs.

Though Flower had access to the main floor, she did not have the authority of Deni nor the status of Star. When Deni or Star spoke to the group, Flower rarely lifted her eyes; she cowered if one of the girls made a disparaging remark. Yet, very discretely, she offered Jess kindness, if nothing more than a slight smile or a tender tone of voice.

That night during a tedious recording session, Rocky, a guard who also recorded, went upstairs "to see if Deni thought any of her takes would work." Jess had come out of her room for water and saw Flower applying makeup. Nearby lay an iPad.

"Where did you get that?" Jess asked.

"Upstairs. It's for online chats."

"So you can surf the net?"

"No. It's on a timer and locked into one site. Child-proofed."

Jess walked to the kitchenette and filled a cup with water. Flower was sitting right behind her. "What's it like up there?" she asked softly.

Flower continued applying makeup, "Like any other home."

"I hear babies."

"Deni's." She ratted up her hair, "I babysit and clean for her."

Rocky came stomping down the stairs at that point, and the recording resumed.

As usual, in the early hours of the morning, the clubbers descended the stairs, but they were unusually subdued. Gloria was not among them. The next day the clubs closed.

Chapter 53

Rocky flicked off the camera impatiently. "What are you playing at, Jackie?" he yelled. "Do you realize who you are dealing with?" Rocky drew his fingers through his hair and pulled in exasperation. "Every time we send Zander your recordings, he gets so pissed. He's getting ready to go after that friend of yours."

Sebastian. Oh, my God, what had she dragged him into? "I'm trying! What more does he want?"

"Get rid of your top."

The disco music continued to play on the laptop. Jess moved off the bed and sat on the floor against the back wall, squeezed between the sidewall and the bed. She felt more protected there, less exposed.

Rocky left the room and, a few minutes later, returned with Seth. Rocky went back to his camera, and Seth sat on the bed near Jess.

"I can't do this shit, Seth."

"If you want to get out of here, you have to."

"Who are the creeps that salivate over these sick videos?"

"Creeps that are willing to pay a lot of money."

Fury washed over Jess. She pushed passed Seth, climbed on the bed, stripped off her top, gyrated, coiled and weaved. Rocky smiled, flicked on the camera and began to record. Seth moved to the door. After a few minutes, she went down on all fours and scowled into the camera, "You're all a bunch of fucking, perverted losers getting off on kids–"

"You're going to get us killed!" Seth said. Rocky stopped the recording and stepped in front of the camera. His well-toned arms and torso bulged through his tight, black tee shirt. He grabbed Jess by the shoulder and pushed her to the head of the bed. Jess sprung into action, blindly swinging and kicking. Rocky grabbed her up again and brought her to her feet on the side of the bed. He shoved her against the wall and kneed her in the gut. Jess bent forward, gasping in pain, but he caught her up by the neck with his forearm and pressed her back against the wall. Jess could not speak or breathe. She felt the edge of a knife near her ribs. "You do what you're told, or you're gone. No one cares about your shitty, little self. And when Zander gives up on you, no one is ever going to find you either."

Jess wheezed, straining to breathe. She wished Rocky would plunge the knife and end her pathetic life. And then a strange sensation washed over her. She seemed far, far away. Away from the stale, grungy room, away from the shouting, away from the pain. It was all an illusion. All fading away. She was safe in her grandmother's bungalow with her grandmother. Far, far away.

Chapter 54

"What the hell have you done to her?" yelled Seth. Jess lay crumpled on the floor. Seth knelt next to Jess and nudged her shoulder. Jess opened her eyes. "She's alive." Rocky moved to the door. Stroking her arm, Seth said, "You'll be okay, Jess. Let me get you up." Slowly Seth got Jess to her feet. He helped her lay on the bed and sat next to her.

"Would you get me a blanket?" he said to Rocky. As soon as he left, Seth whispered, "You can't fight these guys, Jess. I mean, God, what happened to Gloria?" He gently caressed her cheek, "The only way out is to give Zander what he wants and pay off the bogus loans." Jess nodded slightly. "It'll be okay in the end; you'll see." Rocky came back with a blanket. Seth covered Jess and left, softly closing the door.

~

Jess lay on the bed. It hurt to swallow, and her abdomen cramped and spasmed. How had she arrived here? Trapped and beaten? The memory of her grandmother, so vivid moments before, resurfaced. Jess clamped her jaws to hold back her tears. She could not allow herself to cry. She would not cry.

~

The funeral of her father. Refreshments were served in the church basement. Her grandmother turned to hug one of the relatives, and Jess, six years old, walked to the table of bars and cookies. As she considered her choices, a man squatted next to her. Putting his hand on her shoulder, he said softly, "Well, here's the little angel I've heard so much about. I'm your uncle." He stroked her braids and handed her a chocolate cookie. Jess drew away slightly, but her uncle put his arm around her and rubbed her back. Her grandmother materialized next to her, grabbed the cookie from her hand and tossed it at her uncle's feet.

"Get away from her," her grandmother hissed. "You screwed over my son and your sister, but not my Jess. Don't you ever come near my granddaughter!" She grabbed Jess's hand and sailed out of the hall, Jess running to keep up. Jess never saw her uncle again while her grandmother lived. But then she died.

Jess was placed with a foster family who took in numerous children like Jess until other arrangements could be made. Nothing in her new setting was remotely similar to her previous life. She and her grandmother had lived in a small, two-bedroom bungalow, and she had attended the neighbourhood school since kindergarten. Her foster home was large, chaotic and in a completely different neighbourhood. Mid-year, Jess was enrolled in a school near her foster family. Before the next school year, she was placed with her mother and enrolled in yet another school—her educational merry-go-round had begun.

Jess's mother had been studying to be a paralegal before her life unravelled. In order to reclaim her daughter, she cleaned up and got a job as a receptionist at a car dealership. But Jess had spent so little time with her mother, she felt she was living with a stranger... no, worse than a stranger. Jess could sense her mother's anxiety to parent her properly, to make things right between them. The comfortable familiarity at her grandmother's was wanting. Wasn't she supposed to love her mother? Be happy they were together? Jess had always wondered what it would be like to live with her mom. When her grandmother was strict about Jess's bedtime, electronics or chores, Jess would become angry, tell her grandmother how unfair she was and then dream about living with her mother, who would spoil her with treats like she did during her infrequent visits. But now, all she wanted was her grandmother and her old school with her teachers and friends.

Jess and her mother co-existed in their tiny apartment, cautious and civil, until the morning Jess found her on the couch, lifeless, a syringe lying nearby. The morning after a visit from her uncle, Rodolfo Tanis.

Chapter 55

Jess walked slowly from the bedroom to join the others for their main meal. Her gut ached, but Jess couldn't tell how much was from hunger or the blow she had received several hours before. As she eased into the place Deni had designated for her, she noticed there was no bowl of rice. Instead, Star served her a big dish of pasta.

"I hear you've joined the workforce, Jackie. Deni was impressed with what the guys upstairs managed to salvage from your last dance routine. She's named you *The Wasp*. And it's already a hit!" Star laughed, "Who would have guessed?"

Yes, Jess thought, *who would have guessed that men got off on teenagers, beaten and coerced, for their entertainment.* As she slowly ate her pasta, it dawned on her: she now had a persona—The Wasp. No longer would she be expected to play the coy vixen. She could openly rage, snarl and disdain her captors as well as those voyeurs who sought gratification through the nightmare of her existence.

$\sim$

Even though the clubs were closed, the basement routine remained the same: "breakfast" was served in the early afternoon when they rose for another day of work; the main meal arrived around four in the morning when the online sessions closed. Outside of their two meals, their only option was water. After each meal, Star collected the items that belonged upstairs, and Flower began washing the dishes with Jess assisting.

Today Jess rose slowly from her seat and moved to the sink to help

Flower with the early morning dishes. Star went upstairs with her tray, and Coco grabbed a couple of blankets and went to a room to sleep. "Leave some blankets for the rest of us," said Trixie. The two squabbled a bit before Coco entered a room and pulled the curtain. The rest scurried around, taking turns for showers and getting ready for bed.

During the hubbub, Flower clattered the dishes in the sink and whispered, "Are you okay?"

Jess nodded. "It could have been worse. Seth talked down Zander's guard."

Flower shot her a glance, "Is he a boyfriend?"

Jess shook her head. After a few moments, she said, "More like a brother. Lena played us both–" Jess cut off abruptly, afraid she had said too much.

Flower glanced around the room. Someone in the shower was complaining loudly about the damp towels on the floor that she was forced to use. Flower handed a mug to Jess to dry, but when Jess grasped it, she did not let go. Jess looked over and caught a sustained glance from Flower. Flower let go of the mug, turned up the water and leaned close to Jess, "Seth is Zander. Zander is Seth."

PART FOUR

Chapter 56

Several blocks from Gid's house, Sebastian stopped at a bus stop bench; his hands were numb with cold even though he had them stuffed in his pockets. He was rooting through his backpack, feeling for his mitts, when his fingers slammed into something stiff. Cursing, he pulled out the culprit–his photo album, rigid with cold. Sebastian sat on the bench, his back turned against the polar wind, and flipped through several pictures of himself with his dad during their happier moments. He loved his dad. Tears filled his eyes. Then other memories surfaced. Treks with his dad to Gid's, Sebastian shivering in his light jacket. Days of frenetic activity, his dad composing on his guitar, strumming pieces over and over for hours on end, cigarette butts piled around him. Sebastian standing on the kitchen counter, hunting through the cupboard for food. Then days of sleep, Sebastian checking to make sure his father was still breathing, followed by another trek to Gid's. Sebastian watching TV at Gid's until his dad returned with a wad of cash. Repeat until Children's Services arrived.

The last picture in the slim album was one of Sebastian and Jess, grainy, printed on the plain paper of the group home. He could hear Jess saying, "You're dad's in prison because of that bastard." And now Sebastian was heading right back to the bastard, following in his father's footsteps–literally.

Sebastian repacked the album and found his mitts. He stood and turned around. Gid? Not now... not yet.

Chapter 57

Sebastian lost count of the blocks he trudged. He turned a corner, and there, in the midst of a strip mall, was a laundromat. And it was open! As he pushed through the door, the warm air from driers, mixed with the scent of laundry soap, felt like an embrace. A couple of people, tapping on their cell phones, sat in chairs carefully distanced, earbuds in. A squat, middle-aged woman wearing a bright yellow apron and a cloth mask glanced up from her folding. Attached to her apron was a blue plastic name badge boldly stamped, *Elaine*.

"Looks like you have a large load in that pack," Elaine said. "Come with me; I'll get you started."

"Ah, thanks," said Sebastian, hesitating. "Is there a bathroom where I could wash up first?"

Elaine eyed Sebastian top to bottom. "Follow me." She opened a door near the rear exit. "Wait here." When she returned, she had a stack of large, terry cleaning cloths. "They've been washed," and looking up at his hair, "Here's some hand soap to use on that mop of yours." She passed him the cloths, and a plastic bag with remnants of liquid soap settled near the bottom. "It's an insert from the soap dispensers. Just add some water. I usually finish them off in our utility sink back here."

"Jesus, thanks!"

"I have a grandson your age," said Elaine as she unlocked the bathroom door, "Make it snappy and don't leave a mess."

When Sebastian emerged, his wild hair dripping, he carried a small bundle of laundry and his debit card. "Right here," said Elaine pointing to a washer. The soap was already in the dispenser. "Is that all? It's a pretty small load."

Sebastian was already going commando and sockless in order to wash his underclothes. He only had two pairs of pants and three long-sleeved tees, and he had to wear something. "That's it."

"Then why don't you throw in your coat? Might as well. Just clean out your pockets."

After transferring the contents of his coat pockets to his pants pockets and depositing his coat in the washer, Sebastian asked, "How much does it cost?"

"Three dollars to wash, three to dry. But," she whispered, "I'm giving the soap for free." Once the washer began filling, Elaine looked Sebastian over again and patted him on the shoulder. "Much better." Sebastian went back to the bathroom and came out with his backpack and the cleaning cloths, wet and rolled in a ball. Elaine took the cloths and said, "You're a good boy. I can see that." He quickly turned away his head and blinked back tears. She pulled a disposable mask from an apron pocket. "If you're waiting here, we prefer you wear a mask."

Sebastian slipped on the mask and went to the waiting area. Near one chair was an outlet, and posted on the wall was the code for a free Wi-Fi connection. Sebastian planted himself in the chair and pulled out his phone and charger. After several minutes the pings began. Message after message from Mallory, a few from Ms. Willow... none from Jess.

Chapter 58

"Basic and functional," said Officer Wallace when he entered Jess's apartment. Willow followed him through the front door along with one of the Independent Living staff, all of them masked. Once inside, Wallace moved methodically from the living room to the kitchen.

"So nothing's been touched since she left?" Wallace asked the staff worker.

"Jess's caseworker, Paige, gave a look around, but no one after her."

"I called Paige this morning," said Wallace, "and I understand that all her belongings are going to be packed up tomorrow and stored. A new client will be moving in the day after."

"What!" exclaimed Willow. "So when Jess returns, the little home she's made for herself will be gone?"

"Unfortunately, yes," said the staff member. "There's such a high demand for this type of housing that we can't keep it vacant indefinitely. Jess will have to reapply and be reassessed when she returns. Excuse me, my phone is vibrating–I have to take this call," and she walked out to the front lawn.

Willow followed Wallace into the bedroom and watched him open dresser drawers and scan the closet. "Well, it doesn't appear Jess planned to be gone long–her clothes are all neatly arranged in her drawers–no gaps. She's actually quite organized."

As Wallace pulled out a bottom drawer, Willow noticed the corner of a thin plastic folder pouch and pulled it out.

"What do you have there?" asked Wallace.

"Looks like a few pictures," said Willow.

Wallace opened the pouch and gently shook out the contents onto the bed. "Could be family pictures. I know she was raised by her grandmother–this must be her with Jess." There were several pictures of Jess at various ages with an older woman. Then pointing to a couple of others, "These might be her mom and dad."

"I know Jess is PGO," said Willow. "I assume her parents and grandmother are no longer in her life."

"All three are dead," said Wallace.

"My God."

Wallace returned the pictures to the pouch and left them on the top of the dresser. Then he walked to the bathroom and glanced around. "I think we can be fairly certain that Jess did not plan to run away–if, in fact, she did run away." Wallace made a motion with his hands above the bottles, tubes, and jars on the bathroom vanity, "Soaps, deodorant,... all this hair product just left here. And wouldn't she have packed some clothes?"

"I can't imagine Jess running away either," said Willow as she and Wallace walked back into the living room.

"There's no sign of a struggle," said Wallace, giving another look around.

"Could she be in a hospital?" asked Willow.

"We did a province-wide check of hospitals and centres for homeless youth. No luck." Wallace pulled out his pad and flipped through several pages. "You mentioned earlier that Jess was in a performance."

"Yes, she sang with the school choir and also performed solo."

"I understood she was a loner."

"From what I observed, Jess kept to herself, but she has a couple of friends. I've spoken to them, and they say they have no idea where she is. They're really concerned."

"Would you give me their names?"

Willow grimaced. "I don't know... both are rather skittish, and my relationship with them is fledging. Bring a police officer into the mix, and it would be over. They've promised to call me if they hear anything."

"Okay. You continue to stay in touch with them and keep me abreast. If possible, meet with them again and see if there's any detail they may have overlooked. But further down the line, I may have to speak with them personally."

Willow went back into the bedroom and came out with the plastic pouch of photos. "Would you mind if I kept these for Jess? All her things will be packed up tomorrow and put in storage. I wouldn't want these pictures to go missing. It seems they're the only mementos she has of her family."

"Strictly speaking, they should go to her caseworker," said Wallace. "But, quite frankly, you seem to be more connected to Jess." He opened his pad. "I'll make a note that you have the photos."

"And these notebooks and textbooks from school?" Willow continued. "They're here on the table. I can hold on to them." Wallace added them to his list.

"Speaking of school books," said Wallace glancing around, "wouldn't Jess have a laptop? My kids use them for schoolwork."

Wallace and Willow hunted through the small apartment, but no laptop was found. Wallace walked out to the front lawn and motioned to the staff worker.

"Would you hold that thought for a moment?" she said to the caller, "The police officer needs to ask me something." She muted the call and turned to Wallace.

"We can't seem to find a laptop. Did Jess have one?"

"Let me ask my colleague—she's on the phone right now and came to the apartment when Jess was reported absent from school." After speaking for a few moments, she closed the call. "Jess's caseworker may have taken a laptop; she's not sure."

"If Jess had a laptop, we need it back."

"You'll have to ask the caseworker." The staff worker saw Wallace's exasperated look. "It sounds like a runaround, I know," she said patiently, "but we're not the legal guardians of the independent teens who live here. Our program supports their housing needs. We can report our concerns—and we had no concerns regarding Jess—but all decisions regarding a youth depend on the caseworker."

～

Back at home, Willow glanced through Jess's notebooks. Nothing appeared out of the ordinary: schedules, notes, ideas for an essay. As she flipped through a textbook, it opened to a bookmarked page. The bookmark was a business card for Lena Lugine, a modelling agent for InTrend Agency. Willow quickly found their website. The company was located in Toronto, and the contact for children and teens was lena@intrendagency.

Chapter 59

"InTrend Agency, how can I help you?"

"I'd like to speak with Lena, the representative for teens and children."

"Is she expecting your call?"

The receptionist proved to be a formidable sentinel against unsolicited callers. No matter her spin, Willow hit a brick wall of resistance from the guard at the gate. There would be no conversation with Lena. "Maybe you can help me with one question," said Willow. "How often does Lena come to Calgary?"

"Never."

"So if someone from Alberta wanted to be represented by you—"

"All applications are submitted online," the receptionist cut in. "We do have talent scouts, but they circulate in Ontario or, occasionally, a province nearby. No one from our agency travels to Alberta."

"So you're certain that," Willow picked up the business card, "Lena Lugine has not been to Alberta recently?"

"Lena who?"

"Maybe I'm not pronouncing her name correctly. Lugine, L-u-g-i-n-e."

"No one by that name works here."

Willow closed the call and phoned Officer Wallace.

Chapter 60

Mallory walked to the copse of barren trees edging the field behind Riverbank High. She zipped up her winter coat against the raw, north wind whipping across the open expanse. The broad grassy area was dry and brown, awaiting a few weeks of warmth to coax out the dormant green blades. Across the field, she saw a lone figure approaching the trees, shouldering a large backpack–it had to be Sebastian. As he drew nearer, she walked into the field and waved widely. After weeks without seeing him and days without hearing from him, it had been a relief to receive his messages and now a joy to see him face-to-face.

"I know we're supposed to keep our distance, but," Mallory opened her arms, and the two laughed and hugged. "Are you okay?" she asked as they walked toward the trees. "I've been worried."

Sebastian shrugged. "Still got a place to sleep at night."

"What about food?" Before he could reply, Mallory set down her backpack and pulled out a battered, reusable shopping bag. "I made you a few things," she said as she handed Sebastian the tote. "Let me know when you need more, and we can meet up."

"God! Thanks, Mallory!" He hugged her again, wiping tears as he pulled away.

"Still nothing from Jess?"

Sebastian shook his head. "Something's very wrong. Why else would Ms. Willow want to meet up with us?"

"Here she comes."

Sebastian turned, "And it looks like she's brought lunch."

"Sorry to call you out in this cold during your lunch break," Willow said when she joined the two teens. "I didn't know what you drank, so I brought you both hot tea—the regular kind with sugar—and a hot sandwich. I hope you like them." Sebastian delved into his sandwich immediately while Mallory sipped her tea.

"I don't know where we can meet indoors without reams of permissions, so I won't keep you long. If you need help with school, give me a call, but right now, I want to talk about Jess."

"Have the police found out anything?" asked Mallory.

"No. It's like she disappeared. That's why I called you here. I want you to think back. Do you remember anything—and I mean anything— that was the least bit unusual... different—anything at all?"

Mallory sipped her tea, then looked up tentatively at Willow. "What if it's nothing?"

"Then it's nothing. But it could be a tiny something that leads us in the right direction."

"Well," said Mallory hesitantly, "over Christmas break, I saw Jess walking with a lady at the mall. But," Mallory added hurriedly, "she could have been asking for directions."

"Okay, Mallory, this is that 'little something' I was talking about. Do you remember what she looked like?"

"I mean, it was just them walking and talking past one of the seating areas—I was sketching. I just remember thinking she looked like a businesswoman. With long hair, brown—or something darker—not blond."

"Excellent, Mallory. Was she young? Old?"

"She was younger—not old and wrinkly. It was fast. I don't know how old."

Willow turned toward Sebastian. "Anything?"

Sebastian finished the last bite of his sandwich, shaking his head. "Jess really liked living on her own in her apartment. She wouldn't do anything to fuck it up."

"I remember one more thing," said Mallory. "One time, Jess and I were going to meet at a thrift shop, you know, the one not too far from here."

Willow and Sebastian nodded.

"When I got there, she was talking to some guy outside, but it could have been a question he asked, I don't know."

"So what happened when you went over?" asked Willow.

"I didn't. I waited for a little, and they kept talking, so I went home. I didn't want to intrude."

"What was he like?"

"He was really good-looking–older than us," pointing to herself and Sebastian, "but not as old as my dad–he's forty-four."

"Did Jess ever talk about modelling?" Both teens shook their heads no. "Or a modelling agency?"

Again, they shook their heads no. "Never," said Sebastian.

Willow went back to the woman at the mall and the man at the store but could draw out no further details. "Would you like to meet here once a week to update? It should warm up before too long."

Both agreed. "And I'll bring lunch," Willow added.

"I have to hurry back home to sign in for my Math class," said Mallory.

"Yes, we all need to be on our way. Thanks for coming," said Willow. Then she turned toward Sebastian, "Would you walk with me to my car?"

As they said their goodbyes, Sebastian swung on his backpack, picked up the tote of food and walked next to Willow to the parking lot. Mallory trailed along, slipping her sandwich into the wide pocket of Sebastian's winter jacket. He turned and smiled, and she trotted away.

Chapter 61

When Mallory left, Willow veered to a side entrance of the school more protected from the wind. "That's a very large backpack," she observed. Sebastian made no comment. "Everything okay at home?"

Sebastian shrugged, "I guess."

"I noticed you haven't logged in for online school... at all."

"Yeah, I'm working some things out. Trying to get set up."

"Do you need a laptop?"

"I might, yeah. We'll see."

"What does your mom think of online school?"

"What do you mean?"

"Does she like having you home all day?"

"I don't think she cares one way or the other."

"Would you like me to give her a call and see if we can get you set up for school?"

"No, no, that wouldn't be a good idea," Sebastian said abruptly. "She's busy."

"Sebastian, you're going to have to be straight with me. I'm looking at your backpack, and I'm thinking you're not staying at home. Am I close?"

Sebastian let out a sigh. "I'm staying with a friend."

"So why the backpack?"

"I don't want to leave my things at his place."

"Does your mom know where you are?"

"She knows I'm with a friend."

"And she's okay with that?"

"Apparently."

"How can I be sure you're safe?" asked Willow. Sebastian said nothing. "There are other options."

"Yeah, I know all about the other options: youth centres, group homes, foster homes, 'reintegration sessions,'" Sebastian said hotly. "I've done them all, and they always end the same way. I'm better off by myself." He looked straight at Willow. "I'm not going back home, and if they force me, I'll run further away."

Willow considered Sebastian for a few moments. "Let's make a deal. Every day you message me and let me know if you're okay. I'm going to see what I can do to get more gift cards for you. Come back here tomorrow. I should have the gift cards by then. Do we have a deal?" Sebastian nodded yes. "And don't take off. Remember, Jess needs you. If we're going to find her, we have to work together."

Willow watched Sebastian trudge across the field, and then she entered the school. The school's secretaries were taking turns answering the phone; otherwise, they worked from home. To Willow's relief, June Barnes was on duty. She recapped her conversation with Sebastian and asked if there were any more gift cards for groceries. June, quickly and quietly, filled out a form, unlocked a drawer and handed Willow a fifty-dollar gift card, barely making eye contact.

"Have Sebastian sign this form when you give him the card and get it back to me," said June.

"Thanks." Willow paused. "What's up? Something's up, I can tell."

June strummed her fingers on her desktop. "I may have overstepped, and I'll probably get hell for this...."

"This is going to be good."

"I was able to get a SIN card for Sebastian. But he couldn't get paid at work without a bank account, and there was no way for him to open a bank account without an adult. He told me that he couldn't trust his mother to have a joint account—she might take his money. True or not, I don't know. But based on what you just told me, I'm hedging toward true."

"So, let me guess.... You opened a joint bank account with Sebastian."

"Yes. But I told him that if I noticed any funny business going on with his account, I would close it."

"And has any 'funny business' been going on?"

"Last I checked, no. Just deposits from *Strum 'N Drum* and modest withdrawals. I assumed he was home, so I haven't checked recently."

"Can you do it now?"

June went to an app on her phone. "Last paycheque deposited a couple of weeks ago, ninety bucks. Makes sense—that's about the time the stores closed. Small withdrawals—only thirty dollars left."

Chapter 62

The morning newscaster was reciting updated Covid numbers when Oliver walked into his family's double-island, quartz-countered kitchen for a bowl of cereal. His mother stopped what she was doing, intent on the statistics that flashed on the screen. Oliver, instead, went into the pantry, glanced over several boxes of cereal, opted for one, and filled his bowl. When the Covid report was over, his mother carried on with her tasks, but Oliver stared at the screen.

"The Calgary police are asking for your help to find a missing sixteen-year-old girl," announced the newscaster. "Jess Gayle was last seen March 13." A description of Jess was given. "Anyone with information is asked to contact the police."

"Oliver! Pay attention to what you're doing!" yelled his mother as Oliver stood at the counter pouring milk into his cereal, the creamy liquid flowing over the bowl, down the counter and onto the floor. Oliver walked over to the family room area, picked up the remote and replayed the announcement.

His mother grabbed a dish towel and began to sop up the milk. "What are you doing?" she snapped.

"That girl goes to our school."

"Just help me clean up this mess!" Oliver got a cloth. "Down there, on the floor!"

"We need to find her."

"I'm sure the police are perfectly capable—Oliver, wake up! You're just smearing the milk around. Oh, go! Eat your breakfast. I'll finish wiping this up."

Chapter 63

Evening was falling as Sebastian hustled to the laundromat. His phone was dead, and he hadn't sent his daily message to Ms. Willow. Since his first visit, he'd been to the laundromat a few times to warm up and charge his phone–he didn't want to use any more of his limited funds to wash his clothes. Each time, Elaine opened the bathroom door, provided him with terry cloths, and gave him a few snacks as he sat checking his messages.

This evening, he only wanted to charge his phone and warm himself before heading to the chilly garage for the night. Sebastian pulled a ratty mask from his pocket and put it on before opening the door. As he walked in, he saw a woman wearing a bright yellow apron at a side table. It wasn't Elaine. "Can I help you," she asked when Sebastian approached.

"Yeah," said Sebastian, glancing around. "Is Elaine working today?"

"You know Elaine?"

"She's helped me out the last few times I was here."

"I can give you a hand."

"Uh, well, today I just need to charge my phone. I usually sit in that chair over there when I wash my clothes," he gestured. "I won't make a peep."

"Only customers are allowed inside."

"You see, my phone died, and I need to text my mom. She'll be worried."

The woman eyed Sebastian. "You have fifteen minutes."

As the phone charged, messages pinged in. First, he typed a quick text to Ms. Willow and then checked his incoming messages: Mallory and Ms. Willow reminding him of their meeting the next day, Mallory sending memes that got him laughing. Just then, a new message popped up from Logan. *Don't go to garage. Text me when you get to park near our house. I'll meet you there.*

~

Logan stammered apologetically. His uncle and a couple of cousins living at home had been laid off, and the government subsidies had kicked in. With manpower and enough funds to get by, Logan's uncle had a chance to pursue a long-held dream: a skateboard and a BMX bike repair shop. It would be a side business that aligned with two passions he'd had since his youth and would, hopefully, provide extra income for his family. The location: the garage. Beginning that day, everyone in Logan's household had been removing and sorting years of accumulated castoffs and long-forgotten essentials. Sebastian's nightly sanctuary was gone.

"I'm sorry, bro. I was hoping you could have a few more days. But my uncle's still digging through the stuff, and my aunt's right next to him making sure he doesn't get rid of something she still needs."

"Yeah, what can you do?" said Sebastian, masking his alarm. "Thanks for helping me out when you did."

"You gonna be okay?"

"Yeah, sure. There's another place I can try."

Sebastian left Logan at the park, meandering toward the main drag, kicking at pieces of mulch and gravel that had tumbled onto the sidewalk.

~

By the time Sebastian walked to the back entrance of *Strum N' Drum,* the street lights were lit against the fast-approaching night. During the day, the temperature rose above freezing, but it dropped rapidly as the sun slid beneath the horizon. Sebastian rang the bell until his forefinger ached. No response.

Near the back door was a large cardboard recycling container attached by a chain to a wall anchor. Sebastian set down his backpack and reached into the large slot on the front side. The container was nearly full, so by standing on his tiptoes and stretching as far as he could, he was able to pull out several folded boxes. The container was made of heavy metal mounted on rusted wheels, but Sebastian managed to swivel it out at an angle wide enough for him to squeeze behind it for the night. He insulated the ground and sides with cardboard boxes and pulled his sleeping bag from his backpack. With his toque on and the hood of his coat over his head, Sebastian slipped on his mitts, wedged his backpack into the far corner of his shelter, climbed into his sleeping bag, and backed in. He had no intention of sleeping—he sat upright against his pack wrapped in his sleeping bag. His main goal was to stay alive and as warm as possible. A few cars made their way down the alley, and Sebastian pulled in his legs as tight as he could against his thighs, his heart beating rapidly. Each time, his hidey-hole remained undetected. Voices and honking horns from the street occasionally alarmed him, but the voices never made their way behind the store.

Beep, beep, beep! The backup beeper from a delivery truck woke Sebastian with a start. His hiding spot was suffused with daylight. Sebastian quickly rolled forward onto his knees and peeped out from the side of the container. Down the alley, he saw a truck on the side street. He rolled back to a sitting position, wiggled out of his sleeping bag and crawled out from behind the dumpster. Every muscle of his body screamed. He stretched and walked in circles near the rear of the store, trying to ease the pain. As he did so, he noticed a dropbox near the backdoor of *Strum N' Drum*. Sebastian pulled down on the handle, and the chute opened. Small boxes and parcels could fit easily and be delivered outside business hours. He crawled behind the container, dragged out his backpack and rummaged through the front pocket for a pen and a school notebook.

Craig,

Looking for some work. Do you need help? Contact me through YouApp.

Sebastian signed off with his name and *YouApp* handle and dropped the note into the chute.

Chapter 64

Willow waited for Officer Wallace at the Riverbank High School parking lot. She had arranged a meeting between the two teens and the police officer with the understanding that their identities would be anonymous. Wallace pulled in on schedule.

"I checked out Lena Lugine at *InTrend*," he said after exchanging the usual greetings. "No such person. Lena Martin is *InTrend's* child and teen rep. She's never been to Alberta, ever. Her boss confirmed that before the lockdown, she worked steadily from their main office. Lena Lugine is a fraud."

"Did you locate Jess's laptop?"

"Yes and no. The caseworker, Paige, took it from the apartment for safekeeping, but with online school, every available laptop was needed for kids under care, so Paige passed it on. Jess's laptop was wiped and given to someone else."

"Shit!"

"That's putting it mildly. However, my hunch is, most of Jess's communications and searches would have happened on her phone."

"Any luck on that score?"

"No, no sign of her phone and no knowledge of her provider. However, we now know her bank—one of her caseworkers had a direct deposit set up for her government cheques. We've issued a written demand for her account history and are waiting for the document. From there, we should find out her cell service provider and try tracking her phone."

"Jess's friends are waiting for us in the field behind the school. I've promised them they will be anonymous—no names. Do I have your word on that?"

"Yes."

Willow went to her car and took out a large bag and a cardboard cup carrier with two drinks. "Would you help me with this?" she asked as she passed the drinks to Wallace. Together they walked toward the field.

~

Mallory watched Ms. Willow and the police officer approach the copse of trees. Next to her, Sebastian looked like he was ready to sprint.

"Fuck, fuck, fuck," he muttered.

"It'll be okay. Ms. Willow promised no names. If he asks, we leave—simple." When Sebastian had arrived, he stashed his backpack among some bushes, out of sight. Mallory noted he looked more dishevelled than usual. His face and hands were clean, but his clothes were rumpled; his tangled red hair shot out in all directions as if he'd been electrocuted. When she gave him a hug, he smelt rancid. The wind was blowing; hopefully, no one else would notice. Mallory wished she could bring Sebastian home, but her father would never understand, let alone allow it.

~

Willow introduced Officer Wallace and handed Mallory and Sebastian their lunches.

"Thank you for speaking with me," said Wallace. "I know it can be intimidating to meet with a police officer."

Mallory and Sebastian sipped their drinks, barely lifting their eyes.

"I want to go over some information I heard from Ms. Willow." He had Mallory recount what she had seen at the mall and outside the thrift store. Sebastian stated again that he had never seen Jess out and about with anyone. Mallory and Sebastian knew of no boyfriends or any jobs. The last both had seen her was at school that Friday in March. At lunch, she had told them that she was meeting up with her caseworker after school.

"Did she ever speak of a Lena Lugine?" he asked. Both shook their heads.

"Anything about a modelling job?"

"Nothing," both said.

When it appeared Officer Wallace had no further questions, Mallory said timidly, "I saw the TV announcement about Jess on the internet. Did you get any tips from that?"

"Some tips came in, but none materialized."

"Have you found her phone?" she continued.

"No, however, that brings up something you could help us with. Do you know her cell provider?"

"Oh, that's easy," said Sebastian. He named the carrier. "Jess used to brag about the sweet deal she had with them—one with a phone and cheap plan."

"Her phone had a great camera. She kept it in a purple case," said Mallory.

"And she hid her bank card between the phone and inside of the case," added Sebastian.

"Thanks, that's very useful." Officer Wallace looked over his notes, "Well, I'm done unless you have something else to add."

"No." "Not me," said the youths.

"Tomorrow? Same time?" asked Willow. This meeting had been in addition to their regular weekly meeting.

"Yeah, see you then," said Sebastian.

It had warmed up considerably over the previous day, so Sebastian and Mallory walked to where Sebastian had stowed his backpack and sat down to eat the lunches Ms. Willow had given them.

Sebastian opened his bag, "Wow! This is way more than I ordered! Do you want some, Mallory?"

"No, I'm fine. And I have something for your supper." She pulled out a paper grocery bag from her backpack and gave it to Sebastian. "If you ever need a meal, just message me."

"Thanks."

The warm wind brushed their faces and ran through their hair. For a while, they soaked in the promise of summer and admired the buds just beginning to form on the trees. Sebastian finished off his sandwich and pulled out a green salad.

"I've been talking to Oliver," said Mallory at last. "He said that the TV announcement about Jess wasn't enough. I mean, who watches morning news or checks the police social media accounts? I only found out because Oliver's mother had the news on when he had breakfast. We have to get the word out that Jess is missing."

"I posted what you sent me through *Ima-gram,* but it went nowhere," said Sebastian.

"Oliver is very techy. He has some ideas. We could have him come to our meetings with Ms. Willow."

"So you talk to Oliver a lot?"

"He's been helping me figure out the online school stuff, and he really wants to help us find Jess. Asking the cop about the TV announcement and Jess's phone was his idea." Mallory paused. "He's done with Victor and is really sorry he had anything to do with him."

"Yeah, I guess it would be okay. And Mallory, thanks for the food... it's just," Sebastian faltered, "sometimes what I need is a washing machine and a place to charge my phone—"

"I can do that for you! Best time for both is early in the morning, so I can have everything done before noon—on the off-chance that my dad comes home early."

"I'm expecting a message, and my phone is dead."

"Let's go now," said Mallory packing up her lunch. "There's a park a couple of blocks from my house. You can finish your lunch there while the phone is charging. Tomorrow morning bring your clothes." Mallory stopped packing up her lunch and looked at Sebastian. "You know I'd bring you into the house, right? But if my dad shows up...."

"Yeah, I get it."

Chapter 65

The rain began sometime during the night, waking Sebastian from his fitful slumber behind the dumpster. He was protected on three sides from the wind, but nothing overhead. When he set up his shelter that night, he'd been grateful that the temperature was above freezing; he hadn't counted on the rain. Sebastian pulled a piece of cardboard he had placed against the outside wall of *Strum's* and covered his head. The sleeping bag was supposedly waterproof. Tonight he'd find out. The rain was sporadic, pattering on the plastic cover of the dumpster, startling Sebastian just as he was drifting to sleep. Exhaustion eventually prevailed, and he nodded off.

Damp and chilled, Sebastian opened his eyes to a gloomy morning. He checked the time. "Shit!" he muttered out loud. Craig had messaged him the evening before—his phone had been charged, thanks to Mallory. Sebastian was supposed to meet Craig at *Strum's* at nine o'clock. It was a little after eight-thirty. Strictly speaking, he was early, but he'd planned on getting to a supermarket to wash up before the meeting and pick up a warm drink. That wouldn't happen now. Instead, he scrambled to dismantle his shelter. His sleeping bag had proved to be waterproof, but the outside was damp, and the dust and filth from the unswept alley clung tenaciously to the fabric. He had no choice but to roll it up and stuff it into his backpack. Nearby was a sidewall cut off from view by a few scrappy, leafless shrubs growing amid the gravel. Sebastian slid behind the bushes, grateful for the little privacy they offered. He took a leak and walked to the front of the store to wait for Craig.

Craig's truck was already there, the sole vehicle parked in front of

Strum's. Sebastian knocked on the glass door and peered in. The lights were on. Sebastian knocked harder. He was turning away, headed to the delivery bell at the back door, when he heard the door latch turn.

"Craig!" said Sebastian, breaking into a wide smile.

"My God, Sebastian!" Concern flashed across Craig's face. "What the hell happened to you?" He pushed back his cowboy hat and leaned against the open door, "You look like shit. And, quite frankly, you smell like shit, too! My God!"

Sebastian stared at Craig, wide-eyed.

"And am I right in supposing that everything in that pack of yours is in the same condition?"

Sebastian, again, said nothing.

"I've been worried about you, buddy! Don't you ever check your emails?

"Emails?"

"Yeah, you gave me your school email as a contact."

"I never read those."

Craig pulled off his cowboy hat, planted it in his face and shook his head in disbelief.

"What?" asked Sebastian, amused.

Craig sighed and put back on his hat. "First thing we're gonna do is walk across the street and get you something to eat. And then we're gonna talk." Craig locked the store's door. "Just toss that pack into the back of the truck. No one is going to go near it." As Sebastian lifted his pack into the truck, Craig opened a side door and pulled several wipes from a sanitizer container. "Here. Use these on your hands... and give that mug of yours a wipe, too."

~

Though the morning was still chilly, a bright sun had broken through the clouds, warming the picnic table area at the side of the sandwich shop. Once Sebastian had begun to eat his breakfast, Craig said, "I'm going to ask you some questions, and I want straight answers. No bullshitting." Sebastian nodded as he continued eating. "You're not living at home. I can see that. What's up?"

Little by little, with occasional prompting from Craig, Sebastian's story unfolded. "So if I got this right," said Craig, "your dad's in jail on drug charges. He can't seem to kick the habit, so he peddles drugs to get drugs—otherwise, a decent guy who loves music. Your mother's sober but keeps hooking up with losers, the most recent, a well-to-do bully you call Muscle Max who gets his jollies intimidating kids by smashing their keyboards."

Sebastian was finishing the last of his drink. "And I'm NOT going back."

"You've made that clear several times." Craig raised his cowboy hat, smoothed back his hair and repositioned the hat. "What am I going to do with you, kid?"

"Just give me a job. I can take care of myself."

"I can see that. Your hair is the epitome of care." Craig made a motion like an explosion, "Ca-boom." Sebastian finally laughed.

"And he's back!" Craig chuckled, "Have you checked in that mass of tangles recently? Find any animals running around?"

"Just my pet snake. He takes care of the rodents."

"Get your ass in the truck. We're going to grab some new clothes and get you washed up."

Chapter 66

"There's been no activity on Jess's phone, no movement in her bank account since the Friday she was last seen," said Officer Wallace when Willow called for an update. "Her case has been moved to high priority."

"That's good news."

"It's a step in the right direction; however, we have no new leads, and we still have some top priority cases involving minors much younger and less competent than Jess."

"Lena Lugine, whoever she is, has got to be involved."

"Very likely. And very likely, that's not her real name."

"And there was nothing on Jess's phone?"

"Very little. She has a bare-bone phone plan, so I imagine her calls and texts went through apps."

"And?"

"Without her phone, we don't know what apps she used and—"

"I know two for sure, "Willow interrupted, "*YouApp* and *AppChat*. The kids use *AppChat,* and Jess had me use *YouApp* when I needed to contact her for her performance in December."

"As I was about to say," said Wallace, "even if we know the apps used, it's difficult to get access to their data."

"Sorry for cutting in," said Willow. Then after a moment, "What about the woman at the mall, the one Jess was seen walking with? Can't the CCTV footage be examined?"

"In theory, yes; however, the friend who saw Jess with the woman couldn't remember the exact day, had no idea what entrances were used, or if they even entered or exited together. And it was during the height of Christmas shopping. On top of all this, the encounter could have been a passing one, just a question about a store location."

"And I guess the same applies to the guy outside the thrift shop?"

"That thrift shop doesn't even have CCTV," said Wallace, his voice weary. "It's in a strip mall with a couple other small businesses—all in lockdown. A restaurant and camera store have closed for good and are empty. I'm going to push for another news alert and hope it stirs up a few tips."

Chapter 67

Sebastian hadn't shown up with his dirty laundry. He messaged something had come up. Now, two days later, he'd just texted Mallory to meet him at the park near her house. It was afternoon; her dad would be home soon. There was no way she could wash his clothes today. She pocketed a couple of apples and headed out the door.

Mallory hated making Sebastian meet her on the sly, but she had no choice. She and her dad lived on the third floor of a six-plex. An older woman lived beneath them. Her father liked the old gal because she was quiet and kept an eye on the neighbourhood. If she observed anything out of the ordinary, she had a willing listener in Ryder Mudford, nabbing him when she heard him return home after work. Spotting a grubby, wild-haired teen near the property–let alone knocking on Mallory's door–would have the unauthorized security guard conjuring up all matter of evil and imparting her fabrication, embellished with every passing, idle hour, to her dad. *Lay low for a year and a half, then...*, thought Mallory as she turned into the park.

"What the–!" she exclaimed when she saw Sebastian sitting on a park bench.

Sebastian stood and smiled, throwing out his arms and doing a spin. Gone was the over-stuffed backpack, grungy and fraying at the seams. Gone was the sullied winter coat. His over-grown, spiralling hair was pulled back into a stubby ponytail. He wore a lightweight jacket, khaki pants and new shoes.

Mallory threw her arms around Sebastian. "You look great! I came thinking I'd have to tell you to bring your laundry another day, but look at you! What happened?"

Sebastian told Mallory about his meeting with Craig. "He had me dump out my backpack into his truck bed and sort through it all, throwing out anything too cruddy. That ended up being most of my clothes and my backpack—Craig refused to come near any of it," Sebastian laughed. "Just handed me a garbage bag! We swung by a laundromat where we tossed the sleeping bag and my coat in the washer, then off to buy all this," he said, indicating his outfit.

"Looks like you jumped into the washer yourself."

"In the back of *Strum's* there's an employee bathroom with a shower stall. After picking up the clothes, we went to *Strum's*, so I could wash up and get into my new duds. Craig's a real germaphobe. He had me wash my hair with some delousing shampoo!"

"Based on how you looked last Tuesday, I'd say he had good reason."

"That bad, huh?"

"You look great now!"

"And you, too. Did you do something different with your hair?"

"Yeah. Experimenting a little."

The two sat on the park bench, and Mallory pulled out the apples. "Sorry I couldn't bring more. I didn't want to keep you waiting."

"I'm okay for now."

"Here, one each," said Mallory.

As they chomped on their apples, Mallory asked, "Where's all your stuff? I thought you didn't like to leave it at Logan's."

"Logan's garage fell through, but Craig has an RV parked behind his house. That's where I'm staying until we figure something out."

"So he knows about your mother?"

"Yeah. Craig doesn't put up with bullshit, so it was full-disclosure or nix. He said I can do my school work at the store—AND I have Wi-Fi at the store and at his house, AND I can keep my phone charged!"

"Great! You can join Oliver and me tonight on *AppChat*. We are coming up with a plan to get Jess's name out there on the internet."

"For sure. Text me the time."

"She couldn't have just disappeared... someone has to have seen her."

"I know what you mean. I get upset every time I think about her." Sebastian pulled out his phone and looked at the time. "I gotta go. I'm on my way to school to meet Ms. Willow. She has some assignments to help me catch up and a Chromebook—you know, a school loaner."

Chapter 68

"I thought we'd go British today," Willow said after greeting Sebastian. "I brought you tea and a couple of scones. Shall we sit in our regular spot?"

"Thanks... thanks for helping me out like this," said Sebastian as they walked to the side entrance and sat on a step.

Willow smiled at the youth, washed up and in a somewhat stable situation. The day before, she had spoken briefly with Craig when Sebastian introduced him during a phone call. He sounded decent enough. He and his wife had raised three boys, now in their late twenties and early thirties, all out of the house. Seemed to have a soft spot for Sebastian.

"Here's a packet with three projects I'd like you to finish before the end of the school year. You can log into my classes if you like, but you don't have to. Give me a call every morning at eight-thirty and let me know how you're doing; ask whatever questions you have, and then get to work. I'm contacting your other teachers, and they'll put together something similar. Does that sound doable?" Sebastian nodded.

Willow pulled out a Chromebook, a little worse for wear but still functioning. Sebastian set down his drink and signed the IT check-out form. Willow showed him how to navigate to his courses and where to complete his projects. "Everything is saved when you sign out, and I'll be able to see it."

For the rest of their time together, Willow listened to Sebastian chat about the music store, the keyboards he played, the performers he liked and his new "digs." Although upbeat and cheerful, she noticed his foot tapping incessantly and his fingers fidgeting with his jacket, the lid covering his drink, anything at hand. The boy was in constant motion.

"Sebastian," Willow said gently, "you seem really jumpy. What's up?"

"Nothing, nothing," he said, gripping his knees. "Sorry about that."

"There's nothing to be sorry for. You've been through a lot, out on your own... not knowing what's happening with Jess."

Sebastian squeezed his eyes, then burst forth in sobs. For a few minutes, his hunched shoulders shook, and Sebastian wiped away a continuous stream of tears. Willow found the paper napkins that came with the scones and handed them to Sebastian. She said nothing, occasionally squeezing his shoulder. Gradually the tears subsided. "Every morning," he said haltingly, "I'm afraid that Craig is going to tell me, 'Sorry, buddy, can't do this anymore. You gotta go.' Or I'll explode about something, and he'll hate me. It's like it's too good and won't last, and I'm going to be back on the street."

"Sebastian, why do you think Craig and his wife offered you a place to stay? They care for you—you're a wonderful person. I don't think they have any intention of kicking you out. But, if that were to happen, you come to me. We'll figure something out. You're not going back on the street."

"And I'm afraid that we're never going to find Jess, at least not alive."

It was a fear that Willow herself battled against.

PART FIVE

Chapter 69

"Seth is Zander. Zander is Seth."

Jess knew Flower was right. Her acknowledgement of this lurking suspicion had been held off by the dread of losing her only ally in this hellhole... the dread that no one truly cared for her. Beyond providing jobs for human services, she was nothing more than a societal burden, swapped among caseworkers, counsellors and teachers. Her continued assistance depended on the dispositions of government officials who could initiate supportive programs and just as quickly defund them. She despised herself for trusting Seth, for trusting anyone.

Jess never confronted Seth on his duplicity. He came down a few times after she was beaten, always, Jess now noted, when the girls were occupied in the rooms and Coco was out with Star. To observe him keep up the charade, unwittingly making a fool of himself, was a perverse pleasure, but more, it filled her with loathing for someone she had considered an older brother. After a couple of weeks, Seth must have realized the act was over, and he never returned.

Chapter 70

Week tumbled over week, and Jess's persona, The Wasp, continued in popularity. Her original nickname, Jackie, disappeared; Wasp became her name. According to Deni, Jess was slowly digging herself out of debt, but there was always something in addition to their daily expenses that kept the goal just out of reach: upgraded security, car repairs, increase in food prices. Jess realized she would never pay off her "debts" and, even if she did, she would never see a penny of what she "earned." The independence of Star and Lena was flaunted, proof of what they could attain. But Jess doubted their claims. Star and Lena may have begun as clubbers, but, Jess surmised, they were now recruiters–sub-pimps, beguiling the unsuspecting, while Seth and Deni ran the operation. And from what Jess observed, they did it without any sign of shame or empathy for their victims.

One expense Jess kept off her tab was the "vitamins" Deni distributed before and after work: speed in the morning, benzos at night. Most of the girls were hooked. Star often toyed with Coco's addiction, having her perform dog tricks before placing the pills on her tongue. When Deni made her delivery, both Flower and Jess busied themselves with cleaning.

$\sim$

Everyone now was occupied with either live online video sessions or recordings filmed by the guards and uploaded to be viewed at any time for a fee. The back walls of all the rooms were painted bright green, so the backgrounds of the videos could vary. Only one room had a door, the one Jess occupied when she first arrived. It was sandwiched between the padlocked mechanical room and the bathroom and had, most likely, been intended for storage. Because of the noise transfer through the flimsy dividers and curtains, only two live chat sessions could be scheduled at the same time—one in the enclosed room and the other in one of the curtained rooms. Girls with recorded sessions in the other rooms listened to their music through earbuds. Jess wasn't trusted with the live sessions, although a slip from Star revealed that she'd been requested.

Jess noticed another girl who was never put on live: Coco. She was, as Jess's grandmother would say, "slow." Coco would never master the flirty chitchat needed for a live online session; instead, she was part of Star's "escort services," where conversation wasn't necessary. Jess often wondered how Coco had found her way into Seth and Deni's network and, apparently, remained so willingly. But Jess never had an opportunity to ask her. On the occasions when Coco was left among the girls without Star, she rarely said a word, no doubt coached by Star to avoid them—they weren't big earners like her. Aware of her privileged position as Star's pet, Coco strutted among them like a Persian cat, nose in the air. The girls viewed her with amusement or irritation, and she was largely ignored. No one knew for sure if the security cameras were monitored or even worked, but they weren't needed if Coco was around. She was the eyes and ears of Star.

Chapter 71

With Gloria gone, a bed was free, and Belle received the privilege. Jess and Flower remained on the carpet. As the others readied for bed, Jess and Flower scoured the rooms for stuffed pillows used as props. They lay them over the thin area rug to keep themselves off the frigid cement floor. Most nights, they collapsed into a restless sleep brought on by sheer exhaustion and malnutrition. But every so often, Jess would feel a tap on her fingers.

"You awake?" Flower said that first time, her voice barely a whisper. "I can't sleep."

"Same here," said Jess. "I can't calm down."

"My mind is racing, spinning. It's painful."

"On nights like this, I crave benzos. I just want to relax without this... this unending stress," said Jess.

"So why don't you take them?"

Jess studied Flower's face in the dim light. Flower was kind, sure, but Lena and Seth had also been kind and look how that ended. Was this another trap? Yet, Flower had taken a risk to warn her about Seth. Jess could have twisted that information to her own advantage and ratted out Flower. Flower trusted her.

"I wouldn't trust a vitamin C from Deni," replied Jess. Several moments passed. "Drugs killed my parents. My grandmother... my grandmother," Jess's voice trailed off.

"I have a special person, too."

A bedroom door opened, and one of the girls shuffled to the bathroom. Their conversation had been short, perhaps negligible in another setting. But with that brief connection, something shifted, and Jess dozed off.

The whispered carpet chats continued sporadically, depending on their level of fatigue. Sometimes they shared memories from their childhoods; other times, they spit out their hatred for the perversity of johns, and there were the rare moments when the inane behaviour of one of the girls had them quietly giggling. During one conversation, Jess asked about Zander. "All the girls talk about him, Deni as well. How can Seth be Zander?"

"I think Zander is a myth, some boogyman mobster. I've never seen him. From what I can tell, Seth and Deni made him up."

"Are you sure?"

"Seth and Deni are monsters. Beautiful, charming monsters."

"So, no mob?"

"Just the guards. Four of them."

~

One night Jess felt the familiar tap on her fingers. "Do you have anyone looking for you?" asked Flower.

"Unlikely. I had a couple of friends, but what can they do? Who would take them seriously? They're just fucked-up teenagers like me."

"How old are you?"

"Sixteen."

"Shit!"

Flower was silent for some time. Then she slid so close to Jess that the top of their heads touched. "You have to go to the clubs," her voice barely a whisper.

"What?" Jess breathed back. She tilted her head back slightly and strained both ears to hear.

"You'll never get out of here unless you go to the clubs. "

This was different. Although there was a level of trust between them, they both had their limits. Flower rarely talked about her work upstairs. Neither had divulged how they'd been snared. So discussing escape was new.

Jess whispered back, "Aren't the clubs closed?"

"There's talk upstairs that some may be opening soon. Maybe private parties, I don't know—something about live dancing starting up." She paused a few moments. "Clubs and escorting are the only way out."

The stairway door creaked open. Flower and Jess turned away from each other and froze. A guard descended, which was not unusual but hardly necessary; the girls were zoned out on benzos. No, that was not the reason for the check-up. The guard entered a room, the bed creaked wildly, and when he slipped from behind the curtain panel, he was zipping up his pants.

"Christ," whispered Jess in disgust when he was gone.

The two turned toward each other again. "You have to get out of here," said Flower.

"What about you?"

"I'll never get out."

"Why?"

Flower took a deep breath. "I have a son upstairs."

"Fuck!" muttered Jess. It was common knowledge that Flower was the upstairs housekeeper/babysitter, along with her late-night video sessions. And from allusions made by Star, "servicing the boss" was also required. Jess often wondered why Flower had not found a way to flee. She seemed to have the most opportunity and, unlike Star, wasn't seduced by the lure of fast money made from recruiting others. Now she understood.

"What happened?" asked Jess.

"I worked at a restaurant and rented a basement room nearby... and I was pregnant."

"And your boyfriend?"

"By that time, he was out of the picture. I went to a food bank, you know, to try to save a little. I met Star there."

"Star used a food bank?"

"I don't know, but that's where we met. She drove me home with my box of food."

"So she was stalking a food bank."

"We became friends. If I needed a ride, I just had to call her. Star told me how much money I could make at the clubs; I'd be able to buy my own place, take care of my kid. She knew someone who could offer a room and daycare. After my baby was born, I moved in with Deni and Seth. Star and Lena were there, too, working for them. You know the rest. It happened to you."

"It sounds like there's more than one kid upstairs."

"There's two. Deni had a daughter a year after me. Claudia's her name."

"How old's your son?"

"Three and a half. His name is Luxton—it means light. He's my light." Flower's voice cracked, "I can't be with him all the time. If they get mad at me, I'm afraid they'll take it out on him." And for the first time, Jess heard Flower softly cry.

Jess held Flower's hand. When her tears subsided, Flower said, "Seth and Deni sell off girls they don't like, those who don't buckle down."

"Sell them?" Jess broke out in a cold sweat.

"To other pimps. A while back, there were a couple of girls...." Flower wept softly again. After a few moments, she said, "That's my biggest fear. I'll get sold off, and then what will happen to my son?" Flower shifted closer to Jess. "Be compliant and act defeated—you avoid beatings and drugs. Then wait for your chance."

"If I ever get out, I'll come back for you." Flower squeezed her hand. "But," Jess continued, "I need to know your real name and where in the hell we are."

PART SIX

Chapter 72

"I met with Ms. Willow this afternoon," Sebastian told Mallory and Oliver during their video chat. "She said the officer we met was going to get another announcement about Jess on the news."

"When?" asked Oliver.

"Monday, if he could."

"Okay," said Oliver. "We have to get Jess's name and picture out there on social media at the same time."

"I'm doing a course on graphic design," said Mallory. "I can design the post. Something more eye-catching than the blurb we sent out before. Sebastian, do you have a photo of Jess—something that's cool? All of mine are selfies we took when we were goofing off."

"Yeah, for sure," said Sebastian. "I took some pics before our performance together. I have one that's really cool."

"Ms. Willow could get Jess onto the school site, couldn't she?" remarked Mallory.

"Yeah, maybe the teachers can start to post Jess on their personal *Ima-grams* or whatever else they use," added Oliver.

"I'll send it to Logan—he has a big family," said Sebastian. "And I can send it to the group home. Maybe some of the counsellors will put Jess's post on their accounts."

"Hopefully, a lot more people will see the post. It might even go viral!"

"Okay, I think we have a plan," said Mallory.

"What the hell?" exclaimed Oliver.

"Are you okay? What happened?" asked Mallory.

"Sorry about that, guys, but you'll never guess who just texted me... Victor."

"What a downer," said Sebastian.

"I haven't heard from him since–" Oliver paused.

"Since you left the dark side?" finished Sebastian.

"What does he have to say?" asked Mallory.

"His parents bought him a car. He sent a picture of it."

"A Tesla?" asked Sebastian.

"He wanted a BMW. He got a Toyota."

"Oh, the pain and disappointment."

"So why is he telling you?" asked Mallory.

"Who knows. Delete. We have more important things to do. Where were we?"

"Sebastian, you'll send me that picture of Jess?" asked Mallory.

"On it."

"Okay, I'll have Jess's post ready by tomorrow and send it to you guys and Ms. Willow."

Chapter 73

Craig put on his glasses, leaned forward on the kitchen table and picked up a sheaf of printouts. Sebastian scooched to the edge of his chair and looked over at Craig. "Okay," said Craig, "I've done some research about teens leaving home, and this is what I've come up with."

"Well, to be honest...," said his wife, who nursed a mug of coffee across the table.

"Yeah, yeah," snickered Craig, "the research was largely done by Audrey, but you gotta admit," he said, looking at his wife, "I did my fair share of the phone calls."

Audrey smirked. "Just challenging the *I*."

While Sebastian observed their banter with some amusement, he was antsy to hear the results of their research.

"You can leave home at sixteen—you're not breaking any law. What's fascinating is what you can and cannot do without a parent's consent in order to survive. You can legally sign a rental agreement at sixteen, but you can't open a bank account until you're eighteen." Sebastian wiped his clammy palms on his pant legs. "By the way," said Craig as he took off his glasses and leaned back in his chair, "how did you open a bank account?"

"A school secretary opened one with me."

"You have a golden horseshoe shoved up your ass."

"My God, Craig," said Audrey, "Get to the point! Can't you see the sweat on Sebastian's forehead!" She turned to Sebastian, "You're not going to get tossed out of the RV, so relax." Looking back at Craig, "Okay, you can continue. And since I've just prevented a stroke, feel free to take your time."

Craig sighed, sat forward in his chair and put on his glasses. "As I was saying before I was interrupted...."

Sebastian lowered his face to hide a smile, but he was grateful for Audrey's intervention. He could listen more calmly, knowing that his RV accommodations weren't threatened.

"Audrey and I want to set up a rental agreement for the next three months. If everything works out and you want to continue, we can renew the contract."

"Sounds good to me," said Sebastian, brightening.

"This is a rough draft. We'll go through it and edit as we go along. Number one: you can pay for your room and board by your work in the store and at this home. In the store, when we open again, you'll help with keyboard demonstrations, and I'd like you to get familiar with other instruments."

"If you're up for it," said Audrey, "I'd like to get our vegetable garden going again in the backyard. I need help."

"I could do that."

"We're thinking two hours, five days a week—at the store or in the yard—will cover your room and board. You'll get paid for any additional hours. Does that seem fair to you?"

"Sure!"

"Okay, that's settled," said Craig. "Now I know the RV isn't the latest model—"

"It's paradise for me," interjected Sebastian.

"We do have a room in our basement," said Audrey. "It might be more comfortable."

"I really, really like the RV," insisted Sebastian.

"I told you so," said Craig to his wife. "That's fine," he said to Sebastian, "but you need to keep it clean. Once a month, Mama Bear will have a walk-through with you."

"Spic and span, young man," said Audrey.

Sebastian saluted.

"And no one else stays in the RV without my permission," said Craig firmly. "Is that clear?"

"Yes."

"No drugs, no alcohol, no pot. No hanky-panky. If you want a beer, you come and drink it with us."

"Got it."

"We're walking a thin line on what's permitted in the neighbourhood–having you live in the RV. If the neighbours complain, your RV paradise will be nix, nada, zilch. So be quiet. No loud music or carousing, bonfires, fireworks...."

"Got it."

"We have a keyboard in the basement. You can use it in the RV if you like," said Audrey.

"Thanks! That was going to be my first purchase after saving some money. By the way, every week, the school is giving me a fifty-dollar gift card for groceries. I could give them to you to help with the food."

"That's really thoughtful," said Audrey. "But why don't you keep the gift cards to buy breakfast food, snacks, foods you enjoy. We'd like to have you over for supper in the evening, and you'll be at the store for lunch."

"Okay."

"And lastly," said Craig.

"Finally," said Audrey.

"I know you want a career in music."

Sebastian nodded.

"If you want to get into music studies, you need to finish high school." Craig paused and looked a Sebastian.

"What?" asked Sebastian, perplexed.

"*You need to finish high school.* I want to make sure you heard that part."

"Okay."

"So how about doing your classes in the morning at the store. In the afternoon, do some yard work and the rest of the day is yours for music. Just remember, when you're playing the keyboard in the RV, use the headset."

"Yeah, the neighbours," said Sebastian.

Craig turned to his wife, "I told you he was a quick learner."

"How about music breaks during my study time?" asked Sebastian.

"Define 'a break.'"

"Fifteen minutes every hour?"

"Okay. Forty-five minutes of study, fifteen minutes of music."

"We got a deal!"

Chapter 74

"You've done amazing work," said Willow to the small group of students at their weekly meeting. "Thanks for sending me Jess's post. I've sent it out to all my contacts."

Willow, Sebastian, Mallory and Oliver sat on the dry grass behind the school. The trees overhead were close to unfurling their leaves.

Oliver sat with the others, typing into his laptop. "Oliver's keeping track of all our postings," said Mallory.

"How many do we have so far?" asked Sebastian.

"Mallory's posted on four missing person sites and her *Ima-gram* account. You've sent the post to Logan and the staff email of the group home. Hopefully, they'll send it to their contacts. My sister and I have posted it on our accounts. And Ms. Willow, how many contacts do you have?"

"I sent it to all the staff at the school through a group email and my personal contacts."

"What about the students who were part of the *Revue*," said Sebastian. "Can you send it to them?"

"The drama teacher has the complete list of contacts. I'll get ahold of her."

The brainstorming continued: youth centres, homeless shelters, counsellors in other high schools, student groups in universities–anyone who might send out the post or print it out and hang it up.

"You may have seen the TV announcement about Jess on the news yesterday," said Willow.

"Were there any new leads?" asked Mallory.

"Too early to say. By next week I should know more." Willow turned and stood up. "I've got to go now. See you all next week."

The three students remained sitting. Sebastian began to tell them about his new living arrangements but stopped abruptly and looked at Oliver.

"Look, man, I don't know your story, but it's no secret that things have been rough—not being able to contact you, phone uncharged, Mallory worried."

"I haven't told Oliver anything," assured Mallory.

"I promise, what we say in our group will stay here," said Oliver.

Sebastian didn't say anything further about the RV contract but went on about his job at the music store as soon as it reopened and the gardening gig.

"Is *Strum's* online?" asked Oliver.

"Yeah."

"Well, the owner—"

"Craig."

"You guys could make short videos and post them on his website—like you demonstrating something about a keyboard or a guitar. You know what I mean? If you did a couple a week, you would develop a collection, and people might be more willing to buy. You could even ask people for suggestions."

"Or invite people to a Zoom where they can ask questions after the demos," said Mallory, "Like what we're doing at school."

"Or have video appointments for potential customers," said Oliver. "More people are staying at home. Encourage them to learn an instrument."

"Craig's gotta hear this!"

Chapter 75

"You have to meet my friends. They have some good ideas that might help 'drum up' business." Sebastian smiled at Craig. "'Drum up.' You see what I did there?"

"Yeah. Real stand-up comedy material, bud," said Craig as he served up potatoes. "So I give you a place to stay, and now you want to take over my business?"

"Go ahead, Sebastian," said Audrey. "Ignore him."

"My friends, Mallory and Oliver, we're doing whatever we can to find Jess–."

"What? Hold on here," said Audrey. "Who's Jess, and what happened to her?"

"Jess–she's like a sister to me," said Sebastian, and he recounted all that had happened up to that point. "Mallory, Oliver and I are trying to get her face and name out there on social media. We're hoping someone will recognize her and call the police." Sebastian's voice cracked. "How could she just disappear?"

"That's terrible, Sebastian," said Audrey as she got up from her chair and gave Sebastian a hug. "Send the post to me. I'll send it out to everyone I can."

Craig sat back in his chair, "And I can fire it off to everyone on *Strum's* email list."

Audrey returned to her chair, and Sebastian took a few bites of his supper. In a subdued voice, he said, "When we were having our meeting about Jess, I told my friends about your store being online only right now. Oliver said that we could record short videos demonstrating keyboards, guitars and the other instruments and post them on the store's website. You know, just a couple a week. It might increase sales."

"I believe, Sebastian, you are already paying for your keep," said Craig.

Sebastian perked up. "Oliver said he would show us how to do it, and Mallory is willing to help, too. She's an artist and is taking a course on graphic design."

"Have Mallory and Oliver come over," said Audrey. "We could sit out on the deck and talk this over."

"If we meet, it would be easier for Mallory to come to the store—it's closer. Her dad's kinda leery about her having friends."

Craig smacked his forehead as he sunk back into his chair, "What's with you guys?"

"Filters, Craig, filters!" exclaimed Audrey.

"Ah, Sebastian likes me unfiltered. Right, Sebastian?"

Sebastian laughed.

"So, is her father paranoid or something?" asked Craig.

"Ya think?" quipped Sebastian.

"Let's just stick with the Zooming until this lockdown ends," said Craig.

"Zoom," said Audrey and Sebastian in unison.

"Whatever—Zoom, zooming, zoomed. What about this Oliver you mentioned?" asked Craig, "Is he some kind of teen hacker messing around on the dark web?"

"No, he's only interested in skimming funds from big banks," Sebastian laughed. "He might be able to inject some profits into your business."

"Geez!"

Chapter 76

"Dad, I can cook. I want to cook. I'm tired of frozen lasagna, frozen pot pies, frozen... whatever. I can do the shopping. Just give me a certain amount of money each week."

Mallory had brought up the subject before but never with such insistence. Her father worked from seven to three-thirty. In the mornings, he was out of the house by six. Mallory knew he picked up his breakfast on the way to work and often did the same for supper on his way home—she would find the fast-food cartons in the trash. He was rarely at the apartment before five, then he showered and went straight to his video games. Later he would grab something else to eat.

Ryder Mudford considered his daughter's request. "It would make life easier for me, especially when I work on Saturdays.... I'll think about it." A week later, he gave Mallory a debit card. "I've set up a separate account which I'll top to one hundred dollars each week. Groceries and household stuff only. I want every receipt put in this envelope in this kitchen drawer." Ryder held up a manila envelope and then placed it in a drawer. "If there is a discrepancy, it's over."

"Yeah, for sure," said Mallory, non-pulsed. But beneath her deadpan face, Mallory was scoring a major victory. Not only would she submit her receipts, she would take a picture of each one—Ryder Mudford would never accuse her of stealing. And these days, she never knew which version of her father she'd face. He was rattled by the pandemic, swinging from hyper-vigilant to denying its existence. His frequent brooding moods were alleviated only by joining his video game buddies in their alternate reality.

Mallory's goal was to stay out of his way and in her room when he was home. And she was finding more to keep herself occupied besides schoolwork and sketching. She delved more deeply into web design in order to create a web page for Jess and another for *Strum's* instrument demos. And she revived her buried passion, cooking. She'd started scouring online videos for recipes and techniques. Now she could buy ingredients and begin to experiment.

Chapter 77

Officer Wallace shuffled with a mug of coffee to his compact home office and logged onto his laptop. It was Saturday, technically his day off, but with staff shortages due to Covid, he was on call. He'd been shaken out of sleep by crows cawing–his chime for work-related contacts. A missing girl, parents frantic, unrelenting calls.

"Officer Wallace from Missing Persons."

"Oh, thank God you called," said a woman. "I'm Izzy's mother, Evelyn. My husband and I are worried sick.... Roger!" she shouted, blasting Wallace's ear, "The police are on the phone." Then back to Wallace, "I'm putting you on speakerphone." Some rustling and a male voice, "It's about time!" Then loudly into the phone, "What are you doing to find our daughter?"

"Roger, the call centre forwarded the information you gave earlier this morning, and I'd like to clarify a few points before sending your daughter's file to our investigating officers."

"What do you mean, 'before you send the file to investigating officers?'" Roger roared, "Why aren't they working on it now?"

Wallace was prepared for the onslaught of raw emotions from the frightened parents. "Roger, we need to have all the details precise and accurate, so we can proceed effectively," Wallace said evenly. "I want to clarify a few points."

"Well then, get to it!"

"When did you realize Izzy was missing?"

"Around two this morning," said Evelyn. "I got up to use the bathroom and saw that Izzy hadn't come home."

"Hadn't come home from where?"

"Oh, she and a friend were going out for a drive together. They were tired of being cooped up inside—you know, with the lockdown and all."

"Could she be staying with her friend?"

"What! Do you think we're idiots?" barked Roger. "Of course, we called her friend."

Evelyn cut in. "Izzy had a pickup order at the mall. It was one of the reasons she went out. When they got to the mall, Izzy asked her friend to wait while she ran in to get her order. Then Izzy texted that she met up with another friend who was driving her home."

"I'll need the names of both friends and the name of the store."

"That's the point. We don't know the friend who met her at the mall, and I can't remember which store."

"But surely you know the name of the girl who picked up Izzy at your house?"

"Of course!" exclaimed Roger, exasperated. "Evelyn, give him the information!"

After Wallace jotted down the name, address and phone number, he asked, "Has Izzy ever spent the night at a friend's house without telling you?"

"Never! She's a very responsible girl," said her mother.

"You mentioned Izzy texted her friend," said Wallace. "Can you give me Izzy's phone number and carrier?"

"How many times do we have to repeat this!" snapped the father.

"We have to be accurate. When people are upset, sometimes numbers are inverted, so we verify." The information was given. "Has anything out of the ordinary happened recently?"

"You mean outside the pandemic? And the lockdown? And, and—" Roger sputtered to a stop.

"She seemed okay," stammered her mother. "Really excited about going out with a friend."

"I have a few more questions, and I want to emphasize, these are all standard questions we ask everyone. From the file, I see Izzy just turned seventeen. Is she capable of looking after herself?"

"Bloody hell!" Roger blurted. "Of course! Do you think we're still spoon-feeding her?"

Wallace ignored the outburst. "Does she have any medical or mental health issues?"

"She's a healthy, normal girl," growled Roger.

"So she wouldn't be taking any medication?"

"No!"

"Well, only in emergencies," added Evelyn. "She carries an Epi-pen in case she is stung by a bee."

"And Izzy had an Epi-pen with her when she left last night?"

"She carries it with her all the time," said her mother. "I bought her a Coach shoulder bag specifically for the Epi-pen, knowing she would never leave the bag around."

"And she had the bag with her on Friday?"

"Yes. It's a beautiful shade of coral and went so well with the dress she was wearing."

"Any drug or alcohol use?"

"So now you think she's an addict?"

"No, Roger. Like I said, these are standard questions. Has she ever been involved in sex work?"

"God, help me! NO!" Roger shouted. Evelyn could be heard crying in the background.

"It's just a routine question, nothing more. So, to your knowledge, is there anything that could have upset her?"

Evelyn, sniffling, "Like I said, Izzy was quite happy when she left—in a great mood."

"When did you expect her back?"

"Well, we didn't set a specific time. Roger and I went to bed around eleven. I figured the girls had picked up something to eat and were chatting."

"Do you have a recent picture you could send me?" asked Wallace.

"Yes. I took one last evening before she left. Her outfit was so cute," said Evelyn.

"That would be excellent." Wallace gave his number. A few moments later, the picture came through on Wallace's phone.

"Does she have any tattoos? Anything that could help identify her?"

"Yes, she has three little hearts circling her right ankle," said her mother. "And each ear has three piercings."

"Okay, I'll be passing this report to our investigating officers. If you recall any additional information before you hear from them, call me."

"Are you kidding? This is it?" yelled Roger. "Until we find Izzy, I want her photo on the news, on every available platform."

"Yes, I've made note of that and will be passing all this information along within a few minutes."

"Find her!!"

Throughout the morning, Wallace's phone chimed with texts from Roger. He had hired a publicist who was creating a page on numerous social media platforms to alert friends, acquaintances, and the general public that Izzy was missing. Roger let Wallace know when each of them went live. In the latest text, Wallace was informed that the publicist had arranged a brief interview with a local TV station outside their home. Their plea to help find their daughter would air on the evening news and be repeated Sunday morning.

That afternoon Wallace knocked on the door of Izzy's friend. While he waited for the teen to come downstairs, the girl's mother asked, "Are you sure Izzy hasn't spent the night with a friend?"

"Why do you say that?"

"Well, once, after a party, Izzy spent the night with my daughter, and early in the morning, I was awakened by a frantic call from her mother. Izzy hadn't told her mother she was spending the night, *and* her phone was turned off."

When Izzy's friend joined her mother, Wallace asked if Izzy had left her purse in the car when she went into the mall to pick up her package. The teen responded, "Are you kidding me? She never leaves that pink bag anywhere, always strapped over her shoulder. Last night it was bulging—I told her it looked like a stuffed pig."

"How did she respond to that?"

"Oh, she just laughed."

"Does she have a boyfriend?"

"She's been talking to some guy from school, but I don't know who."

~

"Oliver!" hollered his mother from the kitchen. When he descended the stairs, she said, "Listen to this." She pushed play on the remote. An image, frozen on the TV screen, burst into life. A middle-aged couple stood in front of their home holding a picture of their teen daughter, missing since last night. The camera zoomed in for a close-up. The father pleaded with the public to send any news of her whereabouts to the police.

"The announcer said this Izzy is a high school student," said Oliver's mom. "Do you know her?"

"I've never seen her around."

"First your friend..."

"Jess, her name is Jess."

"Yes, first Jess. And now this girl? What's going on with these kids?"

~

Sunday evening, while Wallace watched a movie with his family, his phone cawed. His wife looked over and scowled. Wallace read the text from one of the investigating officers, pressed the call button and walked to his office. As he passed his wife, he whispered, "Izzy's been found."

"Where did you find her?" asked Wallace when the call was answered.

"On her front porch," said an investigating officer. "She spent the weekend with her boyfriend, a kid from her school. According to Izzy, she texted her parents on Friday night but then lost her phone and didn't find it until Sunday afternoon... under the car seat."

"How convenient. And the boyfriend didn't have a phone?"

"He claims Izzy told him her parents were okay with the trip. The boyfriend's parents said he went to Fernie to prep their cabin for the May long weekend. He was going with a friend who, they understood, was one of his school buddies. But since the arrangement with Izzy was consensual, they didn't have a problem with it. They're just upset Izzy's parents weren't informed."

"And Izzy's parents?"

"They believe all of it was a big misunderstanding. Don't believe any coercion was involved."

"So the 'package pickup' was just a ruse to get to the mall to meet up with the boyfriend."

"Seems so."

"Well, I'm glad Izzy's safe, but if those two were my kids, we'd be having a series of very serious conversations."

Chapter 78

Oliver sat at the desk in his bedroom and jotted down notes as his Math teacher on the computer screen parsed through the intricacies of statistics. A ping from his iPad, lying nearby, diverted his attention. He touched the message notification, and an image filled his iPad screen. Written under the picture was the text, "What a slut. You really know how to pick friends." Oliver stared at the image in disbelief. His mind raced, and his heart pounded. *What the hell? What the bloody hell?* Although Oliver didn't recognize the *AppChat* handle, Victor was the first person who came to mind. Just then, another text popped up on Oliver's iPad, "Like I said, a slut." If Victor was behind this, *AppChat* had notified him that his message and pic had been opened. And Victor was in this Math class. Had he timed his text so he could watch Oliver's reaction? *The sadist!* Oliver turned off his video image in the class Zoom. Then acting on pure instinct, he grabbed his phone and focused the camera on the iPad. Oliver knew the *AppChat* image and messages would disappear in seconds. He snapped several pics before it faded away.

Oliver, frozen in revulsion and indecision, remained sitting, staring at his phone with an image of a snarling, half-nude woman—Jess. A deluge of emotions overwhelmed him: outrage, horror, confusion... and sorrow, a deep, heartrending sorrow for Jess.

By the time Oliver refocused, his Math class had ended. What should he do? Whom should he tell? He couldn't share this image with Sebastian or Mallory. Sebastian, like himself, would suspect Victor and go ballistic... and Mallory? Alone with her distrustful and distant father? She'd be a mess. He thought of telling his mom. She knew "that girl from school" was missing and that he and his school friends were trying to get the word out. She even sent the post Mallory designed to some of her friends. But if his mother saw Jess in this lecherous pose—Oliver could hear it already. "What have you got yourself involved in? Who is this girl? And who are these new friends of yours?" His mom would call his dad, and they'd both spaz out.

Ms. Willow—she'd know what to do. He picked up his phone and typed a text.

Oliver's mom was helping his two youngest siblings with their school work at one of the kitchen islands when he bounded down the stairs.

"One of these days, you're going to break your neck running down those stairs."

"I have to go to school to pick up some materials from a teacher."

"What teacher?"

"Ms. Willow."

His mother walked toward Oliver. "Your sister is also in high school, and not once has she gone to school to meet up with a teacher. You go every week."

"It's a different school, Mom, and different teachers."

"I'm beginning to think her school might be a better choice for you."

"I like my school. Besides, one more year and high school will be finished." Oliver lifted his keys out of a bowl near the door, "I'll wear a mask, keep my distance, wash my hands—I know the drill."

～

Oliver pulled into the Riverbank High School parking lot and stood outside his car. He had not waited for a response from Ms. Willow. He had texted her, then emailed the same message: *I need to see you immediately about Jess. It's urgent. I'm on my way to school.* He didn't care if he waited all afternoon in the parking lot. He had to get out of his bedroom, isolated with his secret. Anxiety churned his gut and propelled him to walk in a continuous loop around the parking lot. It was warm for early May but still not quite enough to coax the leaves from their buds. Large white clouds drifted across the sky, causing the school to be bathed in light one moment and shrouded the next. Oliver was insensible to it all. As he walked, he gripped his phone and scanned approaching cars for Ms. Willow.

Chapter 79

"My God," whispered Willow when Oliver passed her his phone.

"What the hell is going on with Jess?" asked Oliver, his eyes misting.

"I don't know. But look at her face, Oliver. She's not enjoying this, not even trying to pretend."

"What do we do now?" asked Oliver.

"First of all, tell me exactly how you got this image."

Oliver relayed what happened during the early afternoon Math class. "I had to take a picture because *AppChat* messages disappear unless you save them to your account. I didn't want to save this picture on my account. I wanted proof that it had been sent. So I took a picture." Oliver wiped his eyes. "I really believe Victor is behind this. What a warped dude. He was always hitting on her."

"So without you taking this photo, there would be no way of knowing it had ever been sent."

"Right. And even with my photo of Jess and the messages sent with it, how do we prove Victor sent it. He can delete this account. Besides, look at the profile picture. It's a headshot of Thor; the handle is *stormbreaker2003*. It's so easy to set up a bogus *AppChat* account. A lot of people don't use their real names or birthdates. And one person can have multiple accounts."

"Have you shown this to anyone else?"

"No. I was afraid if I told Sebastian, he would go after Victor. And Mallory, with that weird dad of hers—"

"Back up there a bit, Oliver. Mallory's weird dad?"

"You don't know?" said Oliver, exasperated. "The guy's paranoid.

She has to watch every move she makes."

"Okay, okay." Willow let a few moments pass before she began again. "For now, let's just stick with Victor. First of all, thank you for trusting me and showing me this photo of Jess. It's upsetting for me, and I see you're upset as well. As bad as it is, at least we know she's alive. (*Or was,* thought Willow, but she kept this to herself.) What about your parents?"

"I haven't told them."

"Why not?"

"They don't know Jess. I don't want them to get the wrong idea."

"Oliver, we need to send this picture to Officer Wallace. He'll want to speak with you. I think it best you talk to your parents. They may be more supportive than you imagine."

"My parents thought Victor was so mature and well-mannered...."

"And you saw another side and found better friends. That's maturity."

"I hope they see it that way."

"Do you want to call your mom or dad and have them meet us here? We could tell them together."

~

Within a half-hour, Oliver, his mother, Officer Wallace, Willow and Frida Quinn, the school principal, were gathered in the school parking lot.

"Victor Dorsey? Are you sure?" asked Oliver's mother. "That Thor character could be anyone!"

"Mom, it's Victor. Believe me. The guy can be crude and mean. I haven't had anything to do with him for weeks."

"Victor Dorsey, you say?" interrupted Officer Wallace. "Where does he live?"

"I'm not sure. His parents just moved to a new home," said Oliver.

Officer Wallace went over all the details with Oliver and forwarded the image of Jess to the head investigating officer on the case. "This changes everything," he said. "Her case will be marked urgent, and the *Internet Child Exploitation* team will be brought on board. It could involve sex trafficking."

"Sex trafficking?" said Oliver's mother in disbelief. "This isn't Thailand."

"No, it's Canada, and, unfortunately, sex trafficking exists locally."

"From what I know of Jess," said Willow, "entering the porn market would not be her choice."

"Having been part of this investigation from the beginning, I would have to concur." Officer Wallace looked over at Oliver and said, "Thank you for coming forward. You could have easily let Jess's image disappear and not been connected with it at all." Turning to his mother, he said, "You should be proud of your son."

~

Willow, Frida and Officer Wallace watched Oliver and his mother drive off in their cars.

"So, where do we go from here?" asked Willow.

"How many Victor Dorseys do you have in this school?"

"I'm only aware of one," said Frida. "Neither Victor nor Dorsey are that common. But with two thousand students, I'll check." Frida sent a text to June Barnes.

"Just like that?" asked Wallace.

"My number one secretary is working from home today."

"She probably doesn't even have to look it up," said Willow.

"But she will," replied Frida. "And coming in... Just one Victor Dorsey."

"We need to find the origins of this image, and it won't be easy if Victor is involved," said Officer Wallace.

"Why?"

"Victor was recently involved in another suspicious incident. You know the girl, Izzy, who was missing last weekend?"

"Yes, I heard about it on the news," said Frida.

"Ads about her were popping up all over my browser," added Willow.

"Well, apparently, Victor and Izzy had a romantic weekend at the Dorseys' cabin in Fernie without telling anyone. The parents of both kids circled the wagons and considered the escapade a mishap of communication. If Victor denies a connection to Jess's picture, his parents will back him up, and any attempt to dig up links to this photo will end before we even get started."

Chapter 80

Officer Wallace parked his car and walked across the quiet street to gaze at Calgary's skyline from the top of the ridge. Below, the Bow River sparkled in the sunlight. Wallace enjoyed this time of year, early May: milder temperatures, daylight extending beyond nine p.m., and summer still to come with even longer days. In a couple of weeks, the trees and bushes in the ravine below would explode in bright green hues, and flower beds would be alive with colour. An accompanying officer joined him at his vantage point.

"You ready?" asked his fellow officer.

"As I'll ever be," said Wallace.

The two retraced their steps to a home facing the ravine and climbed its gently curving stairs to the front entrance. The multi-coloured slate porch led to an arched, wood-plank door with intricate cast iron hinges and a matching door knocker.

"You going to rap that dragon-head door knocker, Wallace?"

"Oh, there's a head I'd like to rap, but it's not the dragon's." He rang the bell. The teen who opened the door recognized Officer Wallace instantly. "Dad," he hollered into the hallway.

"What's this all about?" asked Mr. Dorsey when he arrived. "The misunderstanding with the young woman and her family has been completely resolved."

"Mr. Dorsey, we need to question your son about a concerning photo that was circulated during an online Math class that your son attended."

Mr. Dorsey refused to let his son say a word until his lawyer arrived. When he did, Victor denied all knowledge of Jess's image and the messages that accompanied them.

"Sure, I know the girl... I mean, she's in my English class."

"And you know that she's missing?"

"Everybody does. Some of our teachers have told us about it. But I don't know anything about this picture."

"Why are you singling out my son?" demanded Mr. Dorsey.

"You can understand the urgency of the matter, Mr. Dorsey. Jess is a minor and is likely being held against her will," said Wallace. "We're reaching out to anyone who could be remotely linked to her. We've been informed that in the past, Victor may have shown some interest in Jess."

"Well, it looks like harassment to me."

From the onset, Wallace doubted that Victor had taken the picture, but if Oliver was right, he *had* found it online. If the Internet Child Exploitation team knew where Victor had downloaded the photo, they could hone in on its original source. But with Victor's adamant denial, the hope of such an admission was futile.

Mr. Dorsey was affronted that he and his son had been subjected to the humiliation of a police inquiry "based on such scant evidence." However, Wallace noted Victor seemed disconcerted, unlike the glib, self-assured demeanour following the Izzy escapade. As they stood to leave, Mr. Dorsey turned to his son and said, "I'm done with Riverbank High. You won't be returning next year."

"Well," said Officer Wallace, looking straight at Victor, "let's hope Jess has the chance to return and isn't found in a ditch somewhere."

~

"So that's it?" asked Willow when she and the principal met with Officer Wallace the next day.

"Without proof that the *AppChat* account is actually Victor's, I'm afraid so. The app could be subpoenaed for account information, but if the information's bogus—which it likely is—then we have nothing."

"What about Victor's devices? Couldn't those be searched?"

"If Victor is behind this, he's already wiped and reformatted all his devices. Besides, we'd have to have a stronger case to demand them in the first place."

"Is there any hope that the internet unit can trace the origins of the picture?" asked Frida.

"They'll certainly try. The problem is, this stuff is downloaded from porn sites and posted on other sites. It can take a while to find the original source." Wallace paused and rubbed his forehead.

"Officer Wallace? Is there something else?" asked Willow.

"A guy in the internet unit told me that their caseload has doubled compared to this time last year."

"What?"

"With the pandemic, sexual exploitation online has exploded."

~

That night Crime Stoppers received an anonymous tip. An image of Jess Gayle had been seen on a prominent porn site. She was called *The Wasp*.

PART SEVEN

Chapter 81

Shortly after Flower confided to Jess about her son and her subjugation to Seth and Deni, a new recruit descended the stairs. She arrived in the early hours of the morning, just as their recording and video sessions ended. Deni accompanied her, carrying the main meal. As the girls flocked to the table, Deni said, "Ladies, this is Desme, the newest member of our entertainment team."

Jess didn't know under what pretences Desme had been lured to their lair, but she acted as if she had been invited to join some elite sorority. What astounded Jess was the difference in approach. She had been drugged, threatened, starved and beaten into compliance. Desme walked right in.

To welcome Desme, Deni had prepared an extraordinary spaghetti feast. The aroma from the platter wafted among the young women seated at the table. Jess maintained her indifferent demeanour, but her mouth watered in anticipation. She was always hungry. The two meals they were served each day were high in carbs and low in protein and fresh produce. The amount they received was inconsistent, dependent on the caprice of Deni. Sometimes it was nothing more than a frozen pizza pop each that they heated in the microwave. But today, displayed before them, was a heaping platter of spaghetti studded with meatballs, liberally covered with cheese and encircled by deep red tomato wedges.

"I need to wash up a little before I eat. I've been on the road for almost four hours," said Desme.

Jess saw Deni's jaw tighten, but she replied, "Of course, but don't take too long; we're all waiting for you."

After a few minutes, Desme joined the others at the table and was served a generous portion. While Star dished up the rest of the ladies, Deni introduced them.

"Trixie and Angie will be your trainers," she said. "I've placed them next to you so you can get better acquainted." Trixie gave her an affectionate squeeze. "I have to be getting upstairs," Deni said, like a benign dorm mother, "so I'll leave you to it." Jess was flummoxed.

After Deni left, Angie said to Desme, "You look sleepy."

"Lena and I have been travelling all night. Lena took the scenic route, but," Desme laughed, "we left Calgary so late we didn't see much in the dark. We had fun, though, listening to music, and she brought great snacks. In fact, I'm really not that hungry."

"Oh, don't worry about it," said Star. "I'm sure someone will help you finish what you don't want."

Desme pushed her plate forward, "I don't mean to be rude, but I'm full."

That's unfortunate, thought Jess. *You won't be seeing a meal like this for some time.* Trixie and Angie fished out the meatballs from Desme's dish and passed the remains to Belle.

"Hey, don't forget Coco," said Star, so Belle scraped half into her dish and gave the rest to Coco.

~

Jess was in the shower when she heard the door open. "Go ahead and take a dump," Trixie insisted. "We do it all the time."

There was no lock on the door, and as many as three of the girls could be together in the compact bathroom getting ready for their day's labour. The door closed, and Jess could hear Desme arranging herself on the toilet. Jess kept the shower running and poked her head around the corner.

Desme jerked back, surprised, "What the hell?"

"Just wanted to say hi," said Jess. "Did you sleep well?"

"Yeah, I was tired. I'd been up the whole day before we left Calgary."

"Does your mom know where you are?"

"I'm sixteen," Desme said, defensive, "I can live on my own."

"Yeah, she might get worried, though."

"Not her," said Desme with a short laugh. "She's whacked. Glad to have me off her hands."

The door opened, and Angie yelled, "Get out of there, Wasp, or I'm coming in with you!"

~

Desme's honeymoon ended abruptly during her second week. Unlike Coco, who followed blindly, coaxed by treats and praise, Desme balked at the non-stop, seven-day week, sixteen-hour workday. Gone were the take-out dinners, the snacks, the gifts, and the leisurely camaraderie she had previously enjoyed with Lena. And Desme wanted her phone with her games and music which had been taken "for safekeeping."

After one of their peanut butter meals, Deni announced a house meeting to go over their financial standings. Rocky followed her down the stairs and scrutinized the girls while she spoke. Deni began with the biggest earners and ended with the greatest debt. Unsurprisingly, Desme won the latter distinction. Her extensive list of expenses encompassed the clothes, shoes, meals, and electronics given to her by Lena, plus the copious charges she had accrued since her arrival. Added to her expenses were the dance and modelling lessons Desme received from Lena in Calgary and the additional coaching received from Trixie and Angie.

"Ten thousand dollars!" Desme contested. "Lena gave me that stuff! It's mine! I want my phone! Star has a phone. I want mine!"

In two steps, Rocky was standing behind her chair. He flipped it over, and Desme skidded across the floor. Then he kicked her to the wall. Desme crouched into a fetal position. The other girls watched in stunned silence.

"That's sufficient, Rocky," said Deni. Rocky hovered over the trembling teen, his bulging biceps crossed in front of his beefy chest.

"I don't know what Lena told you, Desme," said Deni in a measured, forbidding tone, "but it's not your stuff until it's paid for and you're a committed member of the family business. You've been free-loading for months."

Deni closed the meeting, and the others, while hyper-focused on the unfolding drama in the room, hurried about their usual tasks. Desme remained on the floor against the wall. Deni signalled Rocky to return upstairs. She pulled up a chair and sat near Desme. Leaning over, she tapped the teen on the shoulder. Desme cautiously looked over in her direction but made no eye contact.

"There is a way for you to pay off what you owe very quickly and then earn big money," said Deni gently. Desme turned over. "Star can make up to a thousand dollars a night, but I'm not sure you're up for it."

"What is it?" asked Desme, sitting up.

Deni stood. "You work hard and produce some good videos, and we'll talk further. For now," Deni's voice grew loud and forceful, "No. More. Bitching! Pick up your ass and get to work, or the deal's off, and you'll be eating rice and sleeping on the floor." Desme stood up. "Don't make me send Rocky down to kick your butt."

Chapter 82

One day Trixie asked Star, "Any news on the lockdown and when the clubs will reopen?" Cut off from the clubs, the basement dwellers relied on Deni and Star for all their information. Some news about Covid filtered in through the online sessions, but it was sketchy since discussing a pandemic wasn't the primary intent of a live-porn viewer.

"The lockdown's still going on," said Star, "but it's not slowing me down. Calls for escorts are growing."

"How did you get so popular?" asked Angie.

"You mean me and Coco? Word spreads. We only go to homes—well, some johns use vacation rentals. We check out the addresses to make sure they're in high-end neighbourhoods. We don't do a thing for less than two hundred dollars."

"Why are these johns willing to pay so much?" asked Trixie.

"Good service and good reviews."

Jess listened as she applied her makeup with the others at the table. Star revelled in her status over the basement girls and often flaunted how successful she was. But why all the particulars? This was new. Jess's gut twisted. Were the details just an added flourish to her usual bragging? Or something else? The worse part of this life was never knowing what was coming up. It was bad already; it could get worse. But you never knew how or when. And with the arrival of Desme, Belle had been sent back to the carpet. The conversations Jess shared with Flower were over.

~

Several days later, Deni called a house meeting. "I hear some of you have been asking about the clubs. They're closed, and there is no sign of them reopening soon." However, she explained, there was a growing market for private parties that offered the full range of entertainment. They'd been exploring the possibilities. "We've been working hard over the past weeks, developing links to various sites that offer exotic dancers for elite parties." Deni told them there would be an all-inclusive cover fee for each party, depending on its length and services. That would go to "management," but everything the girls earned in tips would be applied to their account. The more they hustled, the more they would make.

"Shouldn't we get a cut of the fee?" ventured Trixie. "We're doing all the work."

Deni glared at Trixie. "Who's doing all the promotion? We are. Who's organizing the operation? We are." Deni's voice grew more menacing, "Who is providing transportation? We are! Who's feeding and housing you? We are! Who's giving Zander his cut for protection and his connections? We are! If it wasn't for us, Trixie, you and everyone else here would be doing tricks for some pimp in a back alley for twenty bucks."

Steps were heard on the stairs. Rocky thumped down. "Everything all right down here?"

"Just clarifying a few points with the girls," said Deni. Rocky remained standing on one of the lower stairs, leaning against the wall.

"The first party is next week. New outfits are on the way. They'll be part of your start-up costs." Rocky's presence stifled any thought of protest. "But in the end, you'll be the big winners. These are men with money to spend. You play this event well, we may find others with richer guys. So who's up for it?"

All the girls raised their hands. Jess lowered her eyes and slowly raised her own. "Well, well, well, even Wasp wants part of the action," Deni taunted. "Trixie, Belle and Angie, you're the most experienced. You get the first gig."

PART EIGHT

PART EIGHT

Chapter 83

"Don't bother with that one," said the man, leaning near the entrance of a corner store. He tugged his stained ball cap, pulling it over his eyes and, after taking a drag from the cigarette, added, "Been broke for months."

Another dead payphone. Gloria hung the handset back in its cradle, disappointed. She'd been flitting nervously through the streets of Vancouver's Downtown Eastside in her search for a payphone. Any unexpected movement or gesture set off flashbacks of her assault. Should she consider this an omen and give up?

"Won't find none around here. You gotta go around a hospital." The man took another drag. "That's where I go."

It had been almost five weeks since Gloria had fled Edmonton. By the time she'd arrived in Vancouver that dank, raw March night, she'd already begun to question her decision to leave. But with less than fifty dollars, there was no going back.

For over five years, Gloria had been stringently managed: two years by Deni and three years before that by her boyfriend pimp. She'd been isolated with no resources and no connections—a massive and conclusive blowout with her mother had sent her fleeing as a teen to her coddling boyfriend, who transformed into a controlling, explosive pimp. Living under Seth and Deni had been bleak and punishing, but she'd been off the streets, could bathe, was supplied with pills, and had a subsistence diet that she supplemented at the clubs. She was totally unprepared to navigate the streets of Vancouver, period. With the city in lockdown, it was a nightmare.

~

Gloria met Star at a club when her boyfriend's abuse was intensifying. Star offered to introduce Gloria to friends who could provide safety and a way to gain independence. Star boasted that she already had a car and was working toward an apartment. Gloria bought into the scheme and was relieved to be free of her pimp, but the promised independence never materialized. Each week she handed over thousands to Seth and Deni, but her ongoing "debts" thwarted every effort to reach the five thousand they'd supposedly paid out to her pimp—the amount necessary to release her. Gloria was aware she was being scammed but could see no way out. As Deni reminded her when she was too flippant, her boyfriend pimp was still in Edmonton. Drugs numbed her desperation.

However, Deni's announcement about the clubs closing had pushed Gloria into panic mode. Being trapped in a basement 24/7 under Deni's vindictive control? And forced into online porn or the other "services" Star provided? With Deni keeping track of what they earned? What would happen when she lost the shred of autonomy she had at the clubs? Deni hated her. Frantic, she saw only one option: flee.

During that last night at the club, Gloria's mind raced: work until she had some cash, take what she earned and slip out of an emergency exit near the change room. Beyond that, she had no plan. Her sole aim was to get as far as possible from Edmonton. Although she had long doubted the existence of the elusive mobster, Zander, she wasn't taking any chances, and she was terrified of meeting her old boyfriend.

Around midnight Gloria walked into the club's change room for a bathroom break. Glancing around to make sure no one was lurking, she rushed to a small locker and grabbed her leggings, hoodie and makeup kit that she had rolled into a tight bundle. On her way to a bathroom stall, she snatched a coat hanging on a hook and picked up some dirty socks she had noticed earlier and kicked under a trash bin. Deni didn't provide winter coats or boots. The clubbers were driven to the strip club's entrance, where they disembarked and, at the end of their shift, ran back into a waiting vehicle.

In the bathroom stall, Gloria donned the coat, stashed her stilettos in the coat pockets, and pulled on the socks. A couple of girls rushed in to touch up their makeup. Gloria's galloping heart burst into painful throbs. The girls chattered for what seemed an eternity, then, as abruptly as they entered, they left. Gloria pulled the coat's hood down low, slipped out of the emergency exit and ran down the frigid street toward a brightly lit sign—a 24-hour convenience store. She greeted the attendant, asked for the nearest bus line, then strode to the bathroom. There she dropped the coat, quickly put on her hoodie, pulled up the leggings, wrapped herself again in the coat and left. Two blocks away, she found the bus stop and stood in the shadows, hopping from stockinged foot to stockinged foot until she saw the headlights of an oncoming bus.

As Gloria boarded, she fumbled for a bill.

"It's free," said the driver.

"What?"

"New Covid rules. No fare."

Gloria sat crosslegged on one of the front seats, massaging warmth back into her toes. A lit sign near a shopping centre flashed the time and temperature: 12:36, -24. "Where does this route end?" she asked.

"West Edmonton Mall. But only the casino's open at this hour."

As they approached the mall, Gloria saw a sign for a gas station with a 24-hour shop.

"Could you drop me off at that gas station?" she asked the driver. He glanced down at her stockinged feet and, without a word, stopped the bus near the gas station.

In the store, Gloria took off the socks and stepped into her stilettos, difficult with her now swollen feet. The attendant was bored and seemed happy for her company. He willing made the searches she requested on his phone.

"No buses leave Edmonton until Tuesday morning. You gotta wait for one more day."

Gloria told him about a sick mother and her need to get to Vancouver quickly.

"A lot of trucks stop here to fuel up. You might get lucky and find someone willing to give you a lift to Calgary. Then you can hop on a bus or train from there."

Gloria walked toward the back of the store and counted her cash—just under five hundred. It had been a slow night. She bought some coffee and waited. Around six o'clock, the shop attendant called her over and pointed out a trucker.

"That guy over there, getting coffee? He just told me he's headed to Calgary." Gloria approached the man.

"A ride to Calgary?" he said indifferently as he poured cream into his coffee, barely giving Gloria a glance. "Two hundred dollars."

Gloria's eyes flashed with anger and shock –the price was more than double the cost of a bus ticket. But she was desperate to get out of Edmonton. She moved aside, counted out some bills, then went back to the man with the cash in her hand. He seemed surprised but took the money and pointed out his truck. For three hours, they listened to an audiobook, never exchanging a word until she was dropped off at a truck stop on the outskirts of Calgary. A taxi brought her to the bus station, a tiny office at a mall.

"Bus leaves tomorrow morning," said the clerk when he passed Gloria her ticket. She checked the time: not yet noon. A twenty-hour wait. Although still on high alert, the wild thumping of her heart had eased the further she got from Edmonton and, even more so, when she climbed out of the cab of the semi. Gloria tried not to hobble as she made her way through the mall and into a superstore, searching for shoes and warm socks. She was astounded by the number of shoppers heaping their carts with groceries. Several times she was stalled in clogged aisles on her way to the back of the store.

"I don't know when I'll be able to bring you out again, Mom," said one shopper to an older woman walking next to her. "You better get enough for a month. Who knows how long this Covid is going to stay around."

Another shopper told the children who clung to the cart, "Get a couple more boxes of that cereal. You kids go through it so quickly, I don't want to run out." Impulsively, Gloria reached over the heads of the kids and snagged a box for herself.

Two hours later, Gloria sat in a food court with her feet warming in thick socks and new runners–the cheapest she could find. All her possessions were either worn or neatly placed on the bottom of a reusable shopping tote she had picked up for a dollar. She sipped her coffee loaded with cream and sugar and nibbled on sweetened cereal.

While sitting at the food court, Gloria overheard a woman chatting loudly on her phone. "Can you believe this weather? They say with the wind chill, it's going down to minus twenty-two tonight! In the middle of March! Enough already!" Her comment shook Gloria out of her brief reprieve, and her trepidation resurged. She had another frigid night to survive.

The mall, Gloria was informed, closed at eight. By five, she had

257

scouted out a three-block stretch at one end of the mall and discovered two 24-hour convenience stores—one connected with a gas station—and a fast-food joint that closed at midnight. When the mall closed, she would move among these three businesses until the mall reopened at seven the next morning. When Gloria trudged out of the mall shortly after eight, she had been up well over twenty-four hours. She was too strung out for sleep—that would have to wait for the bus ride. If later on, she needed something beyond coffee to stay alert, she had some speed in her makeup kit, souvenirs from her basement life.

~

Gloria arrived in Vancouver on Tuesday, shortly before ten p.m. She'd planned to find a nightclub that would let her perform and then look for cheap accommodations in the morning. But that plan fell apart after the bus stopped in Kamloops. A pair of new arrivals complained loudly that, due to Covid, all bars and nightclubs had been forced to close—and on St. Patrick's Day, no less.

So Gloria stepped off the bus in Vancouver with no source of income, no education beyond Grade 11, no phone, no map, no knowledge whatsoever of the area. She asked a Pacific Central Station clerk where she could find cheap accommodations. When the clerk found out just how cheap, she directed Gloria to a city bus that would bring her to the shelters in Vancouver's Downtown Eastside. But at the late hour she arrived, the shelters were already filled. Early the next morning, Gloria was found unconscious in an alley, robbed, beaten and raped. She was rushed to a hospital, and when stable, she was sent to recuperate in a women's shelter.

Weeks into her treatment at the shelter, Gloria sat with her counsellor. "How do you know your family hasn't been looking for you?"

"Because my mom told me she never wanted to see me again."

"How many years ago was that?"

"Over five."

"People can change."

So Gloria built up the courage and did an internet search to locate her mother and see if anyone had posted her as missing. That's when she saw it—the notice for Wasp on a missing person site. Jess Gayle, sixteen years old.

Gloria had wondered about the recent basement recruits, in particular, Coco. Until then, the women who arrived were clubbers who had been lured by the safe lodgings and some bogus promise from Seth and Deni. Angie and Trixie told Gloria they had fled an abusive couple who had hired them as nannies... or housekeepers, maybe both. They ran away and clubbed to earn enough money for their return plane tickets and some extra for their families overseas. However, they couldn't rent anything without a visa and references. Star brought them to Seth: once they hit savings of ten thousand dollars, he told them, they could take the money and return to their homeland.

Belle was the first Calgarian and, with Star's coaching, picked up clubbing very quickly. With the arrival of Coco, however, Star stopped clubbing and started arranging house calls with her protégée. Online videos were increased, and then Wasp arrived. The operation was evolving.

Gloria stared at Wasp's posting. She wanted to call in a tip, but not from any phone that could be traced back to her or the shelter. So one afternoon, she left the shelter to hunt down a pay phone—more difficult than she had expected and, in her case, dangerous.

Chapter 84

Trixie, Angie and Belle returned from their first private soiree in high spirits or, as Jess suspected, very high. Not to be eclipsed, Star boasted that she and Coco had quite a lucrative night as well.

"House meeting," announced Deni the next afternoon as the women were busy pouring coffee and assembling their meal of peanut butter, jam and bread. She was unusually pleasant, which set Jess on edge. "Three more bookings have been made for private parties," she happily announced. "Our online videos have a constant stream of viewers, and Star and Coco's clientele is growing. We have many requests for live webcam sessions that we have to turn down—we don't have enough rooms. We need better accommodations." Then, scrutinizing the women closely, she said, "We're moving tonight."

Jess, like most of the girls, looked up from her sandwich, stunned. Deni gazed down at them with a smirk. Each of the women received a grocery tote bag for their few personal items and a couple pieces of lingerie. Everything else was to be packed; the guards would bring down the boxes and tape.

"Flower, you're coming upstairs," said Deni. "Pack up your things now. And for the rest of you, you have five minutes to finish eating, then Star is in charge down here. If you finish early, you might be invited upstairs to celebrate the successful private party launch."

Soon the girls had the room dividers dismantled and the beds and foam pads folded. Everything else was packed into boxes, which wasn't much—mainly blankets, pillows, some dishes and additional lingerie. As the guards hauled it all upstairs, the women were handed a couple pails of paint along with brushes and rollers to cover the bright green back wall.

With the windows sealed, the paint fumes became overpowering. Most of the girls were getting headaches, and Coco threw up. Star, who had to remain in the basement, finally went upstairs, opened the windows, and came back down with a fan. A guard hovered around the open basement door, as if it was necessary. The fear of reprisals kept the women compliantly occupied downstairs.

When the work was done, nothing remained in the basement but the folding table and chairs. "We have a few more hours before the move," announced Deni, "so clean yourselves up. Belle, Trixie, Angie and Coco, you're coming upstairs. Desme and Wasp, you have recordings to do." Desme protested loudly, but the sound of Rocky thumping down the stairs muted her complaints.

~

The recording session was awkward on the bare cement floor with a folding chair as the only prop. Jess felt lightheaded from the persistent paint fumes and apprehensive over the impending move. She went through her routine robotically.

The guard's phone pinged. He glanced at the message, turned off the camera and opened the door. "You're wanted upstairs."

Chapter 85

Officer Wallace picked up his phone. It was one of the investigating officers for missing persons. "Did the internet team find the source of Jess's picture?" he asked.

"No, or at least not yet. I've been told that whoever posted it is no amateur. But that's not why I called. We received another tip this evening. According to the caller, Jess is in Edmonton. Possibly held against her will. The caller said she was in the basement of a house in a residential area but didn't know the exact address. She gave the name of a highway and some streets. Unfortunately, based on what she told us, the house could be anywhere within a huge swath of homes."

"Do you think it's a hoax?"

"The woman sounded convincing. Extremely anxious. Something spooked her, and she cut off the call. Jess's file's been transferred to the RCMP's Serious Crime Unit in Edmonton. And Wallace, this is strictly confidential. We don't want to risk any leaks."

Chapter 86

"I said you're wanted upstairs," the guard growled.

Jess didn't move. "What about Desme? Isn't she coming?"

"Desme has nothing to do with you."

During her entire captivity, Jess had never been out of the basement, had never looked out a window. She fantasized about having an opportunity to flee this hovel, but now, summoned upstairs, she was terrified to leave it.

"Upstairs!" the guard said harshly.

Jess walked barefoot across the cold cement floor in her lacy, black chemise and followed the guard, step by step, up the stairs. He unlocked the deadbolt and motioned for her to go ahead of him. She waited at the top of the stairway, unsure of what to do. "Open the damn door!" said the guard. "What are you, an idiot?"

The door led to a mudroom, and Jess tentatively walked through. "For Christ's sake!" hissed the guard. He grabbed Jess by the shoulder and shoved her until she emerged in a foyer. Bevelled glass doors separated the entryway from an open living area. Jess could make out contorted figures and furniture through the frosted glass, but not much more. Someone approached the doors and opened one. Deni, holding a beer bottle, stood in front of her.

"Well, look who's here," she cooed. "The Wasp." The guard pushed Jess toward Deni. "So you're interested in the private parties." Over her shoulder, Jess stared at those celebrating, packed together on an oversized sectional. Scattered on a coffee table in front of them were bags of chips, containers of dip, beer and liquor bottles. A reality show blared from the TV.

"Seth's in the office waiting to discuss the details."

Maintaining a tight grasp on her shoulder, the guard steered Jess around, pushed her into a small room near the front entrance and closed the door. The "office" was furnished with nothing other than a tightly stretched green screen behind a double bed. Cameras and lights were set up in every corner.

Seth sat on a corner of the bed. It was the first time Jess had seen him without the guise of friendship. He patted the bed, "Have a seat."

"I'd rather stand."

"I'd rather you didn't."

"Seth, don't do this." But the Seth she implored was no more.

"You're a massive disappointment, Wasp. You could have been a key member of the family," said Seth in a low, flat voice. "You're nothing but a slut. No one cares about you, and no one ever will." He reached over and tapped the door. Moments later, two guards entered and forced her down on the bed. The rest was a blur of terror, searing pain, agony and utter helplessness. Jess drifted away. No sound, no emotion, no sense of time. Just images of man after man on top of her and the unwavering red lights of the cameras.

~

Deni was pressing ice cubes on the back of her neck when Jess resurfaced. As soon as she opened her eyes, Deni walked out. Lena entered and tossed some clothes on the bed and shoes on the floor. "I knew all along you were a whore," she sneered, "Didn't even put up a fight." Jess couldn't even muster up a spit. "Get dressed. And hurry, or the guards will be in to do it for you. And they might even dive in for seconds."

Jess slowly pushed herself up. She pulled on the tee shirt and then the jeans, which hung loosely on her bony hips. On the floor were her old boots. How strange it felt when she slipped them on. No one in the basement was allowed to wear shoes except the clubbers and only when they left the house. Laying on the bed was one more item: an old hoodie. As Jess wrapped herself inside it, she remembered Mallory. Had Mallory gone on with her life, forgetting Jess altogether? *Even if she remembered me, what would she think of me now?*

"Speed it up, Wasp," said Deni as she approached the room. When she looked in the door and saw Jess dressed, she scoffed, "You took long enough. Get up. You're going on a little road trip with Star and Coco."

Chapter 87

Jess rose unsteadily from the bed and hobbled, sore and raw, into the foyer. Both doors leading to the living area were now open. The TV continued to blare. Seth and Lena were standing near the sectional, laughing and bantering about some participant in the show, offering Jess little more than a fleeting glance. Next to Lena, joining in on the laughter, was a man vaguely familiar. Belle, Trixie and Angie, wedged among the guards on the couch, averted their gaze from the doorway. As Jess left the area and moved toward the mudroom, she saw the powder room. "I need the bathroom," she rasped.

"Make it snappy," said Deni. "Star's waiting in the car."

Jess closed the door, splashed her face with cold water and then gulped some down. She did not lift her eyes, unable to look at herself in the mirror. From the other side of the door, she heard Deni bark, "Trixie, Angie and Belle—the party's over. Throw whatever is leftover into a garbage bag, sweep the floor and wipe everything down."

Then she heard Seth. "Before you head back to Calgary, give me a hand packing up the last of the equipment. The rest is already in the SUV."

"What are you doing with the sectional?" asked a male voice.

"It's staying. The new furniture's already arrived at the other place."

Deni's voice cut back in, "When they're done, Lena, get them back in the basement and make sure Desme's ready. I'll let you know when it's time to go."

Jess opened the powder room door and looked toward the foyer. A tall, lanky man, following Seth into the "office," paused at the door and ran one hand through his curly hair. "Over here, Jerry," Seth said. "Start by winding up the cords."

Deni turned. "About time, you dolt. I was ready to pull you out." As Jess shuffled slowly toward the back door, Deni shoved her from behind. "Don't be so dramatic."

A dark sedan was waiting in the garage. The motor hummed into action as Deni hustled Jess into the backseat behind Rocky. Star was the driver, with Coco seated behind her. Deni bent her head close to Jess and whispered, "Don't do anything stupid. We still have our sights on your redheaded friend, and Rocky has connections with your Uncle Rodolfo. I understand he would be more than happy to get his hands on you." She stepped back and slammed the door shut. The locks latched, the lights went out, the garage door opened, and the car pulled out into the night.

~

Jess sat in the back seat, reeling from Deni's final warning. Uncle Rodolfo, connected to Seth and Deni? The mere thought threw her again into a state of terror.

Several months after her mother gained custody of Jess, Uncle Rodolfo showed up at their home. Her mom hadn't been able to withstand his charm. In fact, had it not been for the encounter at the funeral and her grandmother's subsequent warnings over the years, Jess may have been less suspicious of her uncle's attention and gifts. Her mother, however, was fighting another demon, and Rodolfo deftly drew her back into addiction. His interest, however, was not Jess's mother but his beautiful and reticent niece. He had made sure her mother was sufficiently high the night he raped Jess; however, he had not anticipated that the heroin he provided would kill her mom or that Jess would be a witness.

Rodolfo Tanis back in her life. No, it could not happen. Jess could feel herself drifting back into her alternate dimension. She pinched her arms and pressed one foot on top of the other. She forced herself to breathe deeply and take in the details around her: Coco ripping open a wrapper, the smell of chocolate as she ate. No, it could not be true. Lena, Seth, Deni, Star—they were all liars. Nothing that came out of their mouths could be trusted. No, she knew Rodolfo was in prison and would be for several more years. The thought lessened her alarm. They were lying, she assured herself. But how did they even know about Uncle Rodolfo?

Chapter 88

A chime rang repeatedly. "Put your seatbelt on," Star said to Rocky. "I'm not listening to that the whole trip."

"Quit bitching. It'll go off in a minute," said Rocky. "I'm so cramped in this car. And this belt is strangling me. Why did you rent this tin can anyway?"

"Oh, poor, little Rocky."

Rocky twisted around in his seat and buckled the belt behind him. The chime stopped. "There," he said, flexing his shoulders, "much better. No more restraints."

Star turned her attention to Jess. "Hey, Wasp. I hear you got a tour of Deni's boudoir."

Rocky laughed. Jess said nothing.

"Ah, she's still savouring the moment," Star snickered. Rocky and Star continued to exchange lewd quips regarding Jess, howling with laughter after each comment.

Jess turned toward Coco. She was sound asleep, her head against the car door, a candy wrapper lying in her open palm.

"Well, they captured it all on video," Star went on. "Ought to fetch them a mint."

"I should get royalties," laughed Rocky. "I paid enough for the honours."

Star giggled. "So generous of Deni to share her studio."

"Share it? Wasp gave the last performance in that place."

"Yeah, I hear Deni has a sweet, little studio set up in the new place," said Star.

"With a garden theme? Eggplant and peaches?" Both cracked up.

When they recovered, Rocky added, "Gotta say, when Deni gets herself decked out, she is something else."

"Oh, so you're ogling the boss's woman?" teased Star.

"Nothing wrong with admiring the merchandise," Rocky snickered.

"Deni makes a bundle on her videos."

"I believe it," said Rocky. "Do you know how she and Seth got together?"

"She was some sort of porn star in Toronto. Seth was one of the video guys on the set."

Rocky made a comment Jess couldn't hear, but it threw both Star and him into another fit of laughter. Usually disdainful and secretive downstairs, Jess was astounded to see Star and Rocky so blatantly glib and full of glee.

Shit, she thought, *they're fucking high!*

Star veered sharply toward an entrance ramp. Jess grabbed the door handle and planted her feet firmly on the floorboards. "Yee-haw!" laughed Star.

Once they were sailing down the highway, Rocky lit up a cigarette. "If you're going to smoke, open your window," said Star.

Rocky fumbled with the controls on his door handle. All the windows started going up and down. "Fuck, the buttons are all screwed up in this car."

"I'll get it," Star said. Latches popped, windows descended; both burst out laughing. Finally, Rocky found the right button. "I got it."

After he tossed out his butt and rolled up the window, Jess asked, "Where are we going?"

"You don't have to worry about a thing," replied Star. "We've got everything planned."

"You booked the motels?" asked Rocky, ripping open a bag and chomping on some snack.

"With Covid, you don't need reservations. Vacancies are everywhere. But," Star said with a lilt in her voice, "on this trip, Rocky Bae, it's vacation rentals all the way!"

"Sweet!"

"Yeah, I thought you'd like that. Hey, don't hog all the chips! I'm the one driving!" Star swerved a little as she reached into the bag. Jess swore under her breath. She was afraid to voice the slightest reaction for the fear that, given Star's giddy mood, she would swerve and jerk just to get a rise out of her.

"You better text Seth before he freaks out," said Star. "You know how he gets when we're travelling, let alone with an export."

"Yeah, yeah," said Rocky. "The guy's so tech-savvy; he's probably got a tracker on our phones." After a few moments, "Okay, done."

"Did Seth tell you when they're leaving?" asked Star.

Jess closed her eyes and feigned sleep, hoping to lengthen Star and Rocky's unguarded chatter as long as possible.

"As soon as he packs up the last of the equipment. I was supposed to go with him but got reassigned when the export came up. One of the other guys is going with him instead."

"What about Deni?"

"She and Lena are going to follow them in her SUV. Did you see all the crap she had packed in there?"

"Props, Rocky, props," Star laughed.

"A whole fucking van full? She had us haul down at least thirty pillows to her SUV, probably fifty."

Star laughed, "I swear she has a pillow fetish. They're everywhere. She's always got to have something crammed between her legs!"

Gut-splitting laughter erupted.

"And," howled Rocky, "she wants to bring Claudia with her!"

"What? Lay her on top of pillows?" she wheezed.

"No room!" guffawed Rocky, "They're packed in so tight on top of everything else that if the sunroof blows, they'll have a pillow ejaculation!" The two roared with laughter. Rocky caught his breath. "If Deni wants to bring the kid with her, she'll have to sit on the floor in front of Lena."

"Not to worry. I'm sure Seth and Deni will be driving like law-abiding citizens–they wouldn't want to get pulled over."

"Speaking of which, shouldn't you be slowing down for the same reason?" Rocky asked.

"Look around, asshole," Star said flippantly. "We got the whole road to ourselves. Besides, we're meeting someone at four."

"Yeah, you're right. We don't want to be late."

"Well, what about the bitches downstairs? And the other kid? When are they leaving?"

"Two of the guys are hanging around until the SUVs return to pick them up."

Star reached over to grab some chips. "What the fuck? You ate them all?"

Rocky laughed. "Don't worry. I lifted about six bags from the party." He ripped open another bag.

"Find something to listen to, would you, Rocky?" Star said as she reached for a handful of chips.

Rocky fiddled with the radio until he came to a station they both liked. With the music blaring, any comments between Star and Rocky were indiscernible. Jess opened her eyes. The beams from the headlights reflected off a highway sign: they were headed toward Grande Prairie.

Road signs flashed by in quick succession as the sedan sped down the highway. The radio pounded out music, Star and Rocky laughed and jabbered, and Coco slept through it all. Jess gazed absently out the window, gutted by shame, hopelessness, and the depravity of those she had trusted. She shuddered with dread of the unknown—the "export" going where? to whom?

Suddenly Rocky screamed through the music. In a flash, the car was catapulting through the air.

Chapter 89

The RCMP Serious Crime investigators combed through Jess's file. The phone tip could prove false, but it aligned with the porn shot Oliver had captured on his phone. There were compelling indications that Jess was being coerced. Based on the streets listed by the anonymous caller, the officers zeroed in on three neighbourhoods. By the early hours of the morning, an unmarked car was surveying the neighbourhoods, winding in and out of the numerous crescents and cul-de-sacs that branched off the main boulevards.

"Nothing seems out of the ordinary," said one officer. "Roads quiet, no one on the streets, occasional TV flickering in an upstairs window. Looks like most people are sound asleep."

"That sounds nice," said the other officer as he took a swig of coffee. "Do you think we got this right?"

Chapter 90

The car hurtled through the darkness, crashing, flipping, tumbling and then landing on its wheels. Jess sat, dazed. The car's hood was crushed into the front seat. Rocky and Star lay motionless, Rocky thrown atop Star, their heads smacked together, the windshield smashed into their faces. Jess turned toward Coco, her eyes wide in shock.

"Undo your seatbelt, Coco," she said as she unlatched her own. Coco did not move. Jess reached over and popped her clip, then turned and reached for the door handle. "Oh, God, open," she whispered. Whether from the force of the crash, some safety feature, or Star's ineptitude when she struggled to lower the windows, the door was unlocked. It moved slightly, then stuck. Jess turned in her seat and kicked the door with both feet. The door squeaked open. "Come on, Coco." Jess grabbed her arm, "Are you okay?"

"Yeah," Coco said weakly.

"We gotta get out of here and fast." Jess stepped out of the car and took Coco's hand. But when Coco put her feet outside the vehicle, she stopped and pulled back her hand, "Where's Star?"

"Look at her, Coco. Star's dead. We need to go."

"I'm not leaving without Star."

Jess took Coco by the shoulders and leaned close to her face, "Star is not coming; she's dead. She was using you, Coco. Using you to make money."

Coco backed into the car. "You're a liar. Star told me you're a liar. You're just jealous."

"Coco, come out!" Jess yelled. She tried to reach in and pull her out but Coco, holding on tightly to the back of the driver's seat, screamed and kicked. Off in the distance, Jess could see headlights approaching. She had to get away. Directly in front of her, Jess heard water. Car lights from the opposite lanes revealed a low bridge. Jess crept and stumbled toward the bank. Just as Jess was about to duck under the bridge, she heard a whoosh. She turned to see flames billowing from under the car. "Coco!" she screamed, but it was too late. The subsequent blast thrust Jess beneath the bridge. Flipping onto her knees, she crawled back to the edge of the abutment. The car was fully ablaze, lighting up the night.

Jess stared in horror. A beam of light from a slowing car snapped Jess back into flight. Half crawling, half walking, she scuttled under the bridge, feeling her way over large stones and gravel. A swath of land separated the northbound lanes from those going south. Walking tentatively among the low-lying shrubs, Jess reached the cover of the second bridge. Looking back, she could see the glow from the flames and heard voices shouting. Tears flowed down her cheeks, and adrenalin pumped through her veins. She had one overriding drive—get away.

The fire, blazing in the darkness, captured the attention of those who slowed and stopped, allowing Jess to flee undetected along the river, away from her tormentors and those in their network. When she reached a stand of willows growing along the riverbank, she was completely shielded from view.

The river curved, and its bank widened. Clouds drifted overhead, and the moon, freed from its misty shroud, gently illuminated the terrain, quickening Jess's flight. Larger trees loomed over the willows as Jess scrambled as quickly as she could on the uneven ground. The sound of sirens in the distance spurred her onward. Ahead, to her left, she could make out a clearing, and as she drew closer, she saw it was a large field, shielded from the highway by the trees' foliage. Jess sprinted across it diagonally, heading toward a copse of poplars. Safe in the underbrush, her heart pounding madly, Jess took in her surroundings. The field she had just crossed was bordered by a dirt road lined with trees—at least as far as she could see. She decided to follow the road, staying close to the tree line, ready to dart into the brush should she see any headlights.

Jess made her way down the road, darting across sections where the trees thinned out or when she could see a farmhouse down a long driveway. She had no idea how long she had pushed herself, running, tripping, desperately moving forward, when she came to an abrupt halt. Before her was a crossroad. Beyond that, a field. In the distance, glimmering through trees, were lights—most likely another farm. Jess bent over, wheezing and cramping. When her breathing slowed somewhat, she cautiously walked to the middle of the road and looked in both directions. To her right, the road disappeared into the darkness. To her left, far off, she could see a few swiftly passing headlights.

"Shit, shit, shit!" she whispered. The road she had travelled ran parallel to the highway; the crossroad led right back to it. She could turn right and follow the road away from the highway, but in this sparsely populated region of northern Alberta, what did she know? It could dead-end at a rutted farm road. Yet, to walk on the shoulder of the highway? At this hour? Not going to happen. Her heart was pounding, her mind spinning.

Jess retraced her steps back down the road, away from the crossroad. The trees and shrubs hugging the narrow road thickened. Jess paused, walked into the undergrowth and sat, hidden among the bushes. *Calm down,* she repeated to herself over and over. She forced herself to slow her breathing. Daylight would come in a few hours. She would wait.

Chapter 91

Early in the morning, six teams of officers rolled into the three identified neighbourhoods and began going door to door. Drowsy-eyed residents, shuffling about getting their kids organized for online school and themselves for work, opened their doors to face two officers.

"Imagine waking up to this," said Officer Dave to his companion as they rang a doorbell.

"They'll recover," said Officer Jan. "Imagine being a missing teen stashed away in some unknown house."

The door opened. "Sorry to bother, ma'am," said Officer Jan. "We're canvassing the neighbourhood after a rash of vehicle break-ins."

The weary mom, a babe in her arms, was continually distracted by a cat determined to escape through the open doorway. "No, problems here," she said.

"No unusual activity in the neighbourhood? People coming and going at all hours of the night."

"Mom, Noah's hitting me!" a boy yelled from inside the home.

"Am not!"

"I'm sorry," said the mom. "What was the question?"

"Unusual activity? Numerous comings and going during the night?"

"At night, the only thing I'm interested in is sleep. I've noticed nothing."

"Well, thanks for your time."

As the officers walked to the next house, Officer Dave said, "This is going to be a long day."

"Let's hope we find a few insomniacs."

~

Officer Jan stretched her head around the porch and looked toward the backyard. Her view was obstructed by a high fence and gate. Officer Dave rang the bell again and knocked on the door. Not a sound came from the other side. Jan checked the time—seven-thirty. "What do you think?" she said when she and her partner were back on the sidewalk.

"A construction worker whose single?"

"That's a lot of house for someone single."

"A couple who hasn't come home from night shift?"

"Or people working remotely at a cabin by a lake?"

The officers stepped onto the porch of the neighbouring house and rang the bell. When the door opened, three school-aged children, curious to see rare visitors during the lockdown, crowded around an older couple.

After explaining the vehicle break-ins, the older woman said, "We don't actually live here. We came last month to help out with the grandkids' online school while my daughter and her husband work."

"Your daughter's lucky to have you."

"We love the kids," said the grandfather, giving one a side hug, "but we'll be glad to be back in our own place after school ends this month."

"Then you kids can come and visit us," said the grandmother.

"Before we go," said Officer Jan, "Do you know who lives next door?"

"I've seen a mom and her little daughter walk to the mailbox occasionally," said the grandmother. "A beautiful young woman."

"Our daughter told us they keep to themselves," said the grandfather.

"We've had beautiful weather lately—the garden is already in and sprouting. Our kids are often in the backyard playing, but I've never noticed anyone next door in their backyard."

"Well, yesterday they were pretty busy," said the grandfather. "Looked like they were moving. A white van came and went, and one of those junk-collecting trucks came by later in the afternoon."

"Did they haul off a lot of junk?" asked Officer Jan.

"I don't know exactly how much—they were pulling the stuff out from their backyard gate on the other side of the house—but it was a fair amount. A couple of buffed-up guys showed up, and they had it loaded in no time."

"When did you see all this?" asked the grandmother.

"I was upstairs reading a book while you and the kids were downstairs doing the Harry Potter marathon."

"Well, thanks for your help," said Officer Jan.

Back on the sidewalk, Officer Jan looked at the homes across the street while her partner scanned the houses on the other side of the vacant home.

"I got one camera over here," said Officer Dave.

"There's three across the street, including the house directly across."

~

"Vehicle break-ins on our street?" said the man who lived across the street.

"In the neighbourhood," said Officer Jan. "We're looking for unusual traffic patterns, particularly at night."

"Have you noticed anything, Darsh? Your bedroom faces the street."

The teen, standing near his father, shook his head. "We could look at the footage from the security camera."

"That would be helpful," said Officer Jan, pleased that the offer came from the family. "Would you be able to download the past couple of days onto this USB drive?" While they waited for the son, Officer Jan asked his father, "Do you know who lives across the street? No one seems to be home."

"No. I hardly ever see them."

~

Back in their cruiser, the officers loaded the footage into their laptop and skimmed through the recorded images of the previous day. The camera's coverage spanned the owner's driveway and sidewalk, the roadway in front of their house and the sidewalk on the other side.

As the grandfather had noted, a white van backed into the driveway and pulled out an hour or so later. Before the van pulled in, an SUV pulled out and backed onto the other side of the driveway, presumably to allow the van to back into the garage. When the van left, the SUV drove into the street, moved to the other side of the driveway and, presumably, back into the garage. After the junk collector left, there was little activity until later at night when the SUV pulled out again, backed onto the other side of the driveway and a sedan backed in.

No further movement was noted until after midnight, when the sedan left, and the SUV pulled back in. A half-hour later, a man came into the field of view and walked down the street. Sometime later, two SUVs drove away, one after the other. All was quiet until the officers saw their squad car pull up.

"What do you think?" said Officer Dave.

"It could simply be people moving out."

"In the middle of the night?"

"Late start? If that's the case, we'll just find an empty house and move on.... I think we call it in and check it out." Officer Jan took out her phone and called the lead of their investigative team, "We might have something worth looking into. I just sent you footage." She gave a summary of the neighbours' observations and pertinent aspects of the video. "We've flagged the footage. We're requesting backup and permission to search the property. It may not have anything to do with the missing girl, but it looks like something shifty could be going on."

"And no one's home, you say?"

"If they are, they're not coming to the door."

"Wait there. I'll get back to you."

Fifteen minutes later, the lead investigator called back. "The house is a rental. The owner's on the way over to open the door. I'm coming with backup. No one goes near the house until we arrive."

Chapter 92

"Best renter I've ever had," said the owner as he passed over the keys. "Never a complaint, pays rent on time, and sees to all the maintenance. In fact, the rent's been paid up to August."

"The name?" asked Officer Jan.

"Beth Spratt."

~

From all appearances, the house was empty. No one responded to the front or back door, and there was no sign of occupancy in the backyard. With backup in place, Officer Jan inserted the key in the front door and turned the lock, but the door didn't budge.

"Christ!" muttered the lead investigator. "Let's try the back."

Officer Jan inserted the key in the back door, turned the lock and pushed lightly. The door opened.

"Police! Anyone home?" No response.

"Beth Spratt?" No response.

Officers swept through the first floor and moved upstairs. "No one up here," reported an officer descending the stairs. "Some pieces of furniture but no personal items."

The same was true on the first floor. A bed was stripped of its linens in the front office. A sectional, a table and some chairs in the open living area. Cupboards cleared out.

"Look at this," said Officer Jan. On the inside of the front door was a heavy sliding bolt, locked. "Just like the bolt on the back door, only it was unlatched."

"The same bolt is on the garage door, latched," said another officer.

"So whoever was here, left by the back door," said the lead.

"There's a deadbolt on the basement door," said Officer Dave.

"Pop it open." said the lead. An officer stepped in with a crowbar.

"Police! We're coming down," yelled Officer Jan.

A stairway of unfinished wood, scuffed and splotched, went down to a small landing, turned and continued to the basement. The basement area, dimly lit from a couple of bald light bulbs, was completely empty except for a battered folding table, several dented metal folding chairs and a utility sink with a counter and cupboards below. A young woman, clutching a child on her lap, sat on one of the chairs. She gazed up at the officers and, without saying a word, tilted her head toward a room adjacent to a bathroom. The officer opened the door and flicked on the light. Sitting with their backs pressed against the back wall were four young women, their eyes wide with fear. The lead investigator turned back toward the woman and child, "Do you know a Beth Spratt?"

The woman looked up, "I'm Beth Spratt."

Chapter 93

Jess woke to a low snarl. Although the early morning sunlight glinted through the trees, Jess couldn't see the animal growling behind the cluster of bushes. Carefully, she felt around for a branch or a stone. Finding none, she grasped a handful of dirt and leaves. Slowly she rose. Immediately a large German shepherd began to bark wildly, lowering its head.

"Go away! Get out of here!" shouted Jess. The dog held its ground. Jess threw her handful of dirt, and the dog ran back a ways. Jess skirted to the side of the bush and reached down for another handful. This time her hand landed on a rock. The dog barked and growled as before but did not come any closer.

A rumbling down the road distracted both the dog and Jess. A dark blue hatchback slowed and stopped parallel to Jess. Jess flashed her gaze from the dog to the car and back again. The side window lowered.

"Eh, girl, that's one mean dog," said a woman with a thick African accent. "You better get in the car."

Jess turned toward the window.

"What are you doing out here all alone so early in the morning?"

The dog snarled and barked and drew closer to the car. "Come! Get in the car before that nasty beast gets you! I'll give you a ride."

Jess pretended to throw the rock and, as the dog turned to run, she opened the car door. The woman in the car looked about the age of Ms. Willow—not old, not young. She was wearing hospital scrubs covered with flowers. Jess glanced in the back seats; they were empty.

"Come, come. I have a daughter your age.... Walking on this road alone—so dangerous," she said as she rolled up the window.

Jess climbed in and shut the door.

"My name is Enuka Abara." She extended her hand in greeting. Jess pressed herself against the door and grabbed the handle. Enuka withdrew her hand and put the hatchback in gear. As she drove up to the three-way stop, the dog barked and jumped at the side of the car.

"That dog should be chained," she said. "Every time I drive this road, it chases my car." Turning toward the highway, she continued, "I work at a hospital not far from here and just finished my shift. I don't usually go home this way, but I buy eggs from a farm down the road and picked some up this morning."

Jess said nothing.

"There was a horrible accident just up the highway. Ambulances were sent out, but I heard everyone died. Seems the car hit a deer, flew onto a bridge abutment and flipped over." Enuka shook her head, "Had to be going at some speed to do that. Police and fire engines are still all over the scene. Only one lane of traffic is allowed going north."

Jess's eyes shifted nervously from Enuka to the highway getting ever closer. When they arrived at the intersection, Enuka asked, "Where do you want to go?"

Jess glanced north, up the flat prairie. Flickering faintly in the distance were the flashing lights of emergency vehicles. "Away from here," Jess rasped.

"I live in a small town about five minutes away. We'll go there and talk." She turned onto the highway heading south.

Chapter 94

Gravel crunched under the wheels when Enuka turned into a narrow driveway and parked at the side of a small white house. "Here we are," she said as she put the car in park. Enuka got out and opened the back door, removing a tote and a carton of eggs. Jess didn't move. "Are you coming in?" she asked gently.

Jess stepped out of the car and scanned her surroundings. No other vehicles were in the driveway. Jess could see neighbouring houses, but they weren't close together like her neighbourhood in Calgary. Enuka walked toward the rear of the house. "The back door is just around the corner here," she said as she turned out of sight.

Warily, Jess followed. Enuka was entering a porch when Jess rounded the corner. "My daughter and I live here. At this hour, she might still be in bed." Enuka unlocked the door and pushed it open. "Come in," she said as she entered. Enuka left the door open, put down her tote and went to the sink to wash up and fill a kettle. Jess stood on the threshold. Seeing Jess's hesitancy, Enuka went into the living room and pulled open the drapes, letting in the sunlight. When she returned to the kitchen, she pointed and said, "The living room is right there. The bathroom and bedrooms are this way. My daughter's room is in the back, my room is up front, and the bathroom is in between." Jess entered the compact kitchen and shut the door.

"You can sit here," said Enuka, pulling out the chair from a small kitchen table near the door. The water boiled in the kettle. "I can make you tea... or coffee... or my daughter likes chocolate milk. Would you like some hot cocoa?"

Jess nodded.

Enuka poured a packet of cocoa mix into a mug, placed a tea bag in another and poured boiling water into each. From the fridge, she brought out a small carton of cream and added some to both mugs. "Here, you stir it up," said Enuka as she placed a spoon and the cup of cocoa on the table. Then she pulled a stool near the kitchen counter and sat. For several minutes neither said a word as they gently stirred their hot drinks and began to sip them.

"What is your name?"

"Jess."

"I want to help you, Jess," said Enuka. "I can see you're scared and hurt." Enuka brushed the side of her own forehead lightly, and Jess mimicked the gesture on her own forehead. She felt a large bump, a small gash and dried blood trailing down the side of her face. "You're lifting your mug with both hands; you're trembling." Jess dropped her hands to her thighs. "It's okay, Jess. I know what it's like to be terrified. Drink your cocoa."

Enuka continued to sip her tea, and soon Jess picked up her mug and drank. When she was finished, Enuka said, "You're hurt badly," and she focussed her gaze toward Jess's lap. Jess glanced down. Blood had seeped through the crotch of her jeans.

"Shit!" exclaimed Jess as she pulled the oversized hoodie around her.

Chapter 95

Seeing the blood, Jess's heart thumped painfully in her chest. Enuka's lips were moving, she was saying something, but Jess understood nothing.

"What did you say?" Jess asked at last.

"I'm a nurse. I want to help," said Enuka. "Do you have someone you can call? Your parents? Relatives?"

Jess shook her head.

"Friends?"

Mallory, Sebastian... they're kids like me. What could they do? Ms. Willow... a teacher of how many? Five hundred kids? She's probably forgotten about me by this time. And besides, what could she do?

"Anyone?"

Jess thought of her caseworker, Annisa. After spiralling from foster care to the group home, Annisa was the first person with whom Jess had connected. With Annisa, Jess was not just a case to be managed–she had truly cared. But even Annisa had left her with little warning. How disappointed she would be with her now. It didn't matter anyway–Annisa was in Vancouver. And Paige? Paige couldn't even remember Jess's name without her computer notes.

"Anyone at all?" Enuka repeated, bringing Jess out of her musings.

"I don't know... I'd like to wash up."

"You can do that, but first, we need to talk a little more. Do you want some more cocoa?"

"Not now."

Enuka refilled her own mug from the kettle. "Jess, I know this is hard to talk about, but I am almost certain you've been raped? Is this true?"

Jess looked away.

Enuka continued softly, "When women come to the hospital after being raped, they have a few choices. They can decide not to report the rape and just get the care they need. This makes it hard to lock up the person who raped them. Another choice is to get a rape kit and collect evidence, then report the incident to the police."

"No police!" said Jess emphatically. There was no way she was going back into the system with complete strangers. Who would believe her, a "fucking runaway?" And Coco, she had left Coco in the car.... Jess sat on her hands to still the trembling.

"Okay, that's okay. No police," soothed Enuka. "The other option is to go to a hospital, ask for a rape kit, but no police, only nurses. At least you'll have the evidence if you need it later."

"What hospital?"

"We could go to Edmonton—"

"Not Edmonton!" Jess said forcefully.

"Okay, not Edmonton. We can go somewhere else, but you don't want to wash up until the evidence is taken."

Enuka leaned back against the counter and sipped some tea. Just then, a young woman in sweats stumbled into the kitchen. "What's going on?" she yawned, looking from her mother to Jess and back again.

"This is Jess," said Enuka softly. "Jess, this is my daughter, Obioma."

The two regarded each other. "Jess has had a difficult evening, and we're trying to figure out the best thing to do."

Obioma continued to stare at Jess, and Jess dropped her gaze. Obioma left the room and quickly returned with her phone. "You are that girl!" she said.

"What are you talking about?" asked Enuka, concerned.

Jess was ready to sprint out the door.

"People are looking for you. They've been posting all over social media. Someone from my university forwarded it to me." Obioma held up the phone to Jess, "Look! Here's one on *Ima-gram*."

Jess gazed at her image from a happier moment; her performance at school.

"There are lots more." Obioma pulled up another chair and sat near Jess, holding out her phone. Enuka watched the interaction with amazement. Obioma clicked the hashtag #FindJessG. Post after post filled the screen.

And then Jess saw a handle.

Chapter 96

Hoodie007. Jess had created the handle for Mallory. "Okay, I get the 'hoodie' part," Mallory had said, "but how does 007 fit in?"

"Because you're always undercover. Get it? Under the cover of your hoodie?"

Mallory laughed, "I like it."

"You really do?" asked Jess. "We can change it if you don't."

"No, no. This is perfect. I'm going to use it for my *AppChat,* too."

~

Jess took the phone from Obioma. She paused for a few moments, her finger hovering over the screen. The handle was right there– *Hoodie007.* Jess tapped the screen. A slew of posts regarding Jess populated the screen. Jess scrolled down. The first had been in the middle of March. Her friends had been searching for her from the start. Tears trickled down her cheeks.

Obioma was gazing at the screen as Jess scrolled through. "You know Hoodie?"

"She's a friend." Jess turned to Obioma. "Do you... do you have *AppChat?*"

"Sure." Obioma brought up the app.

Jess logged in. A stream of unopened messages came up. She recognized Sebastian's handle as well as Mallory's. She clicked on the latest from Mallory, "We're searching for you and won't stop until we find you. If you read this, call me anytime." And one from Sebastian,

"Hang in there, Jess. We're going to find you."

Jess looked over to Enuka, "My friends," she said, disbelief in her voice. "They're looking for me."

"Can you call from that app?" asked Enuka.

"Yes," said Jess and Obioma in unison.

Obioma's finger hovered over the phone icon and looked at Jess. "She'll know you read the messages."

Jess nodded, and Obioma touched the icon.

Chapter 97

Mallory turned over in her bed. The opening lines of "Seasons of Love" played relentlessly. She sprung awake and swatted her hand around her bed until she found her phone. "Hello?"

"It's me. Jess."

"Oh, my God. Oh, my God!" Tears sprung to Mallory's eyes. "Are you okay? Where are you?" She could hear weeping on the other end. "Are you safe?"

Another voice came on the line. "Hello, this is Enuka. Jess wants me to talk to you. She's had a difficult night."

"Who are you?"

"I am a nurse, Enuka Abara. I picked up Jess on the side of the road. She doesn't want to call the police. Can you help her?"

"Yes. Let me talk to Jess."

"Mallory?" Jess whispered.

"Are you safe?"

"Yes."

"What the nurse said is true?"

"Yes. Don't call the police. Please, no police."

"Jess, we've all been looking for you—me, Sebastian, Oliver, Ms. Willow. Don't worry. We'll come and get you. Can you give me the nurse's phone number?"

Enuka came back on the line. Mallory asked for her phone number and address, told her she would call her back in a few minutes, and hung up. Quickly she pressed another contact. "Ms... Ms. Willow," stammered Mallory over the phone, "somebody's found Jess."

Chapter 98

"Yes, we found five women and a child. They're currently in the basement with a couple of officers. We need two vans and an ambulance. One looks sick–flushed and lethargic. Wouldn't be surprised if it's Covid. We'll have to isolate the whole group until we know for sure. Get a forensic team out here immediately. We're taping off the entire site."

The lead investigator ended the call and gathered the group of officers outside who had been pulled from the other two neighbourhoods. "Go door-to-door and get security footage from the entire street. We especially want footage from this morning and yesterday but get as much as you can from as far back as possible."

"I don't think 'vehicle break-ins' will cut it," said one.

"Up the ante: 'Illegal activity in the neighbourhood.'"

He called two of the officers aside. "It's possible someone may have fled over the backyard fence. Go to the next street over and question the neighbours. See if you can get some footage."

~

Back at police headquarters, Officer Jan said, "What Beth is saying pans out. All the women go by pseudonyms. Beth is known as Flower. But look at this." She opened a flow chart on her computer and clicked on an icon with Beth's name, "Rental agreement, bank accounts, car registrations, insurance payments, credit cards–all in Beth Spratt's name. Beth claims she was forced to sign the documents. Either cooperate or be separated from her child–his name is Luxton. She was afraid her boy would be harmed."

"By the elusive Deni and Seth, I presume."

"Beth says Deni and Seth made it seem as if some mob guy called...," Officer Jan looked at her notes, "called Zander controlled the whole operation or provided protection, but Beth doesn't think he exists."

"Do you believe her?"

"I'm inclined to. Even now, sir, she says if Luxton is taken from her, she'll refuse to cooperate."

"And the others?"

"One is quite sick with Covid—hasn't been interviewed," said Officer Dave. "We suspect she's a minor. Two have problems with their work visas, both positive for Covid with mild symptoms. The other teen refuses to talk and is considered a flight risk."

"Beth said the teen's called Desme and came from Calgary," said Officer Jan, "and that's all she knows about her. But wait 'til you hear this. Beth said there were two other women, one called Coco and the other, Wasp."

"So Jess was there?" asked the lead, straightening up in his chair.

"Beth didn't know Wasp's actual name. I showed her a picture of Jess. It's her. Jess told Beth that if she ever got away, she would come back for her. So Beth told Jess her real name. When we arrived at the house, and you asked about Beth Spratt, Beth thought Jess had escaped and tipped us off."

"Do you think Jess called in the anonymous tip?"

"She couldn't have. She left late last night with," the officer referred to her notes, "Star, Rocky, and the girl, Coco."

"Who the hell are Star and Rocky?"

"I'm getting there. But let me tell you this first. According to Beth, Star is running some kind of escort service for Seth and Deni. Jess was never part of that action. So Beth believes Jess was going to get sold off to another pimp."

"Christ!" The lead hit his fist on the desk.

"Beth isn't sure. She overheard something last night, but she said all of them lie, so you never really knew what was happening."

"What do we have on 'all of them' so far?"

Officer Jan went back to the flow chart, and the lead rolled in his chair for a closer look. "From what we've been able to gather, Deni and Seth run the operation. Star and Lena groom and recruit."

Officer Jan reached for her notes, "With the arrival of Coco, Star has focused on the escort service. Lena brings in the girls from Calgary—Beth thinks she's probably escorting as well. Deni oversees the women downstairs; Star assists."

"What about Seth?" asked the lead.

"Beth said he records Deni's videos and thinks he is the one that edits and uploads everything on the internet."

"And this Rocky fellow?"

"There are four other men called guards. They record the videos of the girls downstairs and squelch any dissent if Deni's threats and promises don't work—Rocky is one of them."

"All the names are likely false," said Officer Dave. "We have no photos."

"So what we have are eight phantoms," said the lead, shaking his head. "But footage from the neighbours is coming in, so we should have more to go on soon."

A few moments passed, the lead tapped his fingers on the desk. "What I don't understand is—why would they leave the women behind?"

"They were a liability?" Officer Dave suggested.

"Liability? Do you know how much money each of those girls can bring in?" asked the lead. "I'd wager, in this operation, a minimum 100,000 a year *each* or they're dumped—as Beth said, sold off to other pimps. So, what they left behind is worth at least a half-million... likely much more if there was extensive use of porn sites. Why leave them behind? And where is Jess?" He stood up, "I need to talk to Beth."

292

Chapter 99

"Oh, hello, Jarrett! You're up early. How's my favourite nephew?"

"Not so good, actually. I've got a fever and a sore throat–I might have picked up Covid somewhere."

"Oh, my gosh, that's terrible! And you, working at home, being so careful! Do you want me to drop something off for you?"

"No, no, I'll be fine. I can get what I need delivered. I'll let you know if I feel any worse."

"Make sure you do."

"I just wanted to let you know. We were planning on getting together next week, but I think we should put it off for a while."

"Absolutely, Jarrett. And rest! Even if your symptoms are mild. Close down that computer of yours and relax so you can get over it quickly."

"Thanks, Auntie. By the way, I've been thinking about the student who went missing, the one you told me about a couple of weeks ago. Jess... Jess something?"

"Oh, yes, I remember. The one who sang so beautifully. It's so sad."

"I'm still shocked by the news."

"You have a heart of gold."

"Have you heard anything more about her?"

"Not a thing. No one knows what happened. It's like she just disappeared. We're all trying to do what we can to spread the missing person post about her."

"You let me know if you hear anything."

"Of course. And you take care of yourself. Call me if your symptoms get worse."

Running his hand through his hair, Jarrett paced his apartment. The calming effects of the joint he had smoked when he arrived home from Edmonton were dissipating. He went to his bedroom closet and squatted near a safe. Pressing his thumb on the sensor, he opened the door and pulled out the cash—a nice little bundle. Last night he'd been paid for a few more leads, received a bonus for the last delivery and a good report on the one in the "pipeline." Double had been offered for more like Coco. Wasp, unfortunately, was moving on. Too bad. According to Deni, she'd turned out to be "less malleable than the others."

Personally, Jarrett thought Deni was jealous of Jess—she had more potential than all the others. Seth agreed. He'd seen so much promise, he had even helped with her grooming. But none of them liked the attention she was getting. Jarrett had his aunt to thank for that inadvertent tip a couple weeks ago. Wasp was too much of a risk. She had to go. Their operation was getting more sophisticated and moving to a more suitable location. And his own part in the enterprise was becoming quite lucrative. Jarrett reached deeper into the safe and pulled out a stack of pre-paid credit cards and an envelope of gift cards to his favourite restaurants and stores—he'd been converting his cash slowly and steadily over the past months.

Jarrett stood and walked distractedly around the living area and then back to his room. The celebratory spirit that had sent him flying down the highway with his music blaring had soured. He'd just arrived back in Calgary and lit up a joint when Seth called. Around two, Seth told him, Rocky had texted: they were making good time and should have the "export" delivered on schedule. Sometime after three, before heading back to the house to pick up the girls, Seth texted Rocky to check on their progress, but it didn't go through—common enough in sparsely populated areas with patches of no cell coverage. But repeated attempts, with the same results for both Rocky and Star, had set Seth on edge. He'd searched through highway traffic websites and found a report of a car crash on Highway 43 with three fatalities. Seth was sure it was his crew. He'd called Jarrett.

"How can you be sure?" Jarrett had countered. "The report said the driver and two passengers died. Nothing about a survivor." He tilted his head back and drew heavily on his joint.

"Because I've made that trip. There are patches of no cell service, yeah, but not hour-long stretches. The texts weren't delivered. And

Rocky and Star wouldn't have turned off their phones."

"I think you're jumping to conclusions. I've received texts hours after they were sent."

"Maybe so. But if that crash was them and if Wasp survived...."

"That's a lot of ifs."

"She could lead the police to the house."

"She's not from Edmonton. She doesn't know the neighbourhood."

"Fuck! In just a couple more hours, we would have had the girls cleared out."

"So, what are you going to do?"

"Hold off picking up the girls for a few hours, just to be safe. And I want you to call your aunt and see if she's heard something."

"I can't do that at four a.m."

"No shit! Call as soon as you can and let me know what she says."

~

Jarrett went back to his bedroom and sat on his bed. He had waited until almost eight to phone his aunt. Now he pulled out his other phone and tapped Seth's number. "Yeah, I just spoke with my aunt. No sign of Wasp. So, what's your plan?"

Jarrett listened, stunned, and closed the call. "Fuck, fuck, fuck!" Given what Seth just told him, the accident and its possible survivor were the least of their worries. Jarrett pulled the SIM card from the phone, flushed it and smashed the phone. He put his cash, credit cards and gift cards in a duffle bag and threw in some clothes and toiletries. Making a sweep of the condo with a garbage bag, he tossed in everything perishable along with the trash and sent it all flying down the garbage chute into a waiting dumpster. Then he carefully stowed his laptop and other electronics into a backpack and slung it over his shoulder. Locking the door behind him, Jarrett calmly walked down the stairs of the condo building carrying his duffle bag. Time for a little road trip until things quieted down. If Seth was smart, he'd do the same.

Chapter 100

"I don't think Seth and Deni planned to leave us behind," said Beth to the lead and Officer Jan. Luxton sat close to her, watching a video on a tablet with headphones on. "Deni announced the move that afternoon. But looking back, I can see it was planned for a while. I did all the housecleaning upstairs and helped watch the kids. A couple of weeks ago, Deni began piling up stuff for me to box. She said there was too much clutter, that she was getting rid of junk. After I boxed it, the guys brought it to the backyard. This happened a few times."

"And on the day of the move, what happened?"

"The basement was emptied and painted by the girls downstairs. I packed up the kids' stuff and everything in the kitchen, but after Deni's purge, there wasn't a whole lot. And they never had a lot of furniture—just stuff from thrift shops, and most of that was hauled away in a junk truck."

"Do you have any idea where the new place is?"

"No. They loaded up a van, and one of the guards drove off in it. He was back for the party, but that was hours later." Beth glanced over at Luxton, absorbed in the movie he was watching. "They have two SUVs. One was loaded with all the equipment used for recordings—Seth's stuff. The other had all of Deni's things."

"When did they leave last night?"

"I went down to the basement with Luxton sometime after midnight. The other girls were already down there, except for Coco and Wasp. Deni said they were coming back for us. I figured they'd unload at the new place and return. I heard them leave, but a couple of guards were still upstairs. I could hear their footsteps. The doorbell rang a few times. Then you arrived."

"Why did they wait to move during the middle of the night?" asked the lead.

"I don't know... but that's not unusual for us. We're always up during the night."

"You said something about a party? What was that about?"

Beth's face began to crumble, and she grasped her hands together to keep them from quivering. "They were starting a new thing—private parties. The first one went well, brought in a lot of cash. They were having a party to celebrate. I was upstairs...," she began choking up. "The kids had gone to sleep on some blankets in their room. I sat outside in the hallway, listening.... I heard them bring up Wasp from the basement." Beth turned her back toward Luxton. Her body shook, tears filled her eyes. "They raped her and raped her and went back to the party... laughing... calling out 'Next!'" Beth bent her head into her hands and sobbed.

Chapter 101

"My class plans are prepared," said Willow. "The assignments and resources are posted for every class. Today's Zoom sessions are open for students to ask questions, get coaching–that kind of thing. The sub should be fine."

"So what's happening, exactly?" asked Frida.

"A nurse is driving Jess to Red Deer."

"A nurse?"

"Yes. I checked her out–Enuka Abara. She works at a hospital north of Edmonton. Picked up Jess on the side of a road. She has a daughter a few years older than Jess, Obioma. She's coming with Enuka."

"I hope this isn't some kind of hoax."

"I talked to Jess and Enuka. I think it's legit. All of us have promised not to post anything on social media, not even to close friends."

"So, Jess called you?"

"No, Jess called Mallory. Mallory phoned me. She's begging to come, but I don't think that's wise."

"I agree."

"How did Jess sound?" asked Frida.

"Upset, crying when I said I would pick her up. She is adamant about no police. We'll tackle that problem later."

"Swing by the school, Willow. I'm coming with you."

"God," said Willow, holding back tears. "I was hoping you would offer."

"Maybe I should call the superintendent."

"Don't, Frida. Not until we have Jess and the police have been informed. I have no idea what's going on. And no one else here knows about this except you, Mallory and I. We want to keep it that way until Jess is safe with us."

Frida was silent.

"There's no manual for situations like this, Frida. I'm taking an unpaid leave. This is not on school time."

"I'll see you in fifteen minutes. We'll talk on the way."

~

Willow exited the highway at Red Deer's Gasoline Alley. Amid the numerous fast food joints, one landmark stood out: an enormous windmill perched atop a donut shop. Willow pulled in.

"Where are they?" asked Frida, looking around.

Willow sent out a text. A ping sounded soon after. "Obioma said they're less than fifteen minutes away. I'm texting her the name of the shop and telling her about the windmill."

When the message was sent, Willow got out of her Rav and began to pace back and forth in the next-to-empty parking lot. Every cell in her body felt charged with the anxiety of anticipation. They had worked so hard for this moment, fearing the worst and hoping for this outcome, but now her mind conjured up an endless array of everything that could go wrong. She heard a car door slam and turned. Frida walked towards her.

Willow tapped on her phone. "I'm calling Obioma." A few seconds later, she answered. "Obioma, I'll feel better if I can talk to you the rest of the way. It'll be easier for me to direct you."

"I have the donut shop on the car's GPS. But with you on the phone, we won't be able to miss you."

"Would you pass the phone to Jess?"

Jess came on the line, "Ms. Willow?"

"Almost there, Jess. We're here waiting for you."

Obioma came back on. "Okay, we're exiting. I see the windmill. We should be there in a few minutes. We're driving a dark blue hatchback."

A couple minutes later, the car drove into the lot and parked several spots away from the Rav. A tall woman in flowered scrubs got out of the car and walked toward Willow and Frida. Willow could see passengers sitting in the car but couldn't make out who they were.

"I'm Enuka," said the woman.

Willow introduced herself and Frida, then quickly asked, "Where is Jess?" trying to keep her alarm out of her voice.

"She's in the car, but she's in bad shape. She needs medical attention but says she'll only get it with you in Calgary. I just want you to be aware."

Enuka led them to the car, and the back door opened. Jess emerged gaunt, battered, and bruised; her hair matted; her clothes, a ratty oversized hoodie and pants with bagged out knees. Jess, head bent, slowly raised her eyes to meet Willow's.

"Oh, Jess." Willow opened her arms, and Jess fell into her embrace.

Chapter 102

Officer Wallace entered the downtown Calgary hospital and walked to the designated meeting room. When he opened the door, Willow looked up from a small couch. Wallace sat across from her in one of the cushioned chairs.

"Has she said anything?" he asked.

"Not in the car. She sat next to me and held hands the whole way back to Calgary without a single word."

"How does she look?"

"Beat up, malnourished, bleeding... dazed, devastated. It's heartbreaking. She went straight into the sexual assault unit and has been there since."

"They may want to keep her here for a couple of days."

"She won't stay. She told me that before we walked through the doors. The girl's terrified.... I told her she could come home with me."

"You may need some help with this—counsellors, therapists."

"There's a doctor, nurse and counsellor with Jess now."

"I'm talking about you. By the way, where's Frida?"

"She has a family. I didn't know how long we would be, so I told her to go. She took a cab back to the school."

"It's critical that nothing regarding Jess and her whereabouts gets out. Absolutely critical."

"You made that very clear when I phoned you. Frida was right here and heard the whole thing."

"Yes, I heard her agree."

"Mallory has assured me that she's told no one, not even Sebastian and Oliver."

"Good."

"And you can be sure of Enuka's and her daughter's cooperation. They've been discrete from the start."

"Our team in Edmonton contacted them. This cannot leak."

"And the hospital staff?"

"The protocol here is quite strict regarding confidentiality."

The door to the meeting room opened, and the doctor who had accompanied Jess stepped in. "We've finished the examination. Jess has showered and is getting dressed. However, she has many injuries that indicate another source of trauma. She knows that the police have been informed that she is no longer missing and that an officer is here to speak with her. She does not want to discuss the rape, but she will try to answer other questions. Just remember, Jess is exhausted. Be gentle and stop if she shows any signs of being overwhelmed."

Shortly after, Jess entered with the nurse. The dirt and dried blood had been washed clean, the gash on her head bandaged, her clothing was new and well-fitted, but her eyes were haunted and weary. Jess walked directly to Willow and sat close to her on the couch, linking her arm around Willow's. The nurse put a beverage on a nearby end-table. "Drink as much of this as you can," she said. "I'll be back to see you before you go."

When the nurse left, Jess said, "You need to help Beth and her son and the other girls."

Chapter 103

Late in the afternoon, the lead investigator called his team together. "It's confirmed. Jess Gayle's in Calgary and talking to police." Some of the officers let out a shout while others smiled with relief.

"An officer in Calgary, who's been pursuing this case from the beginning, was able to interview her briefly. Everything he's passed on to us aligns with Beth Spratt's testimony. But there's more. That horrific crash early this morning on 43 north? Jess survived it."

"Shit!" exclaimed a few.

"She said another young girl called Coco also survived but refused to leave the wreckage. Jess couldn't get her to come out. Then the car exploded."

"What the fuck!" exclaimed one officer.

"Exactly," said the lead. "What Jess has been through–" he shook his head. "And absolutely nothing leaves this unit," he continued emphatically. "Nothing! We need to get all the information we can on that car and its occupants. No information on their identities is to be released. No information that someone survived. And no information on the whereabouts of Jess Gayle."

Chapter 104

Jess entered Willow's townhouse and lay down on the couch–she didn't want to be in a room by herself. Willow made her comfortable with pillows and blankets. Suddenly Jess raised herself on her elbow and stared at an arrangement of flower pots on a tiered stand near the front window.

"You gave me those that night."

Willow looked at the plants, now in full bloom. "Oh, the gerberas. Yes, I love them and always make sure I have a pot or two flowering."

"That night... that guy... he was there, too," said Jess, growing upset.

"Hey, hey. Slow down." Willow sat near Jess and put her hand on her shoulder, "What guy are you talking about?"

"You gave me those flowers that night."

"Right! The night you sang, I gave you some of these flowers, yes."

"That guy was there."

Willow scanned her memory, trying to make a connection between the flowers and what was disturbing Jess.

"What did he look like?"

"We were laughing. He was swiping his head, shaking hands. Tall. He talked to me."

Willow paused, trying to conjure up images from the evening. Then it hit her. "The guy shaking hands? Running his hand through his curly hair and shaking with the other?"

"That guy," said Jess as she collapsed back on the couch. "He was there last night. He was there at the house."

Willow racked her brain but could not recall the name of the lanky, curly-haired man she had met before the show. He'd been with his aunt from Central Admin... it had been such a fleeting encounter. She went to her laptop, pulled up a popular social media app and typed in the aunt's name. After several minutes, Willow found her. She swiped through previous profile photos and came across a selfie of the aunt and her nephew high up in the Calgary Tower, a spread of the city in the background. "Overlooking Calgary with my nephew, Jarrett. So glad he's moved nearby," read the caption.

Willow brought the laptop to Jess and showed her the picture. "Is this the guy you're talking about?" Jess nodded and rolled her face into the pillow.

Willow stood up and dialled Officer Wallace.

Chapter 105

Jarrett set his cruise control to just under the speed limit as he headed west out of Calgary. With Covid cases abating, he found some private rental cabins available in the Columbia Valley. He preferred the anonymity of the lower mainland but would wait a little longer. More restrictions, it was rumoured, would be lifting soon.

As he drove, his mind drifted to that night at the bar when he decided to partner with Seth. They'd met during high school in a northern Alberta town and were teens during the oil heyday of the 2000s. With false IDs, they'd entered the crowded strip clubs and witnessed the unbridled spending when the guys were in town from the camps. The economic bust hit just as they graduated. Seth went to Toronto to study film, Jarrett to Edmonton for IT security.

Several years later, Jarrett received a direct message from Seth on one of his apps. Seth had relocated to Edmonton and wanted to meet up. What started as a casual encounter became increasingly animated the more Seth learned of Jarrett's expertise. He'd lowered his voice and related how he had stumbled into adult entertainment trying to earn money to keep down his student loans. While filming, he'd met Deni. By the end of his fourth year, he realized he had enough skills to start his own adult film business with Deni. With the Alberta economy on the upswing, they decided to move to Edmonton—Seth had not forgotten the free-flowing cash in the hands of young workers. Deni worked the clubs, and Seth filmed and edited her videos for the porn sites. He and Deni had plans to expand. Would Jarrett handle the IT part of his business?

Initially, the work was sporadic, supplementing Jarrett's other job.

But as the operation grew, so did the compensation. Jarrett went full-time with Seth. He helped set up several businesses where the legit money from Deni's films, her AppChat memberships, and the like, could circulate with the income from the other girls, laundering it in the process. With all the research he'd done, Jarrett figured he had the training of a finance lawyer.

One summer, Jarrett drove down to Calgary with Lena so she could cash in on the Stampede parties. On the way, she complained about her recent disappointments: girls almost recruited who pulled back, all the time and money she had wasted on them. "You'll make it all back this week," he had consoled her. After dropping Lena off at some corporate bash, he dropped in on an aunt who lived in the city. Once a school teacher and now part of the school district's central administration, she rattled on about lagging students and how she wished more could be done for them, nearly putting Jarrett to sleep. His heavy lids lifted when she described how susceptible they were, many so easily manipulated. The seeds of Jarrett's brilliant plan were sown. If successful, Lena might turn out to be their best recruiter.

Jarrett moved to Calgary—with the internet, his work for Seth could be done from any location—and for over a year, he visited his aunt regularly. He subtly steered the conversation to her teaching experience, was attentive to her past experiences, empathetic regarding current difficulties, and eager to hear her opinions on possible solutions. Her passion was assisting struggling, at-risk students. His goal was accessing their student information; his strategy, patience. He could probably hack into the system. He had the skills and the added benefit of access to her Wi-Fi, but if he could slip in legitimately, all the better. In the meantime, he studied the online manual for the program the district used. His patience won out.

"But how many students are you talking about, really?" Jarrett had asked one day. "Twenty? Fifty? One hundred?"

"It depends on the issue you are looking at," Jarrett's aunt replied. "Poor attendance, temporary guardianship order, behavioural problems, that kind of thing." Her phone pinged, and she looked at the message. "Jarrett, you're here a little early, and I have a report I need to submit. So just make yourself comfortable while I finish it up." She picked up the cup of tea she was drinking and went to her office area in the open living space.

Jarrett pulled out his phone and leaned back on the sofa. His aunt opened her laptop and fumbled with the password. "We have to change our passwords so often; it's annoying." She tipped up the bottom of the laptop and continued on successfully with her work.

The momentary act was not lost on Jarrett. He waited until his aunt left for a bathroom break and took a picture of the post-it note stuck to the bottom of her computer. And with that, he had access to the entire student database in the district. From the manual, he had learned how to run reports, and from his many conversations with his aunt, he knew what he was looking for. Careful regarding the time and lengths of his logins, he'd gradually developed a spreadsheet of potential recruits. These he further screened by searching through social media accounts. And thanks to the school database, he had pictures to identify the person.

Chapter 106

The pounding on the condo door echoed down the quiet corridor. "Jarrett Edgar, Police. We have a warrant to search your residence." A few neighbouring doors squeaked open, and heads peered out to see the source of the commotion so early in the morning.

Wallace signalled one of his fellow officers to open the door.

Once inside, the officers scanned the residence. "No one," said an officer coming out of the bedroom.

One officer dusted for prints while the rest searched the premises. Wallace glanced around. The entire apartment was tastefully furnished. A couple of stunning landscapes hung on the walls, and an edgy, multi-tiered bookcase displayed sculptures of bronze and wood, mostly of women. While the decor smacked of refinement, it lacked anything personal. Not a family picture or personal photo was displayed, nor were any found in the drawers.

A lingering scent of pot hung about the rooms. "I don't think our Mr. Edgar has been gone for very long," said Wallace.

"But it doesn't look like he just stepped out for a walk," said an officer. "There's nothing in the bathroom but cleaning supplies."

"Yeah, the fridge and freezer are completely cleaned out and," he opened the dishwasher, "clean dishes in the dishwasher. Must have started a load before he went."

"Dirty laundry? Garbage?" asked Wallace.

"None. The guy's 'Mr. Clean' in the flesh."

"Yeah, a Mr. Too-Squeaky-Clean," said Wallace. "Sheets on the bed?"

"Ah, let me check. Yes, there are."

"Bag them."

"And there's a safe in the closet."

"It's coming with us."

~

"Jarret Edgar has no priors," Wallace reported to the lead investigator in Edmonton. "His prints have been run—nothing's come up. A hair found on his pillowcase was sent in for DNA analysis. And a BOLO has been issued for Jarrett as a person of interest—photo, description and license plates number. From the looks of his condo, he plans on being away for a while."

"We know he was here in Edmonton on the night Jess was shipped off," said the lead. "Beth Spratt identified him. She said he went by Jerry."

"So Jess was right."

"There's more. With the footage we gathered, we tracked a man leaving the residence after midnight on the night of the move heading toward the parking area of a shopping centre. Wasn't hard to pick him up on their CCTV—the parking lot was almost deserted. The plates match—Jarrett Edgar."

"Should we bring in the aunt?"

"Not yet. So far, there's nothing to indicate she was involved, and she's not a flight risk."

"What about the others in Edmonton?" asked Wallace.

"There were two men upstairs guarding the women in the basement. We suspected they jumped the back fence when they realized police were canvassing the neighbourhood. We were right. With the footage from neighbours on that street, we tracked the two guys to the same parking area Jarrett used and got their plate number. We found them last night at the home of a relative. Both were arrested and their phones confiscated. Neither are cooperating. Beth has identified them as well."

Chapter 107

Mallory got up, peered through a crack in the blinds and watched her father drive away. Though only shortly after six, the sun shone brightly through the green leaves of the nearby trees, adding to Mallory's joy. Jess had been found and was now safe at Ms. Willow's. Yesterday she'd swung from euphoria hearing Jess's voice to alarm over her injuries, dread that something might happen on her way to Calgary, and euphoria again when Jess was safe and cared for in a hospital. Now she was apprehensive about the secrecy. Not even Sebastian and Oliver? What exactly was going on?

~

Willow's phone chimed in a text from Mallory. Six forty-five. Willow looked at the message.

Mallory: *I hope you're not sleeping. How is Jess?*

Willow: *I'm up. Jess is sleeping.* With the help of medication, but Willow didn't add that.

Mallory: *I would like to see her today. Would that be OK?*

Willow hesitated. She'd have to ask Jess, of course. But whether Jess was ready for a visit or not, Willow wanted to check up on Mallory. She'd been focussed and driven in her search for Jess and supportive and concerned for Sebastian—Willow had noticed Mallory slipping her sandwich into Sebastian's pocket. Now Mallory had to bear the weight of secrecy about Jess, unable to share the news of her safety even with the friends who helped spearhead the search. And from what Willow picked up from Sebastian, her father was another burden to be borne. Willow wondered what was going on beneath Mallory's quiet demeanour.

Willow: *Come over this afternoon. We'll see if Jess is up to it.*

Mallory: *Ah... address?*

Willow: *Right.*

~

Mallory stood outside the townhouse, double-checking the address. Ms. Willow opened the door before she reached the doorbell. "I saw you from the window. You're early. Skipping class?"

Mallory blushed, "I can catch up tonight."

"Well, I booked a sub for this afternoon, so we're both AWOL. Come on in. Jess is expecting you."

Mallory entered and looked around the room. Sitting on the couch, wrapped in a blanket, was Jess.

"Jess!"

Jess threw back the blanket and stood, "Hoodie 007."

The two embraced, tears flowing silently. Then Jess eased back onto the couch and patted the space next to her, signalling Mallory to sit. For the next hour, they sat, side-by-side, leaning back on the couch, feet up on an ottoman, holding hands, saying not a word.

~

Mallory gently rose from the couch and tiptoed to the small kitchen peninsula where Ms. Willow worked on her computer. "Jess is asleep," she whispered. The two padded to the back door and stepped out to the deck.

"Can I come back tomorrow?" Mallory asked.

"Absolutely, but I don't want you missing school. Why not come by later in the afternoon? You could stay for supper if you like."

"It's easier at this hour."

"Because?"

Mallory hesitated. "My dad won't understand... I can't tell him about Jess."

"Did he know that she was missing?"

"No, I never told him. He doesn't like... doesn't like me with friends."

"You've never had friends?" Willow asked gently.

312

"Whenever I had friends, he'd move." Mallory turned away. "I don't want my dad involved."

"Fair enough. Come after your morning classes. You can eat your lunch here."

"Don't worry about my lunch. I'll eat during the last morning class."

"Bring your laptop or whatever you use. We'll figure it out."

"Thanks, Ms. Willow. I gotta go now." Mallory walked off the deck and, with a wave, went out the back gate.

Chapter 108

Jarrett backed his car next to the one-room rental cabin, keeping his back license plate out of view. It was the perfect location: a wooded lot close to a main road but not visible; out-of-town but close enough for food deliveries. Jarrett booked a couple of meals online, tipped well through his credit card and left instructions to leave his order on the patio table near the front door. In Covid times, the instructions would be considered merely cautious.

Ironically, it was Covid that caught Jarrett. The symptoms he told his aunt were bogus, an excuse for his early call. However, the fever that had him sweating his first night at the cabin was real. And the following morning, razor-slashing pain had him wincing with every swallow. He called the local drug store.

"I'm so sorry, but we don't make deliveries. However, we do have curbside pickup."

"How does that work?" Jarrett whispered.

"You place your order, pay by credit or debit card, and we'll have it ready for pickup."

"Okay, give me whatever you've got for a cold... I picked up a cold somehow—sore throat and fever."

"You might want to get tested for Covid."

"It's just a cold. I always get one this time of year."

"Okay, we'll get your order together and have it ready in a half-hour. Give us a call when you arrive, and someone will bring it out."

By the time Jarrett arrived at the drug store, a pounding headache had joined his symptoms. With a ball cap pulled low and a mask in place, he pulled up to the curb and lowered his passenger window. Soon a clerk walked out with a bag full of medications and dropped it onto the passenger seat. Jarrett gave a thumbs up and drove away. The clerk watched him pull away and noticed his Alberta license plates. So did an off-duty RCMP officer driving down the street just as Jarrett pulled out of his parking spot.

~

"We have him!" announced Officer Wallace to the lead investigator in Edmonton. "Jarrett Edgar is being driven to Calgary as we speak. We've seized his car, computer and phone and have a warrant to access his finances."

Chapter 109

Jarrett sat on the bottom bunk of his cell, which he shared with another infected inmate. The prison infirmary was filled with more severe cases, so he remained in his cell, locked down the entire day within a quarantined unit. His positive test result was no surprise: fever, chills, sore throat, headache and now a raspy cough. But Covid was a minor issue compared to the charges being filed against him. His criminal lawyer was not optimistic: Jarrett had been identified and captured on CCTV, his finances were being scrutinized, and his car and electronics were impounded.

Jarret mulled over his options. While his computer was highly encrypted, his partners were not. Though he'd never disclosed how he was so successful with his leads, it was no secret that the names came from him. He sold them to Seth and Deni, who passed them on to Lena. His lawyer told him it was only a matter of time before the RCMP specialists hacked into his laptop—he'd be wise to make a plea bargain.

~

The lead investigator in Edmonton called his team together. "Jarrett Edgar gave the names of the other key players and the corporations he helped create to cover their activities and launder money. Let's track them down."

Within two days, Seth and the remaining guard were found and arrested at an acreage outside Edmonton, the new base for their operations. Lena, Deni and her daughter, Claudia, were picked up soon after at a townhouse used as a vacation rental and a location for escort services. Two other properties were seized, one in Calgary, which apparently had been occupied by Lena.

PART NINE

Chapter 110

Mallory baked the cake as soon as she got up—carrot cake. She had made it a couple weeks before to try out the recipe. During a lull in a video game, she had brought her dad a thick slice. He paused to take a bite while she was there. "This is really delicious," he had said with something close to a smile. Mallory considered it a win.

Mid-morning, Mallory arrived at Ms. Willow's laden with a backpack and a tote in each hand. Jess met her at the front door and took a step back. "Well, well, well," she said. "You look amazing!"

Mallory, self-conscious, stepped in through the door. As she placed her totes on the kitchen counter and dropped her backpack against the wall, she said, "Yeah, I've been experimenting with my hair."

"It really suits you, Mallory."

"Thanks. During the day, I've been keeping my hair away from my face, and the acne is clearing up."

"Your makeup is just right."

"I picked up some free samples. And I went to the thrift shop." Mallory pulled off her hoodie and extended her hands. Gone were the sweats. Instead, she wore leggings and a tunic top. "You look great," Jess said as she hugged Mallory.

Despite her encouragement, Mallory picked up an underlying weariness in her voice. "Why don't you sit down," said Mallory. "I have a surprise for you." From one tote, she took out two carefully packed cake layers; from the other, she removed a container of icing and, with the exaggerated flourish of a magician pulling a rabbit from a hat, she drew out a cake decorating kit. "Isn't this great!" she exclaimed, handing the kit to Jess. "Very basic and, most important, very cheap. I found it in the grocery store!"

"You know how to decorate cakes?"

"Experimenting. And today, I'm going to give you a demonstration."

It had been two weeks since Jess had been found. With the key players now in custody, a general feeling of relief replaced the uncertainty and hyper-vigilance of her first days back. Sebastian and Oliver had been informed, and notice of Jess's return had been posted. Willow declared Jess, Mallory, Sebastian and Oliver as part of her "family bubble," and today, in the early afternoon, they were having a small get-together in her backyard.

"Where's Ms. Willow?" asked Mallory as she folded up the empty totes.

"She's in a room upstairs holding Zoom sessions with students who want some help with their work."

"Yeah, we just have to complete our final projects, and we're finished for the year."

"Are you done?"

"No. I did a lot of work over the weekend, though." She handed Jess the folded totes, "Would you put these in my backpack?" As Jess tucked the totes away, Mallory continued, "But I want to finish everything by next weekend and get out of school a week early!"

Jess rested her head on her hand and looked down, "I'm so far behind."

"You'll catch up over the summer."

"I can't even think about school. I can't concentrate. I feel like... numb and dumb."

Mallory looked at Jess anxiously and then began opening cupboard doors. "What are you looking for?" asked Jess.

"I need bowls to divide up the frosting so I can colour it."

Jess got up and opened a cupboard, "Bowls here and," opening a couple of drawers, "spoons and other utensils here."

"Why don't you help me," said Mallory. She took four bowls and put a dollop of frosting in each one. "Blend up four bright colours." She passed Jess three small containers of food dye. "Primary colours—you know the drill. Yellow and red make..."

"Yeah, yeah, yeah," said Jess with a slight grin.

"In the meantime, I'll ice the cake."

Chapter 111

Willow knew the meeting would be emotional, but Sebastian pushed it over the top. "Jess!" he exclaimed as he burst into the backyard. They had spoken through their apps, but this was their first face-to-face meeting. He threw his arms around her and sobbed. Willow was about to ease him off but noted that Jess also clung to Sebastian and cried on his shoulder. Willow, Mallory and Oliver busied themselves at the round table filled with plates, utensils, a salad, chips, buns and all the condiments needed for the hamburgers grilling on the deck.

In a few minutes, Sebastian and Jess walked over to the table. Regaining his composure, Sebastian introduced Oliver. Mallory had already told Jess how Oliver stood up to Victor at *Strum's* and how he'd helped in the search. Jess thanked Oliver, and then an awkward silence enveloped the teens.

"What we need is some music," said Sebastian. "And Oliver and I have come prepared."

Sebastian took out his phone and pulled up a playlist.

"You stream music?" asked Jess.

"Yep, you're looking at an acclaimed musician and employee of *Strum's*." He gave a slight bow. "And Oliver is providing the amplification."

Oliver laughed and pulled out a small, portable speaker. "It's compact, but it does the job."

As the music started, Willow plated the hamburger patties and brought them to the table.

"Dig in, everyone."

Chapter 112

Willow opened the backyard gate for Frida. After greeting the students, she and Willow drew apart, leaving the teens to themselves.

"How's Jess doing?" asked Frida.

"It's hard to know... She is up and about a little more. After school hours we go for long walks. She seems less skittish. I've joined a survivor's support group to learn how I can help her."

"Will she be staying with you?"

"As long as she wants to. Besides, where else would she go? Another group home? No, she can stay with me. She has independent status. She can choose."

Frida looked over at the teens chatting and eating. "What's happened to Mallory? I think this is the first time I've ever seen her eyes."

"Yes, she coming into her own. She's been wonderful with Jess. Visits every day during her lunch break." Willow walked a little further toward the rear corner of the yard. "Did you have a chance to talk to the superintendent?"

"Yes, and it's tragic." Frida lowered her voice, "Jarrett's aunt... You know, Lydia, up at Central Admin?"

"Yes, I've met her."

"Well, she had no idea of what Jarrett was involved in. Lydia's brother is Jarrett's father, and he always considered his sister a bleeding heart. So she was really pleased when she saw her nephew taking an interest in the difficulties some kids face and showing a little empathy. And now, finding out that all along, he was taking her for a ride just to access her data? She's shattered, resigned immediately."

"But how did he do it?"

"Through a post-it note stuck to the bottom of her laptop with her password. The police found a photo of it on Jarrett's phone."

"My God!"

"When they showed Lydia, she was horrified that, through an unguarded moment, Jarrett had been able to violate the very students she always tried to help."

"But why?"

"Seems there's a lot of money to be had."

After a few moments, Willow asked, "What's Lydia going to do now?"

"She has a grown daughter somewhere in the Vancouver area. I wouldn't be surprised if she moves there. Don't think there'll be any more family gatherings with her brother."

Mallory called out from the other side of the yard, "I'm going in for the cake." Willow gave her a thumbs up.

"Stay for a piece of cake," Willow said to Frida. "Mallory's worked so hard on it. Got up early to bake it and came over here early to ice it."

"Of course." And the two walked back to the group of teens.

Chapter 113

Mallory climbed the stairs to the third-floor apartment, happy that the first get-together had gone so well. As she turned onto the second-floor landing, heading up the last flight, the door creaked open, and an old woman peered out. Mallory had gone shopping after the barbecue; her two totes now held groceries. "Want to check out the vegetables I bought?" Mallory asked. The door quickly shut. Mallory laughed to herself as she continued up the stairs and unlocked the apartment door. Her smile faded when she placed her totes on the kitchen counter. Sitting at the dining room table was her dad—home at three.

"Where have you been?"

Mallory slid off her backpack and began removing groceries from the totes. "As you can see, I've been shopping." Then she paused and looked at her father. "Before that, I went to a little celebration for a friend of mine. It was at the home of one of my teachers."

Ryder stared at his daughter.

"You can call her if you don't believe me."

"What's her name?"

"Ms. Willow."

"And does your friend have a name?"

"Jess."

"Why was your friend's party at Ms. Willow's house?"

"Because that's where she lives. Oh, the principal was there, too."

"Aren't you supposed to be doing school work online?"

"It's exam time, Dad. We're all working on our final projects. I'm almost done. We weren't doing anything wrong."

"Well," said Ryder, his voice getting edgy, "I've heard this isn't the first time you've left the house during school hours."

"I've gone for meetings at school every week."

"During the pandemic?"

"Yes. We met outside. Ask my teacher if you don't believe me."

"That's enough!" Ryder shouted.

Mallory resumed unpacking the totes, her hands trembling. "I'm seventeen, Dad. I do all the cleaning, cooking and shopping. I'm not a child."

"Oh, so you think you're big stuff now? Do you pay the rent? The electricity? The heat? Do you *pay* for the groceries? What about the money I gave you for clothes a few weeks ago?"

"I want to get a job," said Mallory, almost in a whisper.

"What? Speak up!"

"I want to get a job."

"What do you know about a job? You think it's sketching all day? You have no idea what it means to work day in and day out. You wouldn't last a week."

Mallory folded up the empty totes and put them off to the side. Her whole body was shaking now, and she leaned hard against the counter to stop it. Never before had she confronted her father as she did today. She knew what his next move would be—a new apartment across town. "I have one year of school left," said Mallory, her voice quivering. "I'm going to finish it at Riverbank High, even if I have to ride transit for three hours each day."

Ryder stared at his daughter. "Where's that debit card I gave you?"

Mallory fished the card from a zippered pocket and reached out to hand it to her father. Ryder whipped it out of her hand, bent it back and forth until it cracked and tossed it on the counter. He glowered at Mallory, "And wash off that makeup. You look like a whore." Then he walked out of the apartment.

Chapter 114

Mallory had planned to come home and study into the night. But after the exchange with her father, she could no longer focus. No sooner would she begin a sentence than a phrase, a glare, a tone of voice would break through her thoughts, and a sense of dread would wash over her. A couple of hours after her father left, she heard the apartment door open and literally jumped. Ryder knocked on her bedroom door, "I've got some hot pizza," he said jovially, "Come out and have a piece." The change of demeanour unsettled Mallory even more. But she didn't want to upset her father, so she went to the kitchen. The warm and inviting aroma of pizza filled the apartment.

"It smells so good. Thanks, Dad," said Mallory, trying to match her father's mood.

Ryder was already plating two slices. "I thought we could use a little treat. This is my favourite pizza."

Mallory had never seen a pizza so laden with meat and cheese. She took a little bite before putting her slice on a plate. "This is sooo good."

"I know my pizzas," said Ryder as he walked to the dining table.

Mallory was well-acquainted with her father's variable moods, but this reversal was the most abrupt ever. Had her father really gotten over their disagreement? What was going on? And eating dinner together at the table? Since when? She cringed at the thought of trying to make conversation. As if reading her thoughts, Ryder said, "Why don't we watch a movie?"

"Sure."

"*Lethal Weapon*. I haven't seen that one for a long time."

"Yeah, why not."

Ryder went to his gaming console, pulled up *Lethal Weapon* on his large monitor and turned it toward the table. For the next couple of hours, Mallory tried to relax, laughing at the appropriate times and glancing nervously every now and then at her father. When the movie ended, Mallory collected their dishes and went to the kitchen to put the remaining pizza slices in the refrigerator.

"So when do you expect to finish up your schoolwork?" Ryder asked off-handedly.

"I want to finish by this weekend if I can."

"I'm sure you will."

Mallory finished in the kitchen and returned to her room, confused and conflicted.

Chapter 115

Jess and Willow walked through the wetlands of Fish Creek Park. The frozen, desolate landscape of winter had thawed, and the dormant remnants of life, protected by the dead overgrowth, had broken through and thrived. The green grasses of the marsh danced with the breeze, and wildflowers cast splashes of colours. Birds flitted from trees to shrubs to grasses, picking at insects and watching over their nests while wildlife scurried beneath the bushes. The entire park was awash with the vibrant greens of early summer. At times the two remarked about something they saw, but for the most part, they quietly walked the trails, soaking in the warmth of the sun and fresh scents of new growth.

After an hour on a trail, Willow said, "We'd better turn around. I don't want you to overdo it."

"Yeah, I think you're right."

"We can always come back another day."

As they were headed back, Jess asked, "Did you have a chance to ask Officer Wallace about the other girls?"

"Yes, I did. I thought I'd tell you once we were home, but I can do it now." She rummaged through the purse she had slung over her shoulder and pulled out a little notepad. "So, there was Beth Spratt and her son, Luxton."

"Yeah, she was called Flower."

"Beth and her son are at a shelter and getting counselling. Then, there's a girl called Belle and another, Desme."

"Belle was addicted to the drugs Deni passed around. She wasn't a big earner, but she could cut and style hair. That's probably why they kept her. Desme was the new girl."

"Both of them are minors and are in a secure treatment facility."

"Desme really bought into Lena's lies. She was convinced she would become a millionaire."

Looking down at her notes, Willow continued, "Angie and Trixie... they're in custody. An advocacy group for foreign domestic workers is trying to help them with their visas. Officer Wallace doesn't know how much counselling they're getting for the sex trafficking."

"They were trying to earn money for their families in the Philippines. Trixie's mom needed some kind of operation. Angie had a daughter she wanted to send to a better school."

Willow put away her notepad.

"What about Gloria?"

"He didn't say anything about a Gloria," said Willow. She pulled the notepad back out of her purse and scanned a couple of pages. "No, he didn't mention Gloria. Who is she?"

"Gloria worked the clubs. She didn't want to do videos or online sessions with johns. On the last night of clubbing, she didn't return. No one knew what happened to her."

"Would you like to talk to Officer Wallace about her? He may know something he didn't tell me."

"Later on, maybe."

They walked on in silence. "And Coco?" asked Jess in a whisper.

"Officer Wallace said there was nothing you could have done. The driver and the passenger in the front seat—"

"Star and Rocky."

"They were either dead or very close to it when the car exploded. Major head and chest injuries."

"And Coco?"

"You told the police that she was kicking and refusing to leave."

"Yes."

"What the forensic team discovered supports that. They found Coco in the back seat, her arms clung around the driver's shoulders with one of the back doors open. By all appearances, she didn't want to leave. And if you had stayed any longer, you might not have made it either." Willow looked over at Jess. "You're going to have to let it go, Jess. It wasn't your fault."

"Was anyone even looking for her?"

"From what I understand, the family situation was chaotic, and

Coco was passed among the relatives and changed schools frequently. No one even realized she was missing. She was only fifteen."

"She looked younger."

For several minutes they walked on quietly until Jess abruptly broke the silence. "Why me? That's something I don't get. Why did Jarrett and Seth target me? Is there something filthy about me that attracts creeps?"

"They didn't even know you, Jess. Jarrett got access to the school records and actually hunted down students he thought would be the most susceptible: caseworkers as emergency contacts, spotty attendance, frequent school changes, independent status, poor grades. Then he tracked down these students on social media. From your uncle's court cases and convictions, he was able to find out about your mother, and God knows what else. Jarrett and Seth are psychopaths. You were targeted, but it had nothing to do with you personally."

"But Jarrett came to hear me sing," Jess insisted.

"You'd been in his sights long before that. He only came to our *Revue* because his aunt had been invited by the drama teacher. And, yes, that night, he saw your beauty and your talent, but his sadistic interest is *his* problem, not yours. You are not defined by Jarrett or Seth or Deni or any of the warped perverts who exploited you."

They walked the rest of the way to the car in silence. As they approached the parking area, Jess said, "During summer break, do you think we could visit Enuka and Obioma? I know we've spoken with them on the phone, but I want to thank them in person."

"I would love to."

"And at some point, I'd like to see Beth."

"You let me know when you're ready. I'm sure we could set up something," said Willow. Jess wiped away some tears. "She meant a lot to you, Jess."

"She gave me hope."

Chapter 116

On Sunday, Mallory woke up abruptly at five a.m. and could not go back to sleep. She'd submitted all of her school work except for one assignment and decided to finish it. Mallory prepared a bowl of cold cereal, grabbed an apple and returned to her room. After a couple of hours, she did a final scan and hit the submit button–her school year had ended.

Mallory closed her Chromebook and stowed it in her backpack between a sketch pad and her modest collection of art supplies. Given her father's current unpredictability, Mallory left nothing she treasured at home.

One day last week, during a lunch hour meeting with Jess, Mallory had carried in two shopping totes. Ms. Willow and Jess were chopping fruit for a fruit salad as she arrived.

"That's quite a load, Mallory. I hope it's not food–you've contributed enough. Stop in for lunch whenever you like."

"No, it's not food. Just a few things of mine I'd like to leave here for a while–my old sketch pads, my icing kit and a few other things."

"Everything okay with your dad?" asked Willow.

"I don't know. He's being super nice."

Willow stopped chopping the melon and looked at Mallory. "Too nice?"

"Yeah, it sounds crazy." Mallory shrugged again. "I don't know. It's probably nothing."

Jess caught the eye of Ms. Willow and shook her head slightly.

"You call me if you need help," said Willow.

During their meal, the mood lightened as they laughed over an episode of a sitcom. As soon as it was over, Mallory said, "I better be going."

Willow walked Mallory to the sidewalk. "If you ever want to talk about what's going on at home, I'm here for you, Mallory. If you don't feel safe, you call me."

Mallory looked down and said, "Thanks," and walked away.

However, her father's upbeat mood had continued. Maybe he finally got the promotion he always wanted, Mallory surmised, received the news while he was out and brought home pizza to celebrate. Maybe. For now, she was relieved she'd finished her schoolwork. As she changed out of her pajamas, she could hear her father lumbering about in the kitchen. She looked at her watch—eight-thirty.

Mallory swung her backpack over her shoulder and went to the kitchen. "I'm thinking of going for a walk."

"You finished all your assignments?"

"Yes. I woke up early, so I finished the last one and just submitted it."

"How long are you planning on walking?"

"A couple of hours. Taking the bus to Glenmore Reservoir—you know, near the hospital. Might sketch out there for a while and then come home."

"Be back before noon," he said as he pushed the start button on the coffee maker and plodded to the bathroom.

Mallory filled her water bottle, grabbed a carrot, buttered a couple slices of bread and walked down the stairs.

~

Mallory glanced at her phone for the time. The buses were running late. She'd planned to be home for eleven-thirty, but at this rate, she'd be skidding in at noon. She jumped off the bus at her stop, three blocks from home, and ran. She slowed to a walk for the last block—she had ten minutes to spare. As she rounded the corner, she saw the rental truck and two young guys heading into the six-plex. Her heart dropped, then a faint spark of hope quickened her step; someone else in the building might be moving.

Mallory raced up the stairs. Their apartment door was propped open, and the two young guys she had seen before were coming out, each carrying one of their large plastic moving crates filled with the items from the kitchen cupboards. She walked through the door and across the hall to her bedroom. Her bed, end table and lamp were gone. The closet was open and empty. In the room were three plastic garbage bags. One contained her clothes from the bins in the closet. Two others held her pillow and bed linens.

Tears smarted Mallory's eyes, her cheeks flushed. She walked toward the kitchen and living area. All her father's electronics were carefully packed, the last things to be loaded. Her dad was in the kitchen checking each cupboard to make sure everything had been removed.

"Well, look who's here," he said pleasantly. "Record time this round—just two and half hours. These two apprentices are the best yet."

"Where are we moving?" said Mallory.

"You're about to find out very shortly."

Mallory's breath was coming quick and shallow, "Why are we moving?"

"Because it's time to go. If you want to earn your own living and get your own place, go for it. If you want a roof over your head and three meals a day, carry down the bags in your room and get in the truck."

Mallory burned with anger and helplessness. She stared at her father, but she could not contradict him—she had no other place to live.

"Now," yelled Ryder. Turning away from her, he muttered, "You're becoming just like your mother."

Just like your mother. Her mother had abandoned her as a baby. Period. Mallory had been told nothing else about her. And now, *just like your mother.* What did that mean?

Chapter 117

With some coaching from Oliver and Audrey, Sebastian completed the schoolwork he received from Ms. Willow and his other teachers. To celebrate, the barbecue was fired up.

"Okay, it's hot enough now," said Craig.

"How do you know?" asked Sebastian.

"You put your hand over the grill about this high," said Craig, demonstrating. "One, two, three, four." He pulled back his hand. "That's how I know. Any longer would have been really uncomfortable."

Sebastian tried. "Yeah. That's a cool trick."

"Or a hot tip!" Craig chuckled at his own joke as Sebastian just shook his head and picked up the plate of raw hamburgers.

"Get those burgers on the grill."

Audrey brought out a couple bowls of salads and set them on the deck table. "Almost ready?" she asked.

"Just a few minutes more."

Audrey went back inside and returned with buns and condiments, and soon all three were seated around the table serving up their meal.

Craig raised his glass and clinked it against Sebastian's and Audrey's. "To Sebastian, on the successful completion of Grade 11."

"And successfully assisting with the garden. The lettuce we're eating is home-grown."

"And to you guys, for helping me out!"

As they ate and chatted, Craig smiled at the lanky teen, relaxed and witty. When the meal was almost finished, Sebastian's phone pinged, and he glanced at the screen to see who had sent him a message. His neck jerked up.

"It's my mom. I haven't heard from her for months." Sebastian opened the message.

"Shit!" His foot began to tap rapidly on the deck.

"What is it?" asked Craig.

Sebastian held up his phone so Craig and Audrey could see. *Your father's getting out of prison in two weeks. Maybe after a stint with him, you'll appreciate Max.*

Chapter 118

"We *are* proud of you," stressed Oliver's mother. Oliver sat across from his parents in his father's home office. The door closed. "All that you did to help find your classmate."

"Jess."

"But your father and I think it's best you change schools. Meet new friends."

"You'll have better preparation for university," added his father.

"And better preparation is, what exactly? Rubbing shoulders with kids whose parents can afford a private school?"

Oliver's mother softened her voice, "Who are these friends of yours, Oliver? Jess—no parents, no relatives. How did she even wind up in... in that... situation? And the others, who are they?"

"If it wasn't for Covid, you would have met them."

"Who are their parents? What do they do for a living?"

"They're my friends, Mom. Have I gotten into any trouble with them? No. All we did was try to find our friend who was missing and, in the process, helped bust a sex-trafficking operation. You know, stuff kids do."

Oliver's dad sighed and sat back in his chair.

"I want to finish high school at Riverbank High."

Chapter 119

"A leave of absence to pursue a post-graduate Special Ed program?" Frida looked up from the laptop at Willow. "So, you're sure about this?" asked Frida.

Willow nodded. "This experience with Jess and Mallory, Sebastian, Oliver—it's cracked open something. I can't just go back to teaching as I did before." Willow got up and walked to the window. "You know that saying, 'The eye can't see what the mind doesn't know.' I want to understand more so I can help more. It's as simple as that."

Frida sat at her desk, Willow's laptop facing her with the email she was ready to send to Central Admin. "Well, in that case, you'll have to hit *Send*." Frida turned the laptop around so that the screen now faced Willow. Willow walked to the desk and touched the keyboard. *Whoosh*.

"I'm sorry to see you go, Willow, but I look forward to your return."

"I won't be returning, Frida."

"What?"

"We've got to help kids like Jess, Mallory and Sebastian long before they get to high school. I'll be going to an elementary school."

Acknowledgements

It takes a village to raise a child is a well-known adage, a truth that cannot be overstated. I want to thank all those who have moulded my understanding of *the village*: my parents and my family that has grown into a clan, and colleagues who have dedicated their lives to the development and education of children and youth, especially those at risk. I'm inspired by specialists whose studies highlight the importance of respectful, caring relationships for children and the impact of key relationships on the developing brain, for better or worse. Their research offers a compassionate understanding of human behaviour and appropriate, empathetic responses needed for healing and growth.

In particular, many thanks go to the persons I consulted regarding specific aspects of this novel: Linden Almer, Brad Dye, Ph.D., R.Psych., Jamie Gramlich, Joe MacIsaac, Damon Mazurek, Mercedes and Steven Smith, Janel Spooner, and the colleagues, outreach personnel, and relatives who picked up their phones for quick questions or fired off text responses.

Much gratitude goes to my beta readers for their time, input and encouragement: Jen and Faith Barton, Sharon Cronin, Dawn Granley, my sister Kimi, my brother, Anthony, my niece, Lisa, and especially, my sister, Nikki, who faithfully reads the first and last drafts of my novels... and some in-between.

To Erik Mohr and his team at Emblem, many thanks for the outstanding cover art and interior design. Collaborating with you is always a pleasure.

To friends, librarians, and booksellers who have recommended my novels, organized book clubs and welcomed me for book signings, thank you.

And to the readers of my novels who have shared their reflections and life stories with me, thank you for your trust and insights.

About the Author

Linda Smith lives near Calgary, Alberta, engaging with children as an educational assistant and enjoying the beauty of the Rocky Mountains. She is the author of *Terrifying Freedom* and its stand-alone sequel, *Dawn Through the Shadows*. *Unknown, Unseen—Under the Radar,* is the first book in her new fiction series.

To arrange a book signing, schedule a book club discussion, or share your reflections on *Unknown, Unseen—Under the Radar,* message Linda through the contact page on her website, lindaannesmith.com.

Land Acknowledgement

In the spirit of reconciliation, we acknowledge that we live, work and play on the traditional territories of the Blackfoot Confederacy (Siksika, Kainai, Piikani), the Tsuut'ina, the Îyâxe Nakoda Nations, the Métis Nation (Region 3), and all people who make their homes in the Treaty 7 region of Southern Alberta.

Manufactured by Amazon.ca
Bolton, ON

40915535R00201